TUTTERVILLE
TIMES

TUTTERVILLE TIMES

Albert D. Audette, Jr.

Tutterville Times
Copyright © 2018 by Albert D. Audette, Jr.

Published by: Lulu Press, Inc.
Cover design by: Sharon M. Gannon
Book design and production by: Sharon M. Gannon
Map cover art by: iStock.com

ISBN: 978-0-359-13318-5

First Edition: November 2018

To my family;
and to the pursuit of imagination,
the mother of invention.

FORWARD

I believe, from my earliest days, that family is the pursuit of God's work throughout the universes. This work is a tale of one such family, conceived on the shores of Maine in the 1700s, and traced into the early west and into the middle of this great country. It is a story of good, and the shadows of evil that grow virus-like in the hearts of mankind. Lives herein are the triumphs of love – the anthesis of evil.

Table of Contents

Forward vii

Acknowledgements x

Upcoming Books xi

Tutter 1

A Man Named Q. 20

Adelaide Magmorth 32

Judge Adelaide Tutter 58

Sweet Merry 76

The Silver Slipper 101

Randolph House 125

Cuenca & Sweet Carlos 145

The Metamorphosis of Dianna 160

Hotel Fortaleza do Guincho 176

Albert and Alexandria and Hosea 197

Code Alpha in Play 213

Master-Dianna 227

Acknowledgements

Special thanks to Ricky J. McRoskey for his technical assistance in basketball coaching.

Upcoming Books

by Albert D. Audette, Jr.

Tutterville Times – Dianna

Tutterville Times – Q

The Sound of a Tambourine

Advice From a Great-Grandfather

CHAPTER 1

TUTTER

Evil and its insidious roots have always been the intercourse of war. As always, its nature of hate and betrayal seep as handmaidens into its aftermath. The discordant threads of peace exist until the origins of good weave themselves into peace's fabric, comforting those who are left to live.

War inevitably succumbs to peace, for as evil tires, its antithesis good does not. Survivors seek the good, since not to do so precipitates the annihilation of specie, and this God will not allow. For, built into all life are the two prime and immutable laws of nature: survival of the individual, and thence, survival of its specie.

The struggle of good men for peace and personal freedom went on for many years after the Civil War. Reconstruction shaped southern habitats so that wearied and broken families could struggle to rebuild their cities and towns, while others traveled for the safety of the north. For many, there was little money, no trade, and barely enough food to help the poorest.

Country families were always in danger. They barred their doors at dusk for protection and many traveled without security. Homesteads armed themselves, and most work and travel was done between sunup and dusk.

The poorest and more troubled families fleeing to the north took the more traveled roads, making their way through forests and hill country during the day. Some sought the secrecy of night's dark, daring risk. Folk with means and families in political trouble sought to go by sea. Ocean passage was expensive and some, hoping for the safety of the sea, traveled along the coast, signaling to coastal cargo schooners for a ride north.

Shippers avoided these signals fearing the risk of picking up pirates; on the other hand, there were some schooner captains prepared for guarded risk. They had experienced so much savagery during the war that the need to help desperate people came first. The Tutter shipping family chose to take the risk. Their crews had been military-trained for rescue work. So it was, on this very summer's eve, when a Tutter schooner caught sight of distress.

Captain Adam Tutter's schooner sailed north along the southern Virginia shore, his right arm cradling the ship's rudder. He had a sturdy ship and enough cargo to make a good profit. He'd seen no distress signals the past few trips, pray God, and as yet, none this afternoon. A steady breeze hung with the wet, foul smell of the dank, coastal summer showers that pushed his ship quickly northeast. Adam tried to keep his eyes from the wild island flats off the coast. Trouble wasn't needed.

All was as it should; the crew was relaxed and Pinkus was asleep, stretched across his boot. Pinkus, the old dog in his late teens, had two homes. His first was on the oldest of the three Tutter ships sailing from port in the morning; the second was in the pier's sail house, waiting for the next family ship to go out to sea. Pinkus was a sea dog, first and last!

Besides sleeping, Pinkus' primary job was ship's compass. No matter the weather, the visibility, or the time, he sensed when the ship was precisely abeam home dock. A throaty bark, tail wag,

2

and most exact of all, his nose was the compass to follow into safe harbor, home.

With a low growl, Pinkus all of a sudden raised his head. Trouble! Adam knew immediately that the dog sensed someone on shore. Was it pirate or family?

"Cap'n Tutter! Dad! Look, eleven o'clock, black smoke. See it? Barely in the tree line?"

"Yeah, I see it Hosea. I was hoping it wasn't real. Tell the boys to lower all but the bowsprit. One sailor stays, the rest of you get ready and keep out of sight. Adam stays with me this time, we'll take her in slow. 'Stow,'" he commanded Pinkus. With no further signal than that, Pinkus walked to the aft cabin where he would remain silent until he heard the proper command.

Hosea, short of eighteen, knew he was considered an equal to his brothers and not 'just' the youngest. He'd proven his maturity many times over. Adam Junior was the older and their father's namesake. To him and to the rest of the family, Adam Junior would always be called 'Tut.' Dad was the Captain, and Tut was his First Mate. The nickname 'Tut' was so very appropriate, since every male-born Tutter was born with a prominent stammer that disappeared at puberty, age twelve!

Adam edged the boat inland between the dunes to his port, keeping the smoke on shore to starboard. The surf was strong enough to hide his sons while they edged over the schooner's side and swam to shore. Surprise was everything and gunshots could mean disaster. Once the swimmers were abeam the dunes, getting ashore was easy. The trick was to keep undercover and to get hidden well behind whoever was involved with the signal smoke.

"They're over the side. All's ready, Captain." First Mate Tut's smile was the thumbs-up signal his father was ready for.

"Secure the ship, I'll get the shore boat. Let's be sure the boys are on the beach before we go." Tut helped him lock the rudder and double-check the heavy lead anchor.

Hosea was first to belly-crawl ashore. Quickly he pulled off the oilskin vest that protected his weapons from the seawater. The vest, snug against the chest, and brief-style trunks helped them swim light and fast. Within seconds the others had done the same. Armed and ready, they slowly moved forward. The four of them belly-inched around the lowest dune. No one was in sight. They ran to the tree line and, as quiet as they'd swam ashore, swiftly moved toward the smell of smoke. Minutes passed. Suddenly the sounds of conversation stopped them. Their older brother George waved them down, and crouching low, he went forward alone. Three bound men lay huddled together in the bush. Within minutes, George was back.

"Looks like some prisoners tied together. They mustn't see us; we can skirt them and see what's what. Let's not be given away, even by accident."

As one, they made a small circle around the brush and toward the beach. Whispers from ahead broke the silence:

"... Only two men in the dinghy, must be more aboard... Billy and Jess should be climbing up the backside of the schooner in a minute or two; they'll take care of anyone still on board. We'll lay low and entertain these two until our boys signal 'all's well' from the ship."

George Tutter pushed his pistols back into his oilskin vest.

4

"I'm fastest and meanest, I'll get back to Dad – wait for my signal, you'll know it – then do what's best to surprise these bastards! See ya…" And he was gone.

The three remaining Tutters hung close to the trees and counted three pirates. Each chose one for himself. When George left, the next eldest brother Michael took command. "Nothing we should do until Dad and Tut get ashore. Pray Georgie is his usual mean best with Billy and Jess."

They could hear the three men whispering as they took positions on the beach: "Pray God we'll see Canada soon, alive and well. This ship can get us home, or it'll get a noose around our necks. It's hell being on the bad side."

"We are not on the bad side, Captain. We did what we were sent to do. We have to believe that we have more work to do for the admiral when we've finished here."

"No more slips – I am not to be called 'captain' until this is over. Canada first and always. We die for home if we have to. Agreed?" There was a unanimous nod of heads. "Now, heaven protect us, let's pray this is a crew of novices and we can get on with it. God protect us; God protect our homeland, and God protect the Queen!"

*

"Hello, shore party! I'm Captain Tutter. Need help?" His voice was calm and easy, but his eyes searched the trees to see his sons. Have to be pirates, he thought, still no sons. "How many are there in your party? Can you swim here to the dinghy?"

"Just three of us, Captain. Thank God you're here. We have an injury. Can you come on in?"

Adam whispered, "Tut, the fire is too bright. Keep your eyes off the flame. Don't get blinded! Let's move in. I'm missing four sons… keep your guns ready."

No one came forward to help Adam beach the dinghy. All three men on shore were clean-shaven, dry, and dressed in the usual sea crew gear. In their forties and dark complexioned from the sun, their leader looked very content with the situation. "Something is wrong," Adam repeated.

"Captain Tutter. Thanks for coming to help." He looked appraisingly out at the schooner then at Tut still on board the dinghy. "I don't see more of your crew, Captain. These are dangerous times for so few men on a class schooner. Why would you risk coming ashore? That's a lovely boat."

Adam stepped into the surf as Tut pulled the boat toward shore.

The three men now stood abreast. "Come to the fire, gentlemen. Get dry. Let's sit for a few minutes, Captain Tutter. We need to talk about a way we can return the favor of your coming to help us." With practiced ease they drew pistols and leveled them at Adam and Tut. "We insist – please sit, gentlemen." He waved a gun at Tut to come ashore.

Adam's steel jaw did not flinch. "You men can't be pirates, everybody up and down this coast knows my boat. You won't get a day's distance to sea!"

"Again, sit down, gentlemen. Please. Again, have your mate step off the boat, Captain." He waved his pistol toward the fire. *There is no need to rush*, he thought; *keep the tension down, no foolish bravado until we're sure Billy and Jess had secured the schooner. Give Billy and Jess time; wait for their signal. With luck there'd be just a few to neutralize on board. Easy pickings for Jess and Billy. If there is no surrender from the ship, we'll have to waste these two and the hostages.*

"You are so right, Captain, your schooner is a familiar ship. When we finish with it, it will be very different – a two-mast gaff rig and new colors. She'll be lovely! We need to get to Canada."

He pointed to a red signal-ribbon just dropped from the schooner's port bow.

"Well for the Lord's sake, gentlemen." The pirate leader's grin was more of a sneer. "My men have just salvaged a schooner lost at sea. The red flag across your bow says your ship is mine. Sea salvage. Good ole Billy! What do you have to say, 'Mr.' Tutter? You're no captain now…"

"My father will always be the captain of his ship. You idiots are as good as dead. Piracy is a hanging offence." Tut's grin was nails and all but pleasant. His fists, calloused and hard, draped like a gunslinger's at his hips. "I suggest you carefully put your guns on the ground and get your hands in the air. I believe you are surrounded!"

The three pirates laughed at Tut's apparent ploy. As Tut spoke, three Tutter men stepped from the trees. Michael's voice was a command: "There's six guns aimed at the backside of each of you, so do as you were told. Ground your guns or we'll split your backsides in two!"

The pirate leader, surprised, swung around. He didn't lose his smile. He shook his head, "No, gentlemen! Checkmate. The boat is actually mine, don't you see? I have two men on board your schooner. I own your boat, and my gun is square on your captain's chest. Nothing you can do to save your boat. As for your captain, you don't want to lose him in the crossfire. Relax gentleman, we need labor; when we sail, you gentlemen can wait for the next ship. At present, I need all of you to re-figure my ship. Work for me or die... simple as that." His grin became more cynical.

Hosea's low laugh raised the ante. "What makes you 'gentlemen' think our ship is yours? I don't see a red flag anywhere, and there's a flare heading this way. I see only one man on our deck and he looks every inch a mean, bad Georgie and..." he took a deep breath, a look of horror replacing his grin, "I don't think... ugh... you'll recognize your Billy and Jess, looks like... ah, ever again." He pointed to froth-white water boiling alongside the schooner. "I think some sharks are feasting." His voice no longer a boy's, "Put your guns down or we drop the three of you, NOW! Spread eagle. Let's secure the prisoners, brothers."

Breathless from shock and disbelief, the leader and then the others dropped to their knees.

Also in shock, Adam whispered, "My Lord and my God!" Looking at his sons, "Harry's on board... the rest of you alright?" Tut took cord from the dinghy and started tying the new prisoners.

Hosea looked at his father. "They have what could be a few refugees tied up and hidden a little behind the trees. Let's take a look."

Adam followed his son into the brush. Refugees were their reason for taking so big a risk in the first place. The war left hundreds of thousands of families migrating to the western and northern states, always for survival and to find a new life. The Tutter family was trained to help where it could. The smoke pots they watched for along the coast challenged both conscience and courage. Adam knew the risk to his family, but what did the Lord want? The haves who have, have to help.

The small circle of brush barely hid the three men tied together. The older broke the silence almost immediately. "We have nothing, please untie us, and there's only old clothes in our gear. We have nothing. Please let us go. We can't do you any harm!"

"I'm Captain Tutter and this is my son, Hosea. We've come ashore looking for refugees. Looks like we hit the jackpot, three pirates and three refugees! Once on board our ship, you'll be completely safe. Can you tell us who you are?"

"Oh, my Lord," a woman's voice sobbed. "Thank God! Are we really saved? Are you going to help us?"

Shocked at finding a woman, Adam smiled the more. "Yes ma'am, we really are; but first let's get you three to the schooner. And then home to a safe port. Anyone else here other than you three?"

The man answered, "We're the Hunter family, my wife and son. Thank you, thank you!"

Twenty minutes later the secured pirates and three hostages were on board and the Pinky schooner headed north again.

Captain Tutter looked at his sons; moist eyes and a grin were all he could muster for a while. "Hosea, you are tough! When you said 'drop 'em, NOW!' they sure did!" The Tutter men's laugh was hard and long.

Their Captain stood squarely before them, hands on hips, serious business on his proud face. "Since the war, this is the third time we've been in real danger. We are a team. I am damn proud of each one of you! Mike, we know what your shore crew did. Everything right by the book. It was precise and perfect, in every way. Serious practice is the reason all of you did your jobs perfectly today.

"And you, George, your decision to quickly return to the schooner was right and quick. It was absolutely the proper decision! Tell us what happened when you got back to the schooner – better tell us now than when we get home. Your mother need know as little of the action as possible." That brought another laugh! They all knew she'd get every last piece of the rescue out of him before she'd let him get any sleep.

George squared off like his father, "Sure, Captain. When I got here I knew there'd be two intruders on board so I hand-over-hand climbed to the deck. No one was in sight. I went over the forward, starboard side just as they finished searching the hold. I crouched low to wait for the right opportunity and that happened as they both tossed a red flag over the bow. There's no place for me to hide on deck. I think he was the one called Jess who saw me first.

"He made a very big mistake. He pulled a knife. Mine slammed into his chest just before he got his ready. He fell backwards, overboard. His buddy dove in after him. It took seconds for sharks to scent blood. Nothing I could do to help."

A whispery voice broke the silence: "Captain Tutter, these men are all your sons?"

"Yes sir, they are, and three more at home! My sons, my friends. They are the best men I have ever known." He grinned again, affirming his words. "By the way, my wife has packed plenty of food; we'll have some nourishment for all of us in a few minutes."

The whisper continued, "I'm Thaddeus Hunter. We're running north because we've lost every farm we've tried to work. All confiscated. Some, ah, some carpetbaggers, we guess, found both north and south soldiers recovering in our barns. They forced us out. We've tried to get more land, but each time it was confiscated." There was a deep catch in his voice. He was silent for a moment.

"We're going north where we can start again." He put an arm around his wife and son, "As Job says in Holy Scripture, 'We came into the world naked, we leave it the same way!'"

His wife tried to stand and balance against the schooner's sea motion. "I'm Georgiana Hunter and this is not our son, it's our daughter, Sally. For obvious reasons, women like us dress as men. These pirates are the reason."

Very surprised, he doffed his cap toward Miss Hunter. "When we get to port, Mrs. Hunter, we'll get everything straightened out, especially these pirates." Captain Tutter motioned toward the three men tied in with the cargo.

"Listen, Captain," the pirate leader interrupted, "I keep trying to tell your men that we are not pirates, we're Canadian agents – my name is Rhue. As I said, we must get to Canada. We are on Canadian duty…"

"I don't care where you're from!" Adam's voice raised in anger, his stress showing for the first time. "You threatened us. You put my sons in danger. You tried to steal my ship. That's what pirates do. You are pirates and we have nine witnesses to prove it. You'll have a few days to plead your story with the judge. As I said, piracy is a hangin' offence.

"I'm sure you've noticed we're flying both red and black signal flags? Black is for prison bound pirates on board, and red is for refugees. By the time we get into port, shore patrol will be waiting. The red flag signals all-hands on shore, with medics ready to help families like the Hunter family, here. We should see port with sunup."

*

While morning mist enveloped his schooner, dog Pinkus had his nose pointing northwest, and with the precision of the best compass the schooner followed his nose snugly into berth.

Roseland Tutter leapt on deck before the first mooring line was tied; within a minute, she scooped up young Sally and her parents, and the four hurried across the pier to the huge Tutter homestead a few hundred yards away.

Coast Guard Commander, Lieutenant Colonel Foster, stood at the ready with four troopers. "You have prisoners, Captain Tutter? What happened?"

"We have three pirates, Commander. My son Tut will help you and your escort to the compound."

A very frightened voice came from the hold, "We are not pirates! We're Canadian special agents and we must have access to the Canadian delegation in Washington!"

"As I was saying, these pirates threatened our lives. Tried to take over our ship, and they held the Hunter family tied and bound, hostage. Two of them went overboard while trying to take over our schooner. One of them was wounded in the action. We believe that sharks got both of them. If it weren't for your special training, Commander, me and my crew would never have been able to turn the table on the likes of these thugs. Every contingency you taught

12

my sons and me helped us work as the finest team I've ever seen. We fought these terrible men and were able to rescue Mr. Hunter and his wife and daughter. Agents, my twittle! Get them hanged!"

Captain Tutter's grin was one of great determination. "George, maybe you should help Tut and the Commander's men. Be sure they are very secure before you take them from below deck; it would be nice if none of them were injured in transport to the compound." He grinned, "Good luck with the prisoners, Commander, and thanks again for all you do for us shippers."

"Commander, we are Canadian agents. I am Captain Rhue. You must help us! We had to do what was necessary to…"

"Agents don't take over a ship, they abide by international law." The guard commander shook his head. "You can plead your cause with the judge. And good luck with that, ladies…" He saluted Captain Tutter.

"Thank you, Captain Tutter. I hope that by weekend we can reenact yesterday's events. As usual, we can include only your crew and my tactics man. A tactical advantage is only successful when we own the plan. Congratulations again, Captain."

It was near mid-morning before the cargo was unloaded and stowed into storage. All ten Tutter men were very hungry when they finally piled into Roseland Tutter's kitchen. She had already placed trays of fish, pancakes and eggs in the dining room. The coffee pots were steaming.

She whispered, stopping them at the door, "You boys have to be quiet. Mrs. Hunter and her daughter are asleep in the guest rooms; and you'll find Thaddeus Hunter waiting for you, Adam, by the dining room. They have already had breakfast and Mr. Hunter will join us for coffee when Mrs. Hunter is up."

When Roseland Tutter cooked, her ten men had their fill and as usual, it wasn't long before the breakfast cookie tray began its round of the table. To Roseland, there were few things more perfect than the lovely sounds of her family at table. The house was her ship, and she was its captain. No one brought a room to silence as quickly as her gentle cough. The hush was almost instantaneous.

"Ahem…" She touched her coffee spoon to its cup. Every eye in the room followed hers toward the parlor. There, dressed as though it was a morning like any other, stood the Hunter family. The silence continued in wonder at Sally Hunter's smile. In moments it conquered the room. Hosea was first to his feet.

Roseland smiled. "Let's join Mr. and Mrs. Hunter in the parlor, gentlemen. Hosea, see to it that Miss Hunter has some tea." Mothers know their children's minds before they themselves do. She barely held her smile as Hosea clumsily rushed toward the kitchen for the teapot.

"Oh Roseland, we, we…" Georgiana began to weep. Her husband, with clenched teeth, held her tightly. Almost unable to control her emotions she kept repeating, "You saved our lives! You saved our lives!"

Thaddeus Hunter led his wife to a chair. "She is right," he repeated, "you have saved us. How do we ever repay you for our lives?"

Roseland's response was sincere and to the point. "Please, oh please don't speak like this. My family was doing its duty. All we shippers, up and down the coast, have been helping families like yours since the war, almost seven years. The Lord is the One to thank! It's Him I trust to keep my sons and their father safe."

Adam interrupted, "You are welcome here until you settle on what you want to do. If you need help getting further north, we can arrange for that. The military coach system is always available at no cost. When you are rested and well enough we'll help you get to where you wish to travel. In the meantime, the Tutter family wants to be your host!"

Thaddeus Hunter's posture stiffened. Could he hope again? He and his family had lost their livelihood many times before; yet, it was the beginning of every prayer. Hope had been swept from them too many times, always to be caught up in tragedy. "We're about as far north as we'd like to be. We have the means to buy a working farm, a place far from corrupt and thoughtless people. We have not had a normal, peaceful life in more than fifteen years.

"It wasn't until we were underway on your ship that a different kind of hope came to us, like, ah… a faith-filled respite. I sensed it in our daughter as she watched your family bring us here. You and your sons exuded complete freedom, even after the obvious trauma of dealing with pirates. It was life-threatening for us, but for each of you, it was freedom as usual. It rubbed off on us in a way we hadn't experienced! It was natural. It was as natural in all of you as it is the nature of the sea and air. God's men, not animals, finally surrounded my family and me. For the first time after all those years we knew a momentous release." Georgiana and Sally hung on each word, frequently affirming him with nods of approval.

He continued, "Maybe one of your sons could help us look for a place in this area. We have funds in our Boston bank…"

Hosea interrupted, placing a tray on the side table next to

Sally, "Here's some breakfast cookies. They are the best part of any breakfast. Mom's best." Not a soul in the room had any doubt that Hosea Tutter's 'lost puppy' look meant that he was completely smitten by Miss Sally Hunter. And in response to the nature of youth, Sally Hunter's cheeks were rose red! The drawn-out glance between the two survived any conversation on any subject.

Thaddeus Hunter continued, "We're looking for about 250 acres of good black land with a sizable homestead. Our intention is cattle and horse breeding, and selling milk and cheese."

Hosea, finally tearing himself from love's sweet fancy, sat on the arm of Sally's chair. "Dad. Dad, that's the farm on the other side of our property! It's perfect! We can put a lunch basket in the big landau for Mom and the Hunters. You and I, Dad, can take the coach…"

*

While both families were making their plans, far to the north in the provincial capital city of Canada, Captain Charles tapped on the door of Vice Admiral Lord Brighton.

"Come in Charlie, what news this morning? Captain Williamsburgh, I hope?"

"Unfortunately, not good news, sir."

"His mission?"

"That was not a success sir; Captain Williamsburgh and his crew did not survive!"

Lord Brighton stood in silence for a moment. With a broad and defiant jaw he nodded to his aide to begin, "Start from the top, Charlie."

"He and his crew of five boarded the Sloop Hemisphere just off the New Orleans shore, well before dawn, and engaged its crew. Reports are that Hemisphere's captain saw that Williamsburgh was about to take his two passengers prisoner and confiscate his ship, so he torched Hemisphere's ammunition cabin. Williamsburgh and his crew could not escape, everyone died in the ammo explosions."

"My Lord, such bravery... that's bravery above and beyond... we have to get to their families immediately. And General Rhue, what of his half of the project?"

"He and his family are hunting in Maine. They will know nothing until he returns on Monday.

"Captain Rhue and his four men did complete their mission. The funds were transferred in full. But," and Captain Charles pulled himself slowly to attention, "the American court records state that Rhue and his men tried to take a U.S. schooner off the coast of Virginia. They boarded it and with force claimed it as salvage!"

"Impossible, Charlie! What in hell was that about?"

"Rhue claimed it for Canada, hoping to sail it home as salvage! Apparently the schooner's captain and men were well-trained to protect themselves."

"Of course they were prepared! What in hell are you saying?"

"In the attack, two of our men went overboard and did not survive. Rhue and the other two were taken captive and delivered to the coastal guard in Virginia."

"What?"

"And tried as pirates, found guilty, and executed!"

"They were hanged as pirates?"

"Yes, my Lord."

"The whole thing was local Virginia – no thought of diplomacy, no thought of military tradition – the locals took everything into their own hands!"

"That's the go of it? Did they divulge their real mission in Louisiana?"

"No, sir. The mission died with them. Rhue was executed first. Before the others were to die however, one of the men admitted their intent was to take the ship for personal gain. Apparently he hoped that a confession would stay his execution. As you and the Director know, two of these men were twin brothers, nephews of General Rhue."

"My God, Charlie. Did it all have to happen like this? What was Rhue thinking? He could have made it home without resorting to piracy. He died a pirate? This is unbelievable! General Rhue will never accept this. Captain Rhue and he are cousins. They volunteered for this mission. The Director chose them personally."

"Yes sir. As you and a few of us also know, General Rhue and the Rhue branch of the family is brash and unpredictable, to say the least. It is a family trait. Whereas, the Williamsburgh side of the family is quite excellent. I could not understand why the Director chose him over others who volunteered."

"Charles," the Vice Admiral reached for his topcoat, "that's why we must get to the Director immediately. Thank God Rhue does not know of this yet. We have little time to stop any revenge he will take, and you know he will. Time for a ruse for a Rhue! What is the name of the ship and its captain who captured Rhue?"

"Captain Adam Tutter. He owns a fleet of three schooner Pinkies. One passenger and two cargo runners from Rhode Island to the Carolinas and south."

"Tutter is as good as dead!"

"In anticipation of this, sir, I have taken the liberty of dispatching a detail south to Rhode Island." Before his Vice Admiral could interrupt, he continued. "I've selected two of my rugby mates, the two best sailors I know. They are instructed to book as passengers on a Pinky and get to Captain Tutter quickly. They will watch his back until this is neutralized…"

"You know, Charlie, besides being the ugliest man I know, you are a most brilliant one indeed! Let's get to the Director."

CHAPTER 2

A MAN NAMED Q

The shadows of fear make faint the heart that cowers in betrayal's womb. Never satisfied, it dreams of the victor's garland wreath, while deep within, its darkness knows no joy. Oft, shadowy-good finds its worth and stills even the hand of death. The man named Q, though dead, lives at the beacon call of intrigue.

*

Older farmers will say that the weather rotates in a seven-year cycle. It crescendos in its seventh and spills its generous bounty of crop, flower and fauna upon the earth; crops are more prolific and nature beams at its very best. This particular summer was the hottest in years, and as if to go one better, fall quickly swept fast and desperate into November. Snow came early to the wet fields of mid-Virginia. By Christmas, Roseland and Georgiana were the closest of friends and the closest of neighbors. The Hunter Homestead was every inch a gracious southern country farm and home. Christmas was the coldest and whitest in memory.

"You boys get your coats on and get to the pier. Pinky II should be here in a few minutes. Get going. I want that log on the hearth and the place cleaned up before supper!" Roseland Tutter's warm and low voice was at the pitch that meant business. Tut and Hosea didn't have to be told twice; their passenger schooner Pinky III was secure at dockside and battened down. Pinky number I was equally secure; she was the older of the first two Pinky cargo schooners, the family's bread and butter ships since the early 1800s.

The Tutter ships made a very profitable enterprise, especially with military and civil clients during the very lucrative post-war years. Adam Tutter's access to the Pinky-style ship was through family connections, and the price for each boat was the most he could afford. His father had fished the waters off Maine's coast with his Pinky and was one of the best known fishermen of his time.

Adam was the last of the family. When his father passed away, he was free to leave the cold waters of the north and take his family to the warm shores of Virginia. He sailed Pinkies I, II, and III to his new dock. Before he set out for the life of a fisherman, he modified the hulls by half more in length, outfitted a deck below for increased cargo and passenger capacity, and added ballast for seaworthiness. He found more reliable work hauling cargo and passengers from Providence to Jamestown and points between. Within months, profits told him where his future lie. It wasn't fishing!

In the coming years, when his sons would be experienced sailors, he planned to crew them with ships proper to cargo and passengers. The Pinkies would stay local and the real future of trans-Atlantic shipping would begin with his son's sons. Today, twenty years later, Tut Jr. was ready, as were George and Michael to captain bigger ships.

Over the years their ships were modified as best they could, designed to maximize space, speed and efficiency. Pinky I and Pinky II were more shallow and wide, with easier access to cargo handling; while Pinky III's passengers enjoyed two fireplaces in a weatherproof cargo-type hold connected to a comfortable but very small crew cabin with its own fireplace.

It was the day before Christmas. Pinky III had docked earlier after an overnight trip to Newport and back. As Pinkies go, it was a comfortable ship, and mid-December had a busy passenger schedule. The Tutter fleet would be in lockup until a few days after New Year's.

Christmas holly decorated the passenger side of the wharf where Tut and Hosea searched the fog for their father's ship, or at best to hear Pinkus' bark announcing that the schooner was pointing home.

"Dad's nowhere in sight, Hosea. Let's wait in the shack till he breaks the horizon." Tut loved being with his youngest brother and knew him to be as tough and hard a sailor as any of them. Every Tutter kid had crewed since he could walk.

*

Pinky II was well beyond the horizon with little wind and traces of ice fog blocking out the sun. Pinkus was curled snugly against the leeward side of the mainsail, his tail tight between his legs. In this kind of weather, wind-buffeted sailors might accidentally step too close – a quick lesson Pinkus learned as a puppy just out of dog puberty. Despite the wind and chill, his rusty-colored coat kept him warmer above than in the damp chill below decks. His namesake, "Pinky," sliced precisely south along the Virginia coast.

A hard-left rudder and tight foresail kept the ship's compass on true south. Pinky was a keen ship, and she was at home in the best of gales. Captain Tutter fed her into the Atlantic current's inland push as freezing winds gusted the sail into fluttery ruffles. The compass led the ship south. Suddenly, with a sharp bark, Pinkus raced to the bow and pointed into the wind – he had scented Hosea and Tut, their arms like waving dots on the misty horizon.

As Roseland had commanded, her men had the Yule Log a-center on the hearth in time for supper. It spit and spewed steam that made the smell of old oak mingle with the aroma of wild roasted boar, potatoes, turnips, and spicy meat pies. She looked down the table at her ten men. Food, talk, and warm-mellow mead could not quench the sweet scent of her homemade vanilla candles intertwined with the holly and red ribbons that divided the table. She caught her husband's eye; he winked, she smiled – *This is truly the day the Lord has made*, she thought, *let us rejoice and be glad in it, for we are each wonderfully made*!

As suddenly as that, the great front door swung open and Georgiana and Sally Hunter, billowing dresses, swept into the great room. "Sally has cookies, special for Hosea!" Georgiana laughed. It was as merry and as wholehearted a laugh as the sweet scent of honey-mead steaming on the hearth.

"Mother, they are for the whole family! Mrs. Tutter, none of these men of yours are about to help with cooking, so I decided to add to your Christmas larder." Before her sentence was finished, Hosea was at her side. At that moment, the whole room changed to the happy tenor of lovers meant for each other since birth.

Mrs. Hunter beamed, "We can't stay, our tree is finally opened and there's dinner yet. Please come over later for some of Thaddeus' Christmas wine. It's wonderfully sweet this year!"

"You go ahead, Mother," said Sally, "let me be with Hosea for a while. I have his present. I'll be just 30 minutes?"

"Hosea, you bring her home," Georgiana smiled with such happiness that not a soul could refuse. Lifting her coat and dress, she went to the door, "See all of you later. Merry Christmas!" And she was gone...

Alone by the fire, Sally pulled a small embroidered sack from her dress. "This is for you, my dearest Hosea." She opened the sack and slid its content into his open hand. "Merry Christmas. Please come back to me quickly, and soon." Soft tears moistened her eyes.

"Oh Sally, it's a locket," He opened it, "you inside." He kissed it, then bent into her lips. Holding her gently, he smiled. "We'll be home before next fall. Maybe sooner with lots of gold and great stories."

"Can you take me home now?" She cradled his face in her hands, "Please?" They slipped from the back door just as the first Christmas snow cast the evening into azure blue. The carriage house and stable were only a few yards away.

"I'll get the pony and you get into the small sleigh. You'll be home in a few minutes." His arms encircled her waist to lift her into the sleigh; he sighed, catching his breath at the sight of her so close. Barely regaining his breath, "It's for sure, I ah, we won't need a blanket..." His voice became a whisper, deep and husky with emotion.

"Please, Hosea, hold me closer. So close, please Hosea, closer... I can't bear to let you go away." Their kiss was the fulfillment of all their yearnings, hungrily freezing them into each other... timelessness. He lifted her into the carriage, breathless and unable to stop…

Much later, when all was quiet, Adam Tutter left his bed to take a last look at Santa's bounty and to stoke the fires. It was almost Christmas. The tree was the tallest and most beautiful of any he could recall. He wasn't alone. He could see the long legs of one of his sons in the 'Great Chair' stretched before the fire, white wisps of smoke coming from his clay pipe.

"Hosea! The youngest of my nine Christmas presents! You're up very late. Lots on your mind, son?"

"Merry Christmas, Father." He handed his pipe to his father and reached for another.

This son was different, somehow more the man; it was the way he sat himself, a difference Adam could not define. "Care for a sip of warm port, son?"

Both men sipped and smoked for what seemed a long time. "Thinking of Sally?"

"Yes, Father," he sighed. "She's all I ever think about. I…" His breath caught in a sigh that was satisfied and fulfilled, the kind of sigh only another man would recognize. His smile absently catching the curls of smoke escaping his lips, he inhaled, drawing slowly. "If it weren't for Tut's excitement about our adventure, I'd sure as heck stay home with Sally and crew with you and the guys. I love the sea."

"Your mother and I think it's a good thing that you go. You'll see life in the wild, and when you get home to us and to Sally, you'll want to stay home."

"At first I wasn't convinced that panning for gold made any

sense at all. Everything we will ever need is right here at home."
He paused, "But Tut and I made the decision a long time ago, and
for better or worse, that's that."

"We, all the family, honor your resolve, Hosea. You are true
and trusted men, and no matter what the future brings, this is your
home. Everything you leave behind will always be here for you and
your brothers.

"It isn't every captain whose sons make up a fourth of his
sailors. You have no idea how proud we are of our children. You
and Tut go, my son. Have a very good time. We'll look after Sally.
You bring her back a keepsake of gold. Any plans for a wedding?"

"Thank you, Father. I'll look after Tut. We should be home
before winter, and yes, Sally is ready to announce everything
tomorrow afternoon at Christmas dinner. How I love that woman!"
He ignored the sharpish pain that flashed quickly across his back.
His father didn't see him wince…

*

While the Director and Vice Admiral Brighton waited for
General Rhue, many miles south in Rhode Island a man simply
known as Q stepped aboard the passenger ship Pinky. Dressed as a
dandy, he daintily stepped around and between the passenger hand
luggage to his seat, nearest the helm. His fur hat, held in place with
a black, jeweled pin, matched his full-length, fur-lined cape. He
had the appearance of a man of means, and the mannerisms of a
patrician. Haughtily, he gathered his fur cloak close and sat cross-
legged appraising Captain Tutter. Leaning to the gentleman next
to him, he pursed his lips, "Is that Captain Adam Tutter, himself?"

"Yes," the gentleman replied, "he's not only the owner of the fleet, but he's also our captain."

Q smiled. "Oh, isn't that too excellent!" He took in his breath as though completely satisfied. The affirmative answer was all he needed.

A few yards away George Tutter sat near the door of the small crew cabin. Nothing anyone could say or do dissuaded him from staying close to his father, since Commander Foster's caution that his father might be in danger as a result of the Rhue capture and death. Where his dad went, he went. He took to sleeping outside with the dogs; were they to be disturbed, he wanted to be disturbed.

This departure from Providence was the first passenger run his father had captained since the warning.

George carefully watched each boarding passenger. Pinkus too must have sensed something for he, usually asleep, sat alert by the mainsail. Only three of the passengers could be considered suspect. He'd never seen the like of a dandy. He had heard of effeminate men, but not of their being dangerous; as a consequence, the dandy made him all the more suspicious. The two businessmen traveling together could be more than they appeared to be. The dandy was closest to his father. The best time to attack would be in the confusion at disembarking, unless, of course, the killer had a more refined plan. The fur cloak could easily hide a weapon.

How could an assassin in such a small space use a weapon and not be apprehended immediately? Because of this question, both Garrison Commander Foster and he believed any attempt would be made in a less obvious place. The questions were, where and how?

George watched the dandy study his father with that strange, woman-like smile. More than once he adjusted his hat, toying with the hat pin. Of a sudden, Pinkus got up and walked directly toward the crew cabin, ignoring the passengers. The dandy kept his eyes on the dog. George looked away and made a cluck-sound motioning Pinkus to come. It wouldn't do for the dandy to see that he was watching him. It was this thought that caused George to break into a smile.

Of course! He thought. Of course! The dandy was the assassin. The hat pin. Six inches long. No noise, slipped into his father's heart through his back. No noise. No blood. His father would slump forward. A heart attack or something similar. Oh, you dandy! George smiled as he ruffled Pinkus and scratched his ears. From the corner of his eye, George watched the dandy move as his father walked cross-deck and away from him. George smiled, biting his lower lip. It was time for the man to do something, and as though on cue, the dandy stood and casually strolled to the opposite railing across from his father, the hat pin missing from his hat. With practiced ease, George slipped his knife from his belt. The dandy was an easy fifteen feet away, daintily gaining his sea legs.

Pinkus sensed his stress. He laid flat, his nose toward his master. The dandy knew where to go. A good seaman would know that the captain would soon come to check the port lines. It was then that the grey light of day glanced momentarily on the stiletto-needle of the hat pin. Within a few minutes Captain Tutter crossed to port and leaned forward to adjust a line. George saw the dandy's left arm pull back, and with that, sent his blade flying forward. It plunged deep into the dandy's back.

At the same moment, Adam Tutter flinched forward and froze in space. The dandy fell dead at his feet. Within moments George caught his father and gently slipped the pin from his father's back, barely an inch from his heart.

"Dad! God, Dad! Are you, all right?" Turning to the passengers he yelled for a doctor.

"I think I'm okay Georgie. What in hell happened to me?"

"I saw that dandy pull his hat pin and I knew he was waiting to slam it into your back. I was almost too late!"

"I'm a doctor. You threw your blade into this man's back. We saw you do it. He's dead."

"I know." George began to pull his father's coat off. "He tried to kill my father with this pin. Please take care of my father." George began to tremble. He leaned into his father to brace him as the doctor made his examination. "Will he be okay, doctor? Was I too late?"

"Another half inch and you would be a dead man, Captain. Your son saved your life. Let's get you to the crew cabin."

*

The operative named Q had made his first and most fatal mistake.

It was just a few moments later that Major General Rhue, Vice Admiral Brighton, and the Director were finally together.

"You have been briefed on this tragic situation, General?"

General Rhue sat rigid. He glanced from the passive face of the Vice Admiral to the Director's cold and inquiring frown. He remained silent.

"It was on your advice that I chose your cousin and your

nephews for this mission."

"My family would die before faulting the Queen's trust. How dare my nephews be tried in an American court! We must get to the American Consul and get to the bottom of this immediately, Director."

"I was informed this morning that HRH-W has assessed the facts as he knows them, and we are to safeguard our Directorate at all costs. He realizes the great trauma to your family. In gratitude, he will have you knighted on the occasion of your next visit to London. Also, as of today, you are elevated to the rank of Lieutenant General."

Rhue's face paled. "Then, our name," he gasped deeply, "our name is not dishonored!"

"On the contrary, my good General. HRH-W expresses his praise for your valor."

Vice Admiral Brighton placed his fingertips together, "Congratulations, old boy. It is necessary that all this be put behind us. We are an apolitical force and must remain so. Our operations are dedicated to the security of this Province; by order of His Grace, we exist. HRH-W has a brilliant young mind. The Director is second only to the Prince himself." Settling back, his expression became most serious.

"We have heard that the life of Captain Adam Tutter is in danger. The Duke will have none of it. We see that you have ordered Q to a special mission?"

"He will be recalled, Vice Admiral."

The Director stood, motioning the two to remain seated. "I am the only one with the authority of command and control.

Neither of you, nor anyone else, may usurp my authority. Is that understood? None of our assets are yours to employ or question. Men like Q are prime assets, and they are mine. Now, gentlemen, with this understood, let's retire to my club for lunch…"

CHAPTER 3

ADELAIDE MAGMORTH

Almost legend now, but stories proven true from county records and many family diaries colored the years with the history of early Americans driving west to birth their country. The story of Adam Tutter, Jr. and his youngest brother Hosea began a very different and more dramatic kind of story. Having left home for what they believed would be a brief sojourn to the gold fields of the midwest, it instead became what neither had dreamed in wildest fantasy. Their adventure would have at best netted them a few nuggets to pay for the trip, or perhaps even better, satisfied the lust for adventure young men of their era could not resist.

Hosea's fantasy was to return with enough treasure to build Sally the home of their dreams. Tut's was to add another Pinky schooner to the fleet, a ship to accommodate passengers in luxury from Virginia, north to Providence and south to Charleston.

Dreams are the cornerstone of more than adventure; they are fundamental to curiosity and thus become the mother of invention. Tut was the more curious, Hosea the more inventive. Together, their love for each other proved a future they could never have expected. Their adventure changed everything. It changed families and foundered new futures that birthed more than a new country; it influenced its very foundation, Phoenix-like, but from the flames of death!

*

Their story begins, they say, just weeks into the mountains that opened the eastern country to the nation's western foothills. Both men were exhausted. The day was half gone. It was a freezing and unusually cold evening. Breathing heavily from the cold, Tut and Hosea sat by a fire near the entrance to the old worked-out mine located low in the foothills, just short of the pass that opened west to fertile flatlands.

The men had mined weeks for gold with no luck. Six other men had joined them some days before and all were bone, dog-tired. It was time to abandon the site and move further west; besides, it was out and out the coldest day of the winter. To a man, everyone agreed to close the mine and move on beyond the foothills into the mountains further west. The six latecomers voted to leave Hosea and Tut to re-close the mine and, if they wanted, to join up when they could.

By mid-afternoon Tut and Hosea had the last planks in place to seal the mine's yawning shaft. Passing his water canteen to Tut, Hosea watched his brother drink deeply. "Tut, it's cold and we aren't real tired. Let's go in a few yards and give it a last go! There's still time till dusk and we can seal her up before leaving in the morning. One last whack a few yards down Tut, and we'll go catch up with the boys tomorrow."

Their pickax and hammer slammed into a shallow crevice in a rhythm only miners know. Not but an hour passed when the jolt from hitting into hard rock suddenly gave ease into the feel of softer rock. Again, soft. And again, a thud instead of the crack sound of hard rock. "Holy crap, Hosea, we've got something! Break it apart,

33

let's see what's in there."

"Tut, it's pure gold! Pure and yellow. Look at that! Pure! Tut."
Tut reached in with a knife and scraped a mark – his knife scraped
against yellow!

Then, with hardly a rasp whisper, "Hosea, this *is* gold…"

Both brothers worked the vein with mouths shut and lots of
sweat; small torches worked until muscles gave way to the need for
sleep. For what had to have been a week or two, they worked alone
and hid the gold in a hole hewn from gravel rock a few hundred
yards away.

The nights between days were giddy with plans and grand
ideas of ships and cities. They slept hard, ate hard, and dug harder.
Their spirits akin to what only brothers could share; together they
would make their family happy, rich, and safe forever.

As must happen, the vein of gold gave out to grey, black rock.
They returned after lunch to make last attempts at other fissures.
The mine was completely worked out.

And on this, the last afternoon, and for sure at the hand of
fate, a tremor hit the shaft with a quake-like force that almost buried
them both where they stood. The mountain had decided to keep
them and hide its treasures.

Hosea managed to pull free and crawl-dig his way to sunlight.
With no hesitation and with bloodied hands, he clawed and dug for
Tut. Every second counted! With animal strength, he dug quickly
until he found cloth and again, the mountain shuddered! More than
desperate now, Hosea clawed, leaving blood and nails behind until
Tut's head was free.

Hosea saw no breath. Tut wasn't breathing! "Come on Tut,

please, Tut!" He screamed over and over, "Come on Tut, I'll save you... come on Tut!" Tugging and pushing he finally pulled his brother free, pounced on his mouth, and blew hard, again harder, again harder, he slammed his chest. "You gotta breathe, Tut! Please, Tut... Tut! You gotta... you... oh! Tut, you're breathing. Keep it up. Let's go!" He screamed louder and louder thinking to bring Tut awake.

Feverishly he brushed the dirt from his brother's face. "Oh, keep breathing dear Tut. We're doin' it, breathe, breathe." Carefully, he pulled Tut toward the campfire. He kept talking. "Come on Tut, we made it. Open those big green eyes!"

At last, Tut began to mumble. But Hosea was hurting bad in the chest. He was barely able to pull Tut at all. He gasped for breath, trying not to look in trouble so as not to alarm Tut. The pain stabbed across his back again then subsided as quickly as it'd come, like always. Something only his mother knew about his back pains until he was twelve. As he grew older he was able to hide the flashes. No need to be different from the others.

"Hosea..." Tut's eyes suddenly flashed open. "Hosea, I, ah..."

"Tut, it's okay, we made it! Can you move your legs and arms?" Hosea gently cradled his brother's head. "Looks like we made it, Tut! Must have been some kind of earthquake or shudder. Let me see you move your hands and arms."

Tut grimaced and cautiously sat up. "I think I'm okay. What about you? You're missing a thumbnail! Better see to it. I think I'm okay, let me get to my feet." Shaking a bit, he shook the dirt away and stood. "Need to wash out my mouth. That was a close call!

"Except for your bloodied hands, Hosea, are you all right?"

He stretched to brush more dirt from his brother's chest.

"Take it careful, Tut. You look okay on the outside, but a lot of mountain fell on your chest."

Gingerly rubbing his stomach, Tut grimaced. "All's okay, we'll probably have sore muscles tomorrow." As he spoke, Hosea stiffened. A searing pain slashed across his back with such violence that Hosea collapsed forward into Tut's arms, his chest burning in pain. "Hosea... What is this?" He gasped!

"I'm okay, I get this pain sometimes. It always goes away quick." He gasped again, holding Tut tight. "Hard to breathe, this time I got a lot of pain, Tut. Why is it in my arms?!" His teeth clenched. "It's in my chest now. It always goes away. Too much excitement!" A few heaving gasps and Hosea Tutter collapsed, dead, his eyes dulled and wide open in surprise.

Tut held his brother in disbelief. "My God, Hosea," he whispered, searching his dead brother's dulled eyes. "Oh, God, Hosea, no. You cannot die. Breathe Hosea!" And he squeezed hard to make him breathe, again and again. "Hosea, don't shit around! You can't be dead like this. You're my kid brother! It's family, Hosea. You can't do this. You can't leave me! You can't leave Sally! No, no Hosea... don't be dead." And he burst into rage. "Help, anybody! Help, somebody!" He screamed on and on into the night, refusing to let his brother fall from his arms. He screamed for help, but none was to be had. Lifeless, Hosea hung limp, his back arched like a fallen stag, his blank eyes looking deep into the heavens.

During the night Tut stripped Hosea and scrubbed the mine's filth clean away. He dressed him proper and put him into his bed as though asleep. Done, he kissed him as in goodnight and took up the

pickax and shovel. The grave he dug was deep and big. Fifteen by
fifteen by ten feet, twenty feet down. In furious silence, he carved a
crypt in the loose stone and filled it with the purest of the gold they'd
mined – some he kept. It was Hosea's after all. It was he who had
decided to try the mine again. It was Hosea's gold, it wasn't his. On
top of the crypt, he carved a door with Hosea's name and covered
it with gravel until it was completely hidden. No one could tell that
a crypt lay below the grave. Next, a few feet above and centered
on the crypt he fashioned a vault of wood that completely hid the
first below. The vault was for Hosea, his burial grave, with a coffin
sized for two. One day, he would lie at rest shoulder to shoulder with
his brother, deep within the rock. No gold, nothing to give away
the fortune that slept beneath Hosea. His anger gone, Tut wept like
a child, cradling himself in a crouch, head buried in his knees, a
brother mourned a brother until he slept, exhausted.

The last night at dusk, Tut took parchment from their writing
box and penned two letters. The first he would place in their Bible
and put it directly on top of the gold in the vault, just below their
double coffin. One day in the distant future, family would find it, and
the treasure would be put to use in Hosea's name. The second letter
was to be kept in the same packet that contained his will. It would
be read only by an heir if the family found itself in dire difficulty;
if not, then 200 years hence on August 4, 2022. He wrote:

> *Beneath my dear and most loved brother Hosea's coffin
> is a sealed crypt, carved from stone. His name is engraved
> on its door. A copy of this will lies within a Bible, just
> inside the crypt.*

I divided all of the gold we mined — one-third I take with me; Hosea's gold is with him in his crypt. Sally Hunter was to be my brother's wife. This gold is for her descendants, for her direct heirs, and no one else!

I am responsible for my dear brother Hosea's death! I love him so, so very much.

This century is a difficult one with few to trust, and so I have delayed making known this treasure, prayerfully hoping that a new generation will honor this will, as my dear Hosea's bequest.

Signed: Adam Tutter, Jr. — Hosea's Brother

This 4th day in August 1822

Finally, with morning gone, the time came to say goodbye. But, how could he do it alone? Hosea lay pale and young, so sleep-like. No one to mourn, no mother or father here to caress their son. Eight brothers not here to mourn; to yearn for the life of their little brother! And Sally. "You, of all of us, should be here," he wept. "I killed him. I took him from you, from everybody. Me, I wanted a last adventure before he grew up. Hosea, I should have died, not you. You, you in all your pain, you saved my life." Tut fell to his knees and across his brother's body. "Oh God," he prayed, "can you take me instead? Pour my life and spirit into him?" He grasped his brother with fierce passion. "Instead, take me, Lord. They will all wish me to have died, not him!"

Fingers almost frozen, Tut placed Hosea's bedroll on the right side of the coffin, then returning to the tent, he carefully carried Hosea deep into the earth and wrapped him in the bedroll. He then placed the second letter in the Bible, wrapped it in oilskin and placed it on his brother's chest. Next, and with a lingering look at his brother, he pulled the coffin's cover closed and carefully wiped any trace that the door to the vault below existed.

Broken in grief, Tut climbed out of the crypt and spent the rest of the day returning the soil he'd dug away until a gentle mound remained. He then littered the area until it blended in to forest floor around the camp.

The grave was a few hundred feet from the mine, a goodly distance from the main shaft. Then Tut rolled a stone to mark the place. Passers-by would see the grave and never dream what lay hidden below.

*

It was not a Tutter thing to do, to run away. He had to face his family, to take the blame and disgrace he deserved. His family would judge him, and whatever that judgment was, he would carry it and live his life for Hosea.

He hid his share of the gold well inside a cave and carried as much as he could in his saddlebags. It took but a few days to find a town with a land office and a bank. His lusty smile and tough appearance made everyone in town believe he'd struck river gold up north. The mine had not been staked so he filed for title ownership along with title to 2,200 square miles of contiguous land. He also purchased a small homestead just out of town.

With papers in hand, signed and sealed, he placed them in the bank's care with what all thought to be the remainder of his gold strike. He deposited a goodly amount, enough to mark him as a man due respect. Taking four copies, he mailed two copies to his father, one to the Land Offices in Washington, D.C., and the other he kept secured in his homestead.

No one in the town's environs could tell Tut the age of the homestead he'd bought. Some thought it was one of the earliest places built before the town settled a mile or so west. It was a plain house of logs and mortar. Two smaller rooms faced out from the great room, its fireplace more than adequate – the length of two men, and taller than Tut by a few feet. The foundation, built of solid rock and heavy mortar, was a food and milk cellar, with its own milk and butter well, and had ample storage space for more than enough seasonal food stores.

Tut sat on the staircase and took in all the possibilities. A family, the size of his own, could survive the worst that any winter could deal out!

The barn was more unique than Tut could have planned in his best dreams! It was twice again the size of the house, constructed of rough-hewn wood plank walls, braced with massive logs of the same oak used for the house. The barn's loft was secure enough for overnight travelers, as well as to provide for livestock feed. A livestock birthing stall with its own well and fireplace took up the rear of the ground floor. Tut stood, amazed. Stored laterally to the tack room he counted three logger wagon frames, probably the same ones used to haul the logs that built the house and barn.

He looked for the wheels; sure enough, twelve huge steel-rimmed wheels were safely stored in the loft. Setting pulley, tackle and line in place, he lowered one to the ground floor, ideas flashing through his mind almost faster than he was able to think.

As the sun set, Tut went to the birthing stall and filled the iron feed trough with fresh, clear water from the well. Stripped down, he relaxed in the coldest bath he'd had since mountain streams. Finally, dried and exhausted, he pushed some straw by the fireplace and slept. Some hours later he woke and looked into the light of a new moon just crossing the open transom above the loft doors.

Oh God, he thought, how many of us are looking at this same moon? You see and know all about us. Hosea is with You, God. For sure that is true. There is much for me to do in Your name and in his memory. You have given me great means and my path looks clear. I know how to haul cargo. Is there a difference Lord, between doing it with a ship and with a flatbed? I don't see any difference. I've smelted lead to repair ship's seals and build worthy anchors. Won't be as easy to smelt gold. And Lord, how hard will it be to build false floors in my logging wagons?

Tut smiled at God and to the moon, and again fell deep into sleep.

By the following evening he had fitted two of the flatbed wagons with false floors; within each he fashioned small storage spaces lined with straw. Once the storage spaces were filled snuggly with gold, he would replace the flooring – hidden and secure.

For the next ten days, he secretly carried his share of the gold to the barn from the cave he had prepared inside the old mineshaft. Well after midnight and before early dawn, he used the birthing room trough to smelt the gold into one-inch thick bars, five by ten-inches. As soon as the bars were cooled, he placed them in the wagon's false floors, snuggled them with straw to ensure no space for movement, and inserted the old wagon floorboards over the gold. It took all three full wagons to store all the gold he owned.

At last, he refitted the wagons and completely rebuilt and installed their huge wheels. Finally, Tut made sure each wagon was safe enough to haul the heaviest of cargo.

The eight draft horses he'd ordered through the bank's agent arrived the following week.

"Fine horses, Mr. Tutter. Bank says yer gonna haul some lumber to your place back east. You be lookin' for some help, Mr. Tutter?"

"Yes sir, I am! I need an expert handler who knows these horses. A lot of horsepower for one man to handle."

"Yep. Deliverin'em here is one thing, workin'em as a team is another!" He put out his hand, "I'm Art. Arthur Thomas. Be thirty-five or some come this summer, don't know exactly," he grunted softly. "I know farmin' and I'm a smithy; my lady, she works cleanin' at the hotel cross from the bank."

Tut smiled, "You work directly for the bank?"

"Sure do. Agent. I do heavy stuff, deliverin', keepin' up the buildin', no paperwork, sometimes wittnessin'. It's honest work, Mr. Tutter. My lady and I don't mind workin'. It's what the Lord settled us here ta do."

Tut felt honest strength in his handshake. "When I get back, maybe we can work something out. Where did you say the horses come from, far from here?"

"Two days ride north, a bit west, foothills. Magmorth Farm. Easy to find. They been raisin' fine draft horses long back as I can recall."

*

A little after noon on the second day, Tut entered the sturdy gates of Magmorth. The spread was clean, well-wooded, and fenced into pasture grids. Two brown painted barns outlined the ranch house centered between them. He rode to the house and tied up where the drive widened before the side entrance. It was a prosperous house. Low and broad, it may have seen two generations.

"Hello! Be with you in a few minutes." A woman's voice, called from his left.

Tut turned toward the far barn and waved an answering doff of his hat in acknowledgment. Surprised, he found himself suddenly absorbed in what he saw. The woman was downright beautiful! Her walk, her gait, athletic and yet wonderfully feminine. Probably his own age.

"Hello, I'm Adelaide Magmorth and this is my ranch manager. What can we do for ya?"

"I'm Adam Tutter, I…"

"Mr. Tutter, you bought all my horses! All of them! Where are they? You keeping 'em all together?"

"Call me Tut." He reached out his hand to take hers. "Yes and yes, a few days southeast of here to my farm. They are brute big!" He laughed. "I need help in managing them."

"I'm Addie. Lunch is ready, let's go inside eat and talk. This is wonderful. I need to know how my children are doing far away from home!" As his horse was led away, he followed Addie into the house.

So taken with her charm and beauty, Tut said barely a memorable word until they sat at table. Finally in control,

"Mrs. Magmorth, ah…"

"It's Miss Magmorth and call me Addie, please, Tut."
She reached and touched his hand. Tell me about the work my,
ah, your horses will be doing."

Her touch was like nothing Tut had ever experienced. His
voice suddenly became thick and dropped an octave. Her eyes, the
greenest he'd ever seen, the warmth of her closeness, all had him
in a state he never experienced before. His throat was unbearably
dry! "Ahem," he coughed. He vowed almost aloud that he would
die before he'd move his hand away. "Ahem," he cleared his throat
successfully. "I plan to move some western oak to my father's place
on the coast, spend a few weeks there and get back home again."

"Western oak is hard wood, browner, a bit honey-colored.
It makes lovely furniture." She had not moved her hand from his.

"Actually, I'm a sailor. I've sailed schooners with my family
since I can remember. We're shippers." He lowered his head as
memories too hard to bear began to form. He pushed them away.
"And, it's time for me to leave that life behind." His eyes returned
to hers, so indelibly green, almost hypnotic to him. Knowing her for
only a short time didn't make any… sense… The intimacy of her
hand on his opened a floodgate. For some reason, he couldn't stop
what he was about to say. "It's more than that, it's more than that."
He looked away, "I lost our brother Hosea in a mining accident a
few weeks ago. I ah, I have to go home and be with the family for a
while." A tear almost escaped, he swallowed hard and returned to
Addie's warm empathy. He forced a smile

"I am so very sorry, Adam. So sorry."

Of a sudden, his feelings rushed back with such fierce pain that he choked a sob. "I killed him! Had I not wanted an adventure, he'd be okay today. I took him away from us and now I have to go home and take the consequences. My little brother is dead because of me." He could not control the tears.

Addie knew the moment she saw this beautiful and perfectly formed man approach her home that something out of her control was happening. The longer she touched his hand, the deeper her awareness of him grew. His face, now in tears, was not at all like that of a youth, but of a man of integrity, of a man loyal to family, a man of traditions. At that moment Addie knew she was completely in love.

She clenched his hand tightly. "I know how you feel Adam. I know how you feel. My father passed away, just after my mother. Since last February I've been alone." Tears fell. "His father, my father and I worked this farm. It's as if… Adam, as if everything I've ever known all of a sudden disappeared within moments. The farm is no longer mine." Addie sat upright and tried to put on a look of confidence. "My family will be here in a few days to take over the ranch." Her sigh was as deep and as profound as his. She continued, "I'm not the direct heir. My father's brother is. He breeds cattle."

"My God," Tut leaned as close as he could, "my God Addie, I'm so sorry. Is that why you sold your horses?"

"Yes. When my uncle comes, I'll go east and find a future." Her smile was forced, her head bent forward, searching his eyes. "And you, Adam, do you have somebody?"

"No, no, just me. Two peas in a pod, huh?" He could not take his eyes from hers, her hand still atop his. "No, just me. I have a little income. I have a farm a few days south of here. I found a couple to work it until I return. It's the bank agent who came for your horses; remember him? His wife cooks and takes care of the house and he works the farm. I made them a lifelong offer they didn't want to turn down." His tears turned to a broad smile.

"By the way, you know that our relationship cannot end any time soon. You are the first one ever to call me 'Adam' since my mother did when I was a boy!" In a low, throaty whisper he added, "and, please don't ever stop." His face could no longer hide his emotions.

Addie took a deep breath, "There is only one person those horses trust enough to do what you want them to do in the time you need them to do it," Her emotions as readable as his, "and that's me!"

"What?" Tut sat up surprised! "You want to do... that means..."

"I know what it means. Tonight they will begin to pack my landau and a few hours after my uncle gets here, we – you and me – are heading south. And we're taking a pack of herding horses with us!"

No one took note of logging wagons leaving the Riverside Sawmill. The tarpaulins, lashed over tons of raw lumber planking, more than protected the real cargo hidden beneath their floors. Nor was it apparent that the four-in-hand lead driver was a woman, a driver with more experience than most. The weather was chilly with showers, and the same weather expected for the three-week journey ahead.

They slept as men would, under the lead wagon, surrounded by the warmth of the horses. It was late when they stopped and early when they started again. Guns were always close, but better still was the peace horses kept when danger did not disturb their safety. The first night out was not in the least awkward. Their happiness made the intense attraction each had for the other a sweet contentment; for they knew, no matter what, they would always be together! A few feet from each other they said good night; then, as when he was alone with Hosea, Tut prayed: "Heavenly Lord, send your angels to protect us this night. Keep all evil from us and forgive us any transgressions of this day. We seek your blessings, and protect us on our journey... sleep well, my dearest Addie."

"Amen, Adam, my sweetest Adam..." As these quiet words of peace were said, a blanket of comfort cooled their passions and brought them to the sleep of innocence, akin to the sleep he always knew at home; just as he had slept protecting young Hosea. Hearing Tut breathe deeply into sleep, Addie experienced a balm-like peace she'd, to this time, never before known. She also knew that this man, so close, would protect her always. So overwhelmed was she in peace that in her heart, Tut's prayer made them, as of that moment, a family. Always to be one. Always her Adam, always together. And Addie slipped into the deepest sleep she had ever experienced...

From that night on Addie and Tut's sleep was never disturbed. During the weeks that passed they grew closer and soon felt that each had known the other all their lives. Though intimacy was always a part of their thoughts, a mutual sense forbade them, reasoning that nothing must disturb their good fortune. The time would come when God and family would give their consent.

On the last night, when the horses were secure, elation kept them awake. Addie whispered, "Adam, will the shipyard need more wood than what we have to build your new schooner?"

"A lot more Addie, this is only enough to frame it. They'll need lots more, and different kinds of wood. Once we've off-loaded the lumber, we'll drive to the bank-side of town, to the delivery doors of the three banks. I don't think they've ever seen deposits like the ones we will make tomorrow. Deposits they've never dreamed of! One third of our load goes into each of the three banks. They will do the rest. How they will do that, I suppose, is the same way the bank did back home. After that, we drive to my father's house."

"Your house, Adam. It's your family. Please don't think of it differently until there is reason to. Your family has lost one son, not two. If they are anything like their son, you, my dearest Adam, they will never want you to leave them."

Tut's smile was one of sad longing. "Maybe, for sure, maybe... someday."

*

Pinkus was unmanageable! His bark, for at least half an hour, was constant and getting hoarse. Pointing toward town, he scratched the pier, yapping in excited desperation. He could smell his Tut a mile or more away and he refused to be quieted! Before he could be leashed, he pulled away, crossed the shipyard and ran until he was out of sight.

Roseland and Adam stood stark and breathless. They too sensed Tut was home. "Oh Adam, please pray that it's our son!" She whispered, "Oh Tut, my little Adam!"

Her husband pulled her closer. "It has to be him, Pinkus knows. Besides, I don't hear him barking anymore." His voice was that of a man desperate with hope. "It has to be our son. Please God. It has to be."

As they prayed, a strange parade began to form in the distance. Pinkus, slow and breathing hard, was first, leading what had to be a huge wagon, the biggest they'd seen. No, there were two wagons! Two four-in-hand wagons. The horses were huge. The horses were dancing! And it was Tut.

Filled with joy and tears they swept their son into their arms. No one could make sense of anything that was said to the other. They wept and laughed at the same time. "Oh Tut," his father held his face in his hands. "My son, my son! Your mother and I have searched for you every minute of the day and night after your letter about Hosea."

Roseland pulled her son from his father and as stern as ice laid into him. "Adam! You and you father and every one of my sons is cut from the same stubborn cloth." She held him by the arms with a vice grip. "Don't interrupt! Were the shoe on a different foot, each of you would blame himself for what happened to Hosea. But," she released her grip, "I knew my youngest son's heart would give him but a short life. He didn't know, but I could feel every pain he endured. When he was born he had no breath in him for the longest time. We were so frightened. And, almost as worrisome, was the fact that unlike every male child born in the Tutter line, until the age of twelve, Hosea never stuttered! You remember."

"Mother, I…"

"I said, don't interrupt!" She kissed his cheek, "when you both decided to make your trip west, I knew it could be his last. But it was his decision. Your father and I have always helped our sons live their good decisions… We love you so very much, Adam. Welcome… welcome home my Adam."

"And Sally?" Tut asked, "what about Sally?"

Roseland, brushing her dress as though to collect herself, answered, "She and her parents have gone to their home near Boston. Sally, like Hosea, was more fragile than anyone thought. It was a few days before she would see anyone. Your father and I went to visit once she was strong enough. They left last week for the summer. So many things remind her of Hosea. It will take a very long time, probably a year before they return."

Adam Tutter held Tut close for a long moment. "Welcome home, son. These are sad times, but life has a way of mending us all. Each day, God expects us to carry on as best we can. Sally will be home when she's ready. Your mother is right about we Tutter men. Guilt seems to enjoy our company; we can certainly wallow in it.

"By the way, you plan to introduce us to the fellow drivin' your second wagon? He handles those horses like they're kittens!"

Pulling her hat from her head Addie leapt to the ground, her auburn hair bunched around her smile, making her tanned face beautiful and fresh.

"I am Adelaide Magmorth. I'm a horse woman and I love your son!" And she ran into Tut's open arms.

At 1:00 PM on Saturday, April 5, 1823, Adam Tutter, Jr. married Adelaide Magmorth at Saint John's church. The bride's family came all the way from Boston and New York to fill almost half the church; the Tutters and neighbors filled every other seat.

A few weeks before the wedding, Adam asked his son about

the best man. "Who have you chosen son?"

Tut smiled in mock surprise, "Why, my best friend, of course. Who else?"

"And which of your seven brothers is the lucky man?" His father asked.

"Not one of my brothers. It's you, Dad, you are my best friend. You are the only man I have ever loved. Will you do me the honor of being my best man?"

"Oh, Tut," his strong jaw clenched in fierce pride, "next to your mother agreeing to marry me, plus the birth of my sons, I'm at a loss. Tut, I am honored to accept, truly honored."

At the same time that Tut was with his father, Addie found Roseland in her sitting room. When she'd learned that her son had proposed, Roseland insisted that Addie call her 'Mother.'

"Mother, I have a small gift for you." Addie held out a small package. It was in a simple wrap and inside was an alabaster casket, carved in rosettes with the most intricate pattern work Roseland had ever seen.

"Is this for me, Addie? I've never seen anything so small and so perfectly lovely. It's beautiful!"

"Gently press the flower, center top." Addie pointed to the place.

Immediately, the casket began to slowly open, as though controlled by secret springs. Fully opened, a leather pouch, the same cream color as the casket, lay carefully held in the center. Roseland, gently at first, then with excited exaggeration, opened the pouch and gasped.

"Good Lord, Addie, it's… it's the biggest pearl I've ever seen! It's magnificent. I've never seen anything like this. It is absolutely stunning."

Addie smiled, "It was my mother's."

"Addie, this will match your dress to perfection. It's the same color. It is simply beautiful."

"It's not for me to wear. It's the focus of tradition among the women in the Magmorth family, and has been since the fifteenth century. The bride's maid of honor is to wear it. She is to keep it and pass it on to the next generation's first bride's maid of honor. And on and on, generation after generation. The pearl is a symbol of unity shared with the women of our family. Family unity, unbroken. To be handed down personally by each bride to the next.

"Mother, I have come to love you as my own mother, would you consent to be my maid of honor?"

"Oh, Addie. Oh my Lord. I would be so honored…" A thread-like platinum chain lay beneath the pearl. Addie picked it up and placed it around Roseland's neck. And they both wept, holding each other.

On Sunday, following an enormous reception breakfast, the bride and groom left by carriage from the dock, just as they'd arrived. Pinkus had no intention of leaving with them – the wheeled thing was not his ship!

The following week, armed with unsigned promissory notes, Tut deposited a copy of his claim along with the purchase receipts of the 2,200 square miles of land he'd purchased. His rather large gift to the U.S. Treasurer, together with signed documents citing that his property would always be open to settlers, assured the property was officially titled Hosea County. Governance would be in accordance with the laws of all counties within the state and its territory.

The horses sensed home two days away. On the last night out, the Tutters feasted on open-fire oven bread, roasted wild mushrooms, and roast trout caught from the nearby stream. Neither was tired. Tut laid on his back, head resting on his folded hands, Addie curled snuggly into his shoulder.

Tut caught sight of the new moon as it crossed the open space in the wagon bed above. He remembered his prayer of months ago when he'd laid his audacious plan before God.

"Addie," he whispered. "This is a God-filled night. A few nights before we met I prayed under this same moon. God has been so good to us! There is a future for us with much to do."

"Indeed," Addie replied. "This is truly a night the Lord had made, let us rejoice and be glad in it."

"Amen!" Adam smiled, and pulled her closer... They did not sleep that night...

*

The four-horse carriage drove onto the pier at precisely 10 AM, thirty minutes before the day's Pinky ship departure to Providence. Sleek, black leather, brass trim and pristine, the coach made its clean circle stop in front of Adam and Roseland Tutter standing in the company of Commander Foster and most of the Tutter family. Commander Foster had set up the appointment, while at the same time booked passage for two VIPs to Providence. Foster's embellishment of the VIPs was such that no one knew what to expect. The family was too curious to miss anything of such importance.

As the carriage came to a stop, a footman had already leaped from his front seat and opened the passenger door. As quickly, a middle-aged man of good fashion stepped from the running board with his hand extended, and before anyone had time to say anything: "You must be Mrs. Tutter!" He took her hand in his and raised it just short of his lips. "I'm Martin Princeton. This is my escort, Captain George of the Royal Navy." The Captain bowed slightly and tucked his hat under his left elbow. "My great pleasure, ma'am."

"You are very welcome, gentlemen. Do you have time for tea before meeting with my husband?" As she was speaking, Mr. Princeton already was clutching Adam Tutter's hand.

"You are very kind, Mrs. Tutter. Captain George and I had tea less than an hour ago. Thank you."

"In any event, Mr. Princeton," Adam suggested, "let's go into my home for a while. I'm sure that you must refresh."

Roseland interrupted. "Since there will be no tea, I will leave you gentleman to your business. I am happy to meet you both." Turning to Commander Foster, "My sons must make ready to sail. Your invitation was to meet our son George as well?"

Moments later Adam Tutter, his son George, Captain George, Commander Foster and Mr. Princeton were seated in the study, the door closed purposely by Mr. Princeton. Taking a letter from his jacket, he handed it to Adam.

"As you see, Captain Tutter, it is dated two days ago and signed by President Ulysses Grant. In short, the President supports our enterprise as does His Grace, the Prince of Wales, who is also mentioned jointly by the President." He watched Adam read.

"This letter is addressed to both my son George and to Commander Foster."

"The content of this letter, along with what I am about to tell you, is considered most secret. I must ask you gentlemen to agree to this secrecy?"

"If my son and Commander Foster agree, I certainly do." He looked at them. Both men were flushed with excitement.

Commander Foster was first to agree. "I am always at the order of my President. Of course I agree! I am amazed that you gentlemen know we exist."

"Oh, we do, gentlemen." Captain George looked at George Tutter, "We do! Q was our best and most experienced agent. You…"

George Tutter interrupted, "Experienced shit! This Q lady, as you call him, tried to kill my father…" Adam Tutter touched his son's arm.

"Q could outfox anyone, in any disguise, in any situation." Princeton smiled broadly. "But not against you, George Tutter. You outwitted him. Q, as with all of us, lived with our risks. You also took a great risk in fighting for your schooner. General Grant admires your way with a knife. So do we. Well done, Mr. Tutter. Can you now consent to our secrecy?"

"Yes, Mr. Princeton. What do you want of Commander Foster and me?"

Captain George spoke. "We are an independent apolitical secret service organization. We have been operating in Canada for the past dozen years or so. The genesis of this organization is the idea and financial charge of the Duke of Wales.

"President Jackson, and now President Grant, want a brother

organization here in the U.S. so that both our countries can act collaterally when necessary. Our purpose and identity is known only to our Director, the President of the United States and the Duke of Wales... we Canadians act only on apolitical orders from our Duke just as you Americans act on apolitical orders from your President."

"And my task, gentleman," Princeton spoke, "is to enlist both Mr. George Tutter and Commander Foster to work directly for President Grant. To form our brother organization in Washington." Looking at Captain Tutter he concluded, "I don't want to go anywhere with this, Captain Tutter, if you do not fully support your son, should he agree to join us."

Adam had been watching Georgie carefully throughout. His son's excitement was identical to Foster's broad grin. "I will always support the decisions our sons make. George and his brothers are the truth of our family. Their mother and I will always respect their independence."

"We are about to sail, are we not, Captain? By the time we reach Providence, I hope that the President of the United States will have his own team..."

George Tutter interrupted, his smile a little twisted in irony, "This Q person, is this, is this an example of your work?"

"Yes, it is, Mr. Tutter, let me explain. Until a few months ago our agents acted under the Intelligence Command. The three men your Virginia courts hung as pirates were on a mission to New Orleans. It was successful; however, the three your father captured had gone rogue and tried to hijack your ship. As it happened, two of the deceased were nephews of our General Rhue, a member our

Intelligence. On his own, he ordered Mr. Q to retaliate. When we'd learned what he'd done, it was too late to call off Q. As of that time, all our agents now react only to one person, the 'Director,' a man appointed by our Prince. Q had a two-fold mission that day: exposing an enemy agent, an actor, in Providence (approved by the White House), and then to avenge General Rhue. None of this will ever happen again. By the way, Mr. Tutter, our Mr. Q was a very close friend. A man's man, his skills were especially unique – a replacement will be extremely difficult. Perhaps you, Mr. Tutter, or you, Captain Foster, may qualify to be your president's Mr. Q."

George and Foster were first to the schooner. They both sensed the enormity of their new adventure. A new beginning!

CHAPTER 4

JUDGE ADELAIDE TUTTER

Judge Adelaide Tutter locked the heavy oak door to her courthouse chambers and left through the private exit convenient and secure to the few who had keys. She walked to the side lot and then up toward the path that led home. The late afternoon breeze from the west always had a scent of hickory from the trees that guarded the mountain hills way out beyond the river. Most everyone fondly called her Addie, because to native Tutterville citizens she was a living symbol of their history. School children watched her with curious interest.

Her great-grandfather, almost three times removed, with no other force or power than himself founded every last foot of the Tutterville towns. As if to reign over all he'd founded, generations of Superior Court Judge Tutters replaced one after the other – a few appointed in the early days, the others elected during the past three generations. The people loved their Judge. They loved the romance that clung close to the Tutter fame. Book after book had been written about their founding horsewoman, and the golden touch of her lover, Adam Tutter. Not only did the two of them generate wealth and power; they did it themselves. They tilled, they mined, they hauled freight, and they did whatever their neighbors needed of them. In return, they were loved. They built schools, roads, and municipal parks; they built the finest hospital that today is as timely as the best. Young Adam Tutter wanted his children safely born!

Their first child came so quickly that it was delivered in the barn's birthing room stall. Well into her ninth month their baby decided she wanted daylight *now*. Mrs. Thomas, their cook and also the best midwife around, arrived in time to cut the umbilical cord. Not so for the next eight children. Their coming was a chore, each one!

The family cemetery included the Tutter Mine in the foothills beyond West Tutterville. In its center stood a huge and perfectly square rock. Pristine simplicity and peace drew people to it, as did its history and too, most families from the Tuttervilles found their final rest in the various sections of the park.

In simple golden letters only one name was inscribed and centered on each side of the great rock: Hosea. The founder of their county. The founder who inspired his brother-founder to build cities and farms; the founder of what everyone now called home.

The municipal shrine was open to the public at certain times of the day. Visitors could actually walk down a broad and beautifully designed staircase into the tomb below the huge rock. Inside and on a low pedestal, rested a simple sarcophagus, a seamless grave for three: the first from the entrance lay Adam Tutter, Jr.; in the center, Hosea Tutter; and in the third place lay Adelaide Magmorth Tutter. They slept shoulder to shoulder forever.

The story of Hosea Tutter became everyone's story. The hero idol who gave himself to save his brother, a story of a brother's love so great that it reminded others of their own courage, that deep inside courage that thrives on responsibility, selflessness, and dignity. The Tutter blood, they claimed, mingled in everyone's veins throughout his county, their county.

School children came to see this monument dedicated to love.

Families sought burial there as a sharing in bravery and daring. Simply said, 'if you lived in the Tuttervilles, you had to be part Tutter!'

To those who came before her court, Addie was always referred to simply as "Judge." She was the last of the Adam Tutter line, the end of five generations.

Addie crossed the street and began her way home. The day was far from over. The city planners had their first meeting of the year at eight. In ten minutes she would be home, just time to shake her mind free of work and wait for the first aroma of Miss Lilly's cooking. The house was the Tutter home since the first Tutters settled the town in 1822; rambling and shuttered, it had the look of old settler's times. It was very sturdy, and built to serve its generations. Addie's bedroom was adjacent to the kitchen on the original two-room foundation – now twelve rooms and seven fireplaces. Just off her bedroom was the family parlor, big and warm, with the patina of tough times: of rugged founders, scars from skates and toys, and the stuff from happy children of the past.

Her will left the property to the county for use as a public library to be named after her family. As far as she could see, though she was the last, she'd marry, and the family would continue.

Tonight's meeting was all about the County Fair, the biggest celebration the Tuttervilles had, and Addie was co-chair. The fair began back in the late 1800s, on the weekend closest to June eighth, the incorporation day of the county and its townships.

Miss Lilly had just placed the soup on the table. Hearing the door unlatch she called, "Addie! Hi. I'm told you had no lunch today. You're only ten minutes from there to here!" Lilly had been with the family long before Addie was born. She was her nurse and now, literally her keeper. So much did they love each other that as Addie closed the door, she mouthed every word Lilly'd said. Lilly knew everything, Lilly remembered everything, and her curiosity was legendary. You could never tell the woman a fib or exaggerate; if you did, her lower lip would curve like her eyebrows. If one were in or near trouble, it was best to avoid Lilly at every cost.

Addie kissed her on the cheek and enjoyed the solid hug she got in return. Cooling the soup with a breath, she looked toward the kitchen, "Was today the big day at the Botanical Gardens? Get any good cuttings?"

"That zoo is unbelievable, so many visitors! I was surprised to be the only one in the Botanical Gardens. Except... there was a lovely couple visiting with one of the keepers. Not interested in plants. I wonder why they were there?" She queried inquisitively. "Yes, I did. I have a strangely lovely chute from their only Chinese Elm bonsai."

"I love Elm bonsais – feathery, aren't they? Anything else? Had you seen the couple before?"

"Yes, dear, just a few shoots of a long-leafed Drynaria rigidula white. No, not the woman..." Lilly held her spoon to her lips. "Not the woman..." She hesitated. "But the man, very attractive, a businessman from near here, I think. Not her, lovely figure. Don't know her." She elongated her last word, as she did when things were curious.

*

Earlier in the morning, a graceful commuter jet swept low

and inside the hills west of Tutterville. It was scheduled to land before eight, in time for Ussie Rhue to become Ussie Willow, and change for work at the Fox Glove Inn. She wasn't scheduled for duty for another twelve hours, but much had to be done before noon.

Ussie tightened her seatbelt; her smile almost a laugh. Well-proportioned and quite beautiful, her face gave way to lines that betrayed little to no emotion. Almost the stare of a psychotic – vacant yet intensely interested. Her smile was always calculated, as if to keep prey aware of the fringes of tragedy, but more than that, it anesthetized the beginnings of suspicion.

For the past few days all she could think about was the incredible plan they'd pieced together. Precise, timed to the minute, like a puzzle to a faultless picture. Piece by piece, the plan was intricate and daring; best of all, it was all hers to activate. Yes, and a mystery. Why was her best friend so interested, as though she were the one with most to gain? Dianna, the goddess of women and the goddess of the hunt. Dianna the political. Was there a political end to this adventure, had Ussie missed that part of the equation?

Money. Lots of money; money is the goddess's endgame. Political? Maybe… after all, money and politics look to similar ends. Ussie laughed almost aloud. Dianna was the dearest and closest friend she'd ever had. To the goddess, everything was easy. Dianna's artistry found its elegance in simplicity. Danger was the greatest of her fixations. "What," she'd said, "was a life or two when so much was to be gained?"

Vengeance! More vengeance, and lots of money! Money that was by right hers to begin with. Her side, the Rhue branch of the family, inherited a pirate's hanging; Merryweather Williamsburgh's side, the money. Poor, sweet, old maid Merry. Never too late to undo injustice; but then, there was so much more to it than that. And, the weapon – oh, how perfect! Ussie was giddy with lust.

*

Miss Lilly fluffed up the 'Great Chair' by the fireplace and insisted Addie relax with the paper before leaving together for the meeting. "Oh my!" She said aloud. "That was Happy! And, that was not his wife…"

"What… who?" Addie asked absently.

"The woman at the zoo, dear."

At eight o'clock Addie was in her seat ready for the kick-off meeting. She sat in the jury box with the five Town Selectmen, leaving the most prominent place to Doc Harry Hendricks, this year's Fair Chairman. Addie was familiar with most who came into the room, folks nicely representing the five towns: Tutterville Falls, North Tutterville, West Tutterville, East Tutterville, and Tutterville City, the County Seat. What would have been South Tutterville was a vast county complex of sports fields: Hosea Stadium, the swim creek and of course, the huge County Fair fields of display barns and game fields. Hosea Stadium was host to all the schools as well as the University itself.

The committees were traditional. Chairmanships passed from one generation to the next, and thank goodness for that, because nobody ever wanted to volunteer for the work involved. Instead, families volunteered for whatever seemed best and more interesting for them at the time.

Lots of weddings found their origin as a result of the annual fair, as did many birthdays in common (they say) – these babies alone were tradition enough!

Addie couldn't keep her eyes from Harry Hendricks. He was tall, not at all lanky, but solid and completely his own man. He was also the County Coroner in his off-time, and consequently a frequent witness before her in court. Handsome? She smiled. Definitely. Since grade school. Of a sudden he turned to look at her with that 'all's okay' smile. In a few weeks, they must make a very big decision…

Picking up the agenda from the table, Doc Hendricks brought silence with a slam of the gavel. After opening amenities, he recognized a citizen whose hand was always first for recognition. As he recalled, she never had a positive word – maybe this time… With his best bedside smile, he began, "The Chair recognizes Millicent Grove."

Hair tucked behind her ears, her eyes close-set under level eyebrows, and comfortably dressed in a bulky jacket, she stood adjusting her hair. "Ahem." She cleared her voice, looking to be sure she had the room's attention. "This has never been brought up at any meeting to my recollection, Doctor Hendricks, and I've been here as long as you have. There are lots of folk in the county who just won't pull their fair share to help us. Ahem. And, I believe they should. We all work weekdays, most on weekends, but those of us here all give to make the fair a success. Religious issues notwithstanding, I have an idea that might inspire everyone in the county to join in the work." With that she pulled her head aloft quite imperially. "An incentive program!" She paused, folded her arms at her waist, and to the surprise of everyone in the room, she actually smiled.

"Why Ms. Grove, please continue."

"My cousin works in a metal and die shop over on Conure Street, you know... Smitty Die? Well, she and Smitty have made a commemorative medallion. It was my idea, of course." Her cheeks pinched with a faint flush. "The size of the medallion would equate to the number of hours a volunteer worked. That, with a certificate, would be awarded at the Ball. If the Committee agrees with the plan, the certificates, design, and production of the first 100 medallions will be at no cost. Ahem..."

Ms. Grove quickly sat down, eyes straight at Harry, obviously a little embarrassed.

Harry, sensing a first for this heretofore quiet, almost spinster woman, put on the best smile he could muster. "Millicent, we've never done anything like that before. I think it's a fine idea. In fact, it would be great were you to chair a committee to set up a commemorative program. Would you agree?"

Millicent Grove nodded approval.

"Ms. Grove, thank you." Turning to his committee, "Approve? Looks like yes, Ms. Grove. Congratulations!"

"May I add something to the project?" A woman, just behind Ms. Grove stood. "I'm Merryweather Williamsburgh and I'm from Canada. I visit quite often, especially for your extraordinary fair. I wish to underwrite Ms. Grove's project completely, and I'd like the medallions to be of gold. If the committee agrees, of course."

Some applause and a general gasp. "Very generous, Ms. Williamsburgh. Please meet with Ms. Grove when we break into committees. That's very generous."

"Does that mean, Doc, we should invite Canada to exhibit? Lots of us ski in Canada!" The voice, hidden in the crowd, was a happy shout. "Can we bring it up in committee?"

"Absolutely, sir. Did you bring your skis along?"

Addie watched the room smile and felt the undercurrent of excitement that was the nature of the Tuttervilles. Harry stretched his legs and tapped the gavel.

"May I say something, please?" A hand waved.

"Of course you may, Ms. Thorp."

"As you know, I love teaching the seventh grade at Hosea Middle. The children sometimes ask why some are so concerned with a nation's flag; especially the reasoning for prejudice. Prejudice is akin to injustice, and I am thrilled when someone makes as public a stand as we've just heard. Liberty and justice prevail when reason prevails. Can we affirm the gentleman's comment about Canada in the minutes?"

Before Doc could respond, Ms. Williamsburgh stood. "My country has nothing to do with my gift. I do it in memory of my late fiancé who died saving my life. Everything I do is in his memory. He was from Tutterville Falls." She touched a handkerchief to her eye. "I would love to see my country's flag flown at your fair. From my point of view, I cannot distinguish a Canadian from an American...!" And, she sat.

"I want to say something, too."

"Yes, Miss Lilly."

"Well, as I see it, we should vote now on the gentleman's recommendation. If the vote is unanimous, perhaps Ms. Williamsburgh, a Selectman, and a committee representative should visit Canada with a Tutterville invitation, and report back to us at the next General Committee meeting."

Lots of applause met Miss Lilly's words, and the subject quickly moved to toddlers' games at the fair. The biggest issue before closing was selecting the King and Queen for the fair's Grand Ball, which was postponed until the next meeting.

It was ten o'clock before Addie and Lilly closed the chamber's door for the second time that day. "My land Addie, Tutterville folks make me feel so good. Imagine the good that comes of it!"

Addie smiled, "I'm very proud of you, Lilly. Some tea before we turn in?"

"Yes, and let me tell you, I intend to get the White House involved!"

*

Ussie was no longer the elegant woman on the commuter jet. Her makeup was gone, and she wore a housekeeper's jacket and skirt. Merryweather Williamsburgh was her first cousin in flesh only. Neither side of the family had exchanged a pleasantry in memory. Perfect. I'm just the hotel housekeeper... Shortly before dawn, she tapped gently; hearing nothing she turned the maid's key and was in Merryweather Williamsburgh's room without being seen nor heard. She walked to the bed and for a moment watched her cousin as she slept; then went to the opened suitcase and luckily found what she was looking for – Merry's passport. She looked with distaste at the expensive leather valise and matching jacket. A few minutes later Ussie stood in the ground floor hall, watching for the moment she could slip unobserved into the business room for hotel guests. With no lights, she placed photo paper in the copy tray, and lay the passport photo of Merry, face page open and down, then pressed six copies. She knew, after copying her own passport, that Merryweather Williamsburgh's would copy as well as hers. It did. Within minutes she replaced the passport and was safely, and unseen, back in her own room. Tomorrow was almost as exciting a part of her plan as was the endgame. Tomorrow's task was to find a deliciously handsome mortician.

He would be her unwitting accomplice. A mortician. That could be very exciting, especially were she to find the 'perfect' man. He will, she knew, be in store for the best time of his life... except for the bitter end, of course. Female spiders notwithstanding... or, reptiles! She would begin visiting mortuaries right after lunch.

The first establishment did not suit her taste. On her second try, she rang the visitors' entrance to H. Alcuette Funeral Home. A young woman answered the door. "May I meet with the Director?"Ussie smiled.

She was brought to a well-appointed mahogany office, leathered and not at all morbid.

"Hello, I'm Hap Alcuette. How can I help you?" His eyes appraised her a little more than casually. Ussie could read his pleasure at meeting an attractive woman. If only he were the one – he's gorgeous! She sat, very slowly crossing her legs and let her gaze match his apparent interest.

She smiled, held his glance, and he did not falter. Her smile became more open. "Hap? Please call me Ussie. I'm new to Tutterville City. I'm here seeking a place to refer my family when the time comes. I think it is always smart to be prepared. One will always need funerary services, so…" Her glance searched him. "I've been looking for the right place." She sighed, purposely breathing heavily.

"I know for a fact that you've found it, Ussie. We've been here for almost 75 years. We are definitely competitive… All we need is your name and phone number, and the rest will fall into place 'every time' you call me." His body language was every bit obvious.

"I adore simple solutions," she leaned toward, equaling his best intention. "In any case, perhaps we'll get to know each other socially." Ussie stood to leave and tugged at her necklace as though it were uncomfortable. She watched him stand as she did, her eyes always on his. "I think we have a deal. Brochures?" She extended her hand. Instead of taking his, she moved closer to him and began to unbutton his jacket. "My, your biceps take a woman's breath away. They are really big. I like people who see the value of a good workout. I'm a mess if I miss a single day. I am impressed, Hap. All right to call you Hap?" She whispered.

"Any chance of seeing yours…?" He put his hand on her arm.

She pressed against him, hoping against hope he'd do more than just fall for her advances. He did.

"Let me be sure we won't be interrupted," he turned the door latch and returned to her embrace, his hands taking advantage of her closeness. They weren't interrupted.

A bit later, "Oh Hap, at last I think I've found someone like myself! If it were up to me, I'd like to meet every night for a few days. I could pick you up. Different places… we can keep this very much between us. See how it works out…" Ussie's smile answered every question Hap might have had.

"I'm game. Perfect. I can do whatever you want!" He laughed softly, "It would be a lot of fun to keep this to ourselves. But, no strings attached, right?" He returned her smile hungrily. "How about ten tonight? The library on Bradley Ave; I'll be parked way in back."

"Yes, oh yes, Hap. I'll be there. And... as you say, no strings attached. This is the kind of relationship I've dreamed of." She laughed, "A real man, on call! And Hap, no phones – can't we just arrange things each time we meet?"

*

Merryweather Williamsburgh's wealth had made her a virtual prisoner. Her first and last attempt at marriage was her last. Her fiancé, an American exchange student from Tutterville Falls, had died saving her life on a Toronto street. It happened in an instant as he dove between her and a runaway motorcycle. She took him home with his family, and since then, nothing it seemed could cool her ardor to be where he'd lived, if only to pretend she could feel him near. She could hold out for three weeks and sometimes four to be driven to his grave. He had loved the restaurant/bar at the Fox Glove Inn, and that's where she would sit each night before dinner, knowing, knowing that he'd walk in and whisk her away. She could see him in the faces of the men in the room, everywhere. After a few days she'd leave, sated as it were, for Toronto, her awful need never fulfilled. Was it wrong? Could she pretend? Just for one night, with another man? Maybe then... Maybe then she could return home and stay home.

The handicap stall in the ladies room was space enough for

Ussie to change. She changed into clothes that helped her appear a little older, in as nondescript an outfit as she could find – a simple grey skirt with a matching sweater, low heels and muted makeup. She added a hairpiece to make her appearance as neutral as possible. For the final touch, rimless glasses instead of jewelry. She left the stall and went to the mirror looking stern and business-like. Washing her hands, she looked into the glass well-pleased. Dianna couldn't have done better. A woman in disguise must not be in disguise! Plain and unidentifiable looks are difficult to recall. Ursula left the ladies' room and entered the bar. "Williamsburgh," she whispered the name distastefully to herself, was seated perch-like at the middle-end of the bar.

Pursing her lips, bag in both hands and held a timid-bit too high, she approached. "Miss Williamsburgh, isn't it?"

"Yes, hello." Merry looked somewhat surprised. No one had ever come up to her at the Glove. "How can I help you?" She asked, her voice a bit too loud, thinking the woman a little older.

Leaning forward, purse a little higher, more nervous than moments earlier, she smiled gratuitously, "I am Ursula. Call me Ussie. You look very familiar. Perhaps it's because I see you here so often." Ussie hunched forward, appearing more relaxed. "It's such a nice place. May I buy you a drink? That, I think, would be very nice." She pursed her lips again and nodded with a helpless kind of smile.

"That would be very nice, although I must go in to dinner soon."

Ussie carefully placed her bag on the bar between them both, and with delicate ease settled herself, properly adjusting her skirt.

"Ahem… yes. Thank you. I have a feeling you think of me as an interfering woman." She settled comfortably and took bills from her purse.

Merryweather smiled, "Oh no, not at all. This isn't really a drink. I'm a ginger ale person. I just love to sit here at the bar for a few moments. I love to watch Tutterville Falls people."

"Really? I'm a rye and soda person. And what's so special about the people of this town? I'm a Tutterville person."

"My late fiancé was a Tutterville Falls man," she laughed self-consciously "I just think he'll walk through that door one evening, at any moment. Crazy. But he is, was, my best friend…"

"Oh, Ms. Williamsburgh, that's hardly crazy. How long has it been?"

"Over three years, Ussie. Silly. I should be quite used to all this by now. As you see, I sit facing the door." She sighed deeply, a winsome smile escaping her sadness. "Please call me Merry."

Ursula had just discovered the success she needed for the next step of her plan. She equaled Merry's sigh with more exaggeration, looked at the mirror on the wall, and knew her plan had now fallen into lovely shape. "Merry, I'm a widow too. Ahem. I know exactly how you must feel."

"I'm so sorry Ussie. How long ago? What happened to your husband?"

"An airplane crash. He was alone. It was the first time… I ah. It was the first time he went without me. I had a terrible flu… had I gone with him. I've always believed he would never…"

"It's all right, Ussie. It's nice to be with a person who understands."

Ussie sat up straight. Pulled her shoulders back and smugly forced a smile. "Know what?" She turned to Merry, leaning forward into a whisper, "This bar taught me how to live with it!"

"What?" Merryweather put her hand up in surprise. "What do you mean?"

Ussie continued to whisper, her hand covering her lips. "Last Thanksgiving eve I came in here as lonely as hell. I had just ordered my drink when the bartender told me that it was already paid for. He had a strange smile and nodded to a man further down. I looked at him. My lord, Merry, he was so good looking! All my grief seemed to disappear in a moment. I had to smile back. I didn't know what else to do. No one has ever bought me a drink!"

Merry sat mystified. "Really?"

"Yes. He came over and asked me if I worked here. At first I didn't know what he meant. 'Wanna go to my room?' His smile was devastating, Merry, and I said yes."

"You did not!"

"Yes, Merry and it's the best thing I've done to cope with being alone. That night, I kept my eyes closed and all I could feel was my husband. The way we always were. Now you think I'm the crazy one.

"It's worked you know. We meet here once a month when he's in town, always on a Wednesday. Our monthly anniversary. He is beautiful. He is single. Maybe one day I'll say yes… maybe…

"Take it from me Merry, a man will help. Just close your eyes…"

Merryweather shuddered. "It's time for me to eat," and walked away.

Ussie sipped, smiled and watched poor, sweet Merry run away.

"The seed is planted," she said almost loud enough for anyone to hear. Her clenched jaw sealed her cynical smile. "Hap will have his cupcake, or two."

*

The library parking lot was empty but for a small green coupe and two other cars parked inconspicuously in the corners. Ussie pulled to the driver's side of the coupe. Hap smiled back, opened his door and slipped in beside her, barefoot and in walking shorts and a t-shirt. He kissed her cheek. "Somehow, I knew you'd come!"

"Twice in one day is very exciting Hap. You look better in a t-shirt than in a suit." She returned his kiss... won't your wife miss you?"

"She and her therapist won't miss me at all. It's too involved to understand, Ussie. She spends a week every month with her mother. Something about mood swings for them both."

Ussie felt his touch and leaned into his arms. "Hap, you are so perfect."

"Ha, not me, Ussie, it's you; the second time around is best."

She tickled his chest and felt him quiver. "Hap. One of these days I will introduce you to an acquaintance who lost her fiancé a few years ago. One night with you and she'd forget she knew him." She laughed, hoping he'd not see it as a joke.

On the contrary, "A threesome?"

"No, silly. She needs to get back to life. You know what I mean."

He nuzzled her neck. "Of course I do. A gentleman always comes to help a lady in distress."

Ursula Rhue scented the sweetness of success. The goddess would be proud. Poor sweet Hap. Poorer sweeter Merry. She enjoyed Hap's warm lips and fumbling hands…

CHAPTER 5

SWEET MERRY

Some days later, in the park by the river, Hap opened the passenger car door and found Ussie pensive, quiet and resting on the wheel. The full moon shone on her hair adding mystery to her silhouette. For Ussie, everything was playing out to perfection. The pleasure of her thoughts made her shiver, ever so slight, but enough to make Hap think he was the cause. Far from it, she thought. Such a boy. So deep and over his head. How can a man let himself be so manipulated? Sex? Loneliness? Hap was pouting – no, not pouting, he looked very worried. She studied him for a few moments more to prolong the pleasure of seeing him changed from the once happy Hap of a few weeks ago. The boy-look of his obvious discomfort roused her passion – just a bit. She moved over to him and stroked his brow.

"Dear, dear Hap, you look so blue. I thought Merry would be a good thing for you. What's wrong? Remember what I told you the day we met?" She laughed, curling his hair. He faintly smiled. "We women love a man with big biceps. Well," she pinched his arm, "what did Merry have to say? Is she not a class act?"

"She's different, Ussie. So innocent. It was her first time ever… I felt like an intruder. Like I, like I had no business there. It was like intruding on a privacy that's inviolable. At first she was scared to death. Then something took over, as though I was someone else…"

"Oh Hap! Didn't you both enjoy yourselves? Does she want

to see you again?'"

"Yes. We've met twice since."

"When will you see her again?"

"Day after tomorrow. She returns on the evening flight to Ontario. She is so, so sweet. So unlike anyone I've met before."

Ussie moved closer and placed her head on his shoulder, a little jealous. She tickled his chest to feel the familiar tremble. "Hal, you are doing a good thing. Soon she won't need to come back at all. Does she know about your wife?"

"No. I felt dirty telling her anything about my family… about anything. She thinks of me as a Tutterville Falls 'man of the night' – ha, that's what she calls me. We don't talk about anything but what's happening at the moment… It frightens me a bit. Can you understand that?"

"Hap you are the perfect 'man of the night'! Let's stop talking about the Williamsburgh woman. Let's talk about us." Ussie laughed. "I'm sorry I pointed her out to you. I think you prefer her to me and I won't have that. Now kiss me again, and again! Oh Hap. It is hard not to fall in love with you!"

*

Hosea County stretched beyond and well into the protecting foothills to the west. Seasonal weather was just that. Fall was colorful. Spring was as an apron of wild flowers overhung with oak, birch, and aspen red-hewn tree leaf buds leaping across their time to bloom for Easter. Summer was hot. The river's deep slice through the hills became more and more rapid with snow's melt, especially from late winter into late spring. Snow runoff and mountain streams fed into Miner's Creek. This time of year it was a dangerous rush of frothy waters, swollen and deep; centuries of its might had carved shelf-like slate steps along its grey banks. The three-mile sweep down and over to Tutterville Falls was a sight to see. Frothy, cold, and cresting with rainbows, it fell beneath the bridge and some twenty meters into the creek below.

Made more violent by its fall, the river made its way east and southeast into the great Hosea County Park called South Tutterville by most. The river swept over the falls, silver and dark, feeding the great swim holes that dotted its path through the park before moving southeast into fertile fields far away.

Miss Lilly and the Fox Glove Inn went back many years, back when the McCalley sisters, Millie and Grace, opened the inn with their first breakfast. No one on this green earth made better tasting waffles than the McCalley sisters. It had everything to do with Grace's very secret wild flower stamen she pestled into the flour.

Lilly pushed her plate back. "That, was a breakfast, Hadley!" She squelched a healthy burp. "I could go back for a bit more!" She laughed ever so modestly. "If you go back, please bring me just a touch of that breakfast pudding. I can't get enough of it. I understand why the girls don't write a recipe book; if you can make it at home, why eat it here, I suppose?" She conjectured.

She sat back quite comfortable, watching her brother Hadley. Yes, before Addie, he was completely her love. The dear never, never missed taking her to the inn for her birthday breakfast. Their ritual began when Lilly was widowed and had gone to work for the Tutters just before Miss Addie was born. She had married young and widowed young and not much, if anything, missed her inquisitive nature.

The Fox Glove was perched high on a hill a few miles before the highway bent up toward the mountain pass near the old mine. The sisters fashioned it to be a lovely, window-boxed, Alpine place that overlooked all of Tutterville Falls and beyond. The six bedrooms upstairs included a small, hideaway bridal suite.

But for the overhang above their breakfast window, Lilly and Hadley had a picture card view. A car pulling by the inn's garage interrupted her thoughts.

"Hmmm, look there Hadley." Lilly pointed. "That's the County Coroner's car coming from the back of the inn, and his ambulance, too. What's going on?" Lilly waved to Millie who was standing by the reception desk. Lilly pointed to the ambulance as it turned out of sight.

Millie, mid-sixties, slender, a skier's tan, and lithe for her years, followed Lilly's finger.

"One of the housekeepers found a guest dead in her bed – apparently she died early this morning. Williamsburgh, Merryweather Williamsburgh, Canada. Must've gone in her sleep; late thirties maybe. Poor dear, she came here every few months or so."

"Mind if I go up for a moment? You know the Judge; she'll want to know everything. When did she check in?"

"A few days ago, just after dinner, with a few bags. Gracie took her to her usual room. She reserved it for all her visits. Poor dear. We'll miss her terribly."

Lilly and Hadley got to the room just as the housekeeper pulled her cleaning cart to the opened door.

Lilly smiled broadly as she approached her. "It must've been a real shock to find her like that, are you all right dear?" At times, Lilly sounded a lot like sweet empathy come alive. "Mind if I take a peek? Did you notice anything unusual?"

"No ma'am. She must have died real peaceful. She was laying there, covers and bedspread folded across her chest like the bed was just fresh made. Her hands were folded peaceful-like. I hope I go peaceful like that. Ah, even a touch of makeup and lovely hair." Her tone of voice had become like Lilly's.

"What do you mean by peaceful, dear?" Lilly coaxed.

"Oh, ah, like she was asleep, her hair so nice, like just combed, blankets pulled up like the bed was just made, and her hands, folded so nice. I thought she was asleep!"

Lilly looked at the bed and night table. The overnight was the only bag opened; the others were closed. Perched on the edge of the bedside night table was a restaurant teacup, the only sign of life in the room. Lilly gently picked it up with the napkin – the greenish liquid looked like the tea she usually made, only a bit darker. She saw no teabag and to her surprise, the teacup was still very warm. Nothing left to see, she thanked the housekeeper and headed to the hall where she'd left Hadley.

"For the life of me Lilly, why do you always have to nose around? The coroner will tell the Judge what she needs to know." He was used to her ways and his grin had a way of saying so.

Lilly was perplexed. "I'm anxious to hear what Doc says caused her death. More pudding, dear? Let's! It's my birthday, and I need to be spoiled more than you and Addie have spoiled me already!"

*

Judge Addie could not believe a month had passed since the County Fair planning meeting. Chair Harry Hendricks was trying his best to get the meeting to order – the members were a little excited since this was the night they had to elect the King and Queen. Finally, he slammed the gavel so hard that silence began to settle in.

"Well, tonight's the night. Advertising for the fair begins tomorrow, right, Simon?" Simon Jenkins had a printing company and always volunteered to do the advertising: TV, radio, press, posters, everything needed to get attention. "Just waitin' for you to say go, Harry!"

"Soon as we get nominees, Simon; the floor is now open for nominations." Harry banged the gavel again.

Before Harry finished the question for nominations, a portly, impeccably dressed gentleman declared in a voice equal to his flawless presence:

"Ho sir! I am Bebe Pipo. I am the University Chancellor. I wish to be recognized."

"Mr. Pipo." Doc Hendricks was happily surprised. "Tutterville University always makes a spectacular presence at the fair, in many ways. We thank you, Chancellor. You are recognized."

As Harry said his words of compliment (Pipo preferred the common title of Mr. rather than Doctor), he bowed ever so slightly. Chin up and leaning forward, he began. "Usually, and in the way of tradition, worthy citizens have been recognized and given public accolade. This, as I said, is tradition. We at the University," and he stood more erect as he said the word, "present something new for this great and most august honor." He coughed slightly as if to make his pronouncement all the more significant. "The University is internationally known for its innovation in chemistry, especially new drugs that are a blessing for saving lives. The Board of Directors and I wish to place into nomination the University of Tutterville's School of The Sciences as King of the fair." Mr. Pipo bowed again slightly as if to receive an automatic agreement of the committees.

"That, Mr. Pipo, is an excellent and most appropriate idea. The nominations committee is pleased to accept the nomination as you have stated. Thank you, Mr. Pipo." Glancing around the room for other nominations he saw Rabbi Cluny, Chair of the Nominations Committee, lift his hand. Harry nodded to him in recognition.

Rabbi Cluny stood slowly, glancing across the courtroom. He was a popular man and revered throughout the county. Raising his hand toward Mr. Pipo, he began, "You have read the committee's mind, Mr. Pipo. The University itself is a formidable entity. Thank you."

Returning his attention to Harry, "Presuming there are no further nominations," he looked across the room, "we've lots of input and recommendations from across the county, and of course, we've met with each of the other committees. We have all come to about the same conclusion. Most everyone in town is of like mind. It's a big honor for the winner who will represent all of us, not only as a moral guardian, but also as a good example for our youth. Someone who has a reputation for doing things well.

"We unanimously agree," he paused to savor the tension in the room, "that Maude Checkhaus is our candidate!"

With that the room leaped to its feet with thunderous yeas and applause. Harry's gavel finally broke the noise; Lilly's hands were as red as most everyone from clapping. Unless anyone was as observant as Lilly, the casual smiles exchanged by Bebe Pipo and the Rabbi went completely unnoticed.

"Well," Doc Hendricks was ready. "Any more nominees? Any more?" He looked around the room, then to the jury box where all five Town Selectmen were seated. "All heads seem to be nodding yesss! Nobody else? No one? Hearing none, I declare, on behalf of this great and honorable committee, that Maude Checkhaus is elected this year's Royal County Queen!" More applause.

"Few in this county are more worthy," Harry continued, "and here are a few reasons why Maude was chosen. She graduated from Tutterville schools and from Hosea County University of Science, Tutterville University. Then, having won quite a few scholarships, she went on to Oxford in the UK from which she was hired – before graduation I must add – by an international pharmaceutical company, and the rest is history! She developed meds that are now standard therapies. East Tutterville has always been her home; she has endowed the Children's Hospital, and her pride and joy, the University, and a lot of other places she keeps to herself.

"All that's left is to get Maude's consent. Maude?" Maude was standing already, amidst extraordinary applause. By standards she was remarkably lovely. Not beautiful as beauty goes. It was everything about her that people fancied; she was likable on sight. Her hair, usually plaited back, exposed an ivory neck and framed her soft eyes. Her very pink flush only added to the admiration of the crowd.

"Thank you, Doctor Hendricks, and all of you for this, this, breathless honor. I am at a loss for words. And me, only a doctor!" She smiled broadly. Some giggles and knowing nods helped her to go on. "And, I do, I do accept, but with one very big stipulation."

Her hands went to her chin, her smile faded to a grimace.

"You may recall that my father had a tremendous stroke just after George, our youngest brother, was born. Mother had six of us, along with Dad, to nurture and care for. She went to work: had two jobs, sometimes three, and babysat 'for bread money,' she used to say. Totally alone, she brought us up until Dad was on his feet again, which took years. She would never ask for charity; it was her family and we were her keepsakes. She and Dad had difficult times but they sent us all to college. We're all professionals: two teachers, one lawyer, two medical doctors, and me." More firmly she went on, "I accept this nomination only if my parents, for all that they have accomplished, are honored instead of me. They should be King and Queen, and not me." Stunned silence followed.

Well, as Miss Lilly will later repeat, again and again, "My land! My land!"

If a mouse would have crossed the courtroom at that moment, you would have heard it. Stone silence, and then a voice. "That's fair, I buy that!" The gavel was the only thing to get order again.

"All those in favor?" The yeas were resounding. "It is my honor," said Chair Hendricks, his voice cracking like a kid's, "it is my honor, and on behalf of this great County, to declare Justin and Elvira Checkhaus, King and Queen of this year's annual Hosea County Fair!" Well, if you think the shouting was fierce before, now the Chair's gavel went unheeded.

It was ten-thirty when Addie and Miss Lilly closed the Judge's private chamber door in back of the courthouse and climbed the path toward home.

"My land, Addie, that Maude is quite the one," she laughed,

"when Elvira hears this, she'll just pitch a fit! She'll absolutely just die on the spot. Yes!"

Addie continued the thought, "I would not want to be in Justin's shoes when the newspapers get to him. Lilly, this is a very nice county, very nice indeed." Silence.

"Had to return a few cuttings to the botanical this morning. I just love those gardens."

"Do we need more?" Addie interrupted.

"No, nothing was left; they appreciated what I returned. Do you know, déjà vu, that couple was there again?" She hesitated. "The man was very attractive."

Lilly touched the Judge's arm, "Has the County Coroner talked to you about the Fox Glove yet? I'm beginning to believe there is more to this untimely death than a natural one. Warm teacup and all! Something is wrong, and I will bet my last slice of orange cake that the cause of death will be 'natural causes.' No, no, no…"

*

A world away, Principessa Anna Maria Elizabeta Valois do Emmanuel carefully slipped from her bed. The nude leg of Albert Williamsburgh lay carelessly draped across her side of the covers. He groaned as she moved, a small snort of comfort escaping his well-heeled and very spoiled lips. Soon they would shower and head for the Dolomite ski slopes. The snow was powder and fresh. Anna Maria opened the terrace door and felt the freeze of morning air shiver her completely. Of a sudden, cold, she flew to the warmth of the bathroom.

Ortisei, a small, very rich and touristy town, sat just on the lip of the Italian Olympic Ski team's practice slopes. Invisible from her balcony, a red and elegant ski lift at the edge of town carried its passengers to the crested edge of the most beautiful and natural bowl nature could create, a vast bowl set in the base foothills of the Dolomite mountain range. Grey and solid, the flat iron-like mountains perched on the southern edge of the Alps like a comma of limestone that God absently etched from the great Alpine Range – as though an afterthought of utter beauty.

Pre-dawn darkness was not black at all, but more of a deep powder blue that blended the rooftops into a collage of velvet shapes. A figure, impossible to notice, crouched silently below the balcony, well out of sight of the Principessa. Completely at ease with the silence and its precarious hold, the figure slipped over the balcony rail as the door to the bathroom closed. As darkness itself would, it slid softly across the room to the bed. The figure looked casually at the unclothed male, unsuspecting victim. It whispered, almost silently, "A better cause needs your estates. You would never in a million years give them to us… Sleep, my dearest boy…" As the shadowy figure whispered, it touched him with a gloved finger so fine that Albert felt nothing; in less than three seconds, he was dead. First, Merry; then, Albert… no more Williamsburghs…

The deep blue figure from the night disappeared as quickly as it had come.

The next morning had a hazy, azure beginning. Light breezes from the mountain pass were cool and insistent; early birds were quick to inhale and feel its freshness cool their breasts.

*

Tutterville City is bigger both in geography and population than each of the other Tuttervilles, not just because it is the County Seat, but because of the few thousand students and faculty living and studying within the twelve city blocks owned by the Hosea County University of Science (HCUS), known as Heycus around the world.

Its reputation is unique because it was founded on a new concept of education heretofore much different than any other. Now that the system is accepted and in operation, it has become a template for education systems that begin with pre-school education and continue all the way to post-doctoral diplomas. Simply put, it is a return to classical education with science as the handmaiden to philosophy.

Actually, Venus d'Sicily-Pipo's brainstorm fed upon the innovation that children brim with curiosity. They feed on the wonderment of unfettered imagination, and as will always follow, bursts of invention bring creation; for nothing is impossible when ideas are borne of their curiosity. Venus and her developmental psychiatric staff carefully structured safe methodologies to bring curiosity to life through hands-on classroom applications, adding such things as speed-reading, and meticulously integrating the various curricula with state accreditation. Schoolwork has to be exciting.

She'd spent almost every dime of her family's wealth. She and her husband Bebe recruited the best corporate scientists and set about the task. Child, youth, and adult admittance was selective and only a few students were admitted beyond Hosea County. Developmental psychiatrists populated each phase of the university's growth.

On this particular morning the campus was fresh and crisp. Weeks had gone into preparations for rush week student activity, and to rolling out the red carpet for registration week.

Bebe Pipo pushed aside the massive brown velvet drapes that hid the university's lavish boardrooms from any viewer. The campus had much earlier come to life, its shaded intertwining pathways were a fantasy of gardens and shrubs, too irresistible to avoid.

Bebe looked toward the university gym complex. This was the real reason he'd arrive early each morning – to watch Judge Tutter and Chief Cutter disappear into its side door. Almost twice their age, his reclusive nature, birthed in tutored private schools, yearned for the public social normalcy he'd never known. Impossible to recapture his youth, he decided to risk a very safe alternative: observing rather than doing!

Since their friendship's beginning at the university, Addie and Joanna Cutter planned their daily basketball workout to coincide with the Police Department's midnight-day shift change. After 20 minutes of one-on-one hoop brawling (that's what they called it), Deputy Chief Mont Westerly with five first-shifters joined Addie, Joanna and a few friends for a winner-take-all workout. The Chief and the Judge were university varsity players; the guys didn't stand a chance unless, of course, Mont faked a few and hooped a tiebreaker.

At the end of the workout, Dr. Pipo just happened to be sitting in the coach's chair when the women left their locker room and joined the officers just leaving theirs.

Beaming, hand out and on familiar terms, he greeted them all. "Joanna, Addie, Mont old fellow, coffee and danish next door?

On me, I insist!" No need to coax them, he led the way.

Pointing to a huddled figure at the far end of the gym he asked, "Who is the 12-year-old? He's been sitting on that top bleacher since before I got here." Joanna had also noticed, but no one knew.

As they stepped into the morning sun, Mont's phone buzzed. "Yeah, Hullo? Yeah, of course, put her on." Cupping his phone, he whispered to Chief Cutter, "Chief, let me take this, I'll meet you in a few minutes, if I can." He pressed the phone closer.

"Good morning Deputy Chief, this is Lillian Atterby, hope you are well this morning?" Her voice always tensed him more than just a little.

Miss Lilly never ceased to surprise him. She's looking to visit he thought; he cleared his throat, "Good morning Miss Lilly, all's fine here. How can I help you?" Lilly's voice was one of her sweetest, "Well, Deputy Chief, it may not be important, probably not, but then I'm a little concerned about a confidential matter. Will you be available around two, after lunch tomorrow? Just for a few minutes?"

"I'll have some tea ready," he answered.

"Oh, thank you Chief, you are so kind, ahh, umm, not green, if that's alright with you?"

"See you at two tomorrow afternoon, Miss Atterby."

Mont caught up in time to order an English muffin. "Mustard?" asked the waitress, always pained by his unusual taste.

"One little pat of mustard is good." Turning to Addie, "that was Miss Lilly. She wants to come by tomorrow. Anything I should get ready for?"

"I think it has to do with the dead woman at the Fox Glove Inn.

She's going there again this morning. 'Peculiar,' she says, 'too many things in question.' She probably wants to pump on you a bit!"

The game was hotter than ever the following morning, lots of sweat and a lot of shoves and few hoops. At one point, one of the guys on Addie's team came down awkwardly on his right ankle after attempting a layup and slid to the floor holding his foot. Everyone stopped to see if he was okay.

"I'm fine," he said, "but better hang it up till tomorrow."

Everyone looked at each other in resignation; the game was done for the day. They started to head for their gym bags on the sidelines.

"No!" Came a piercing cry from the boy in the bleachers. "I can roll with you guys. I can take his place. I can!" He tore off his jacket as he leaped from the benches. "I can ball. I play point guard for my school's team."

Someone smirked. "You're probably pushing 12, son. Maybe on a slower day." Some of the other players chortled.

"I'm not 12!" He insisted. "I'll be 18 and a freshman here next semester. I can handle it," he smiled, a crooked and imp grin, his lips pulled to the right, under a squinting left eye. "I can take on the judge and her guys. Unless you're all a bunch of wusses and don't want a 'kid' to show you up." His imp smile made his five-foot-four-inch frame look even shorter.

Then, grabbing the ball, he launched it toward the hoop from the sideline—at least 30 feet out—without a pause or aim. The ball splashed through the net. Before Mont could get to the ball, the kid had beaten him to it. Then he crossed the ball over between his legs, did a quick spin move, and released a beautiful finger roll that kissed off the glass before falling through. The onlookers stood agape.

"Wanna play, or just stand there?"

Ten minutes later, there wasn't a dry shirt on the court; the game was over. The 'kid' had bagged ten shots to their zero through a flurry of pull-up jumpers, reverse layups, skyhooks, bank shots, three-pointers, and fadeaways.

"I'm here tomorrow if you can't get another cop… Park's my name, Hunter. I just love basketball!"

From that day, and for quite a few years, the university gym was never the same. Mr. Hunter made an indelible mark on the game, as well as the school.

*

Miss Lilly knew that the water had not been steeped but then, these days, is it ever? Appearing not to notice, she leaned across to the arrangement of tea bags and slipped one into her cup.

Chief Detective Westerly watched Lilly as she fussed politely with the tea. His smile wasn't a condescending smile so much as one of polite dismissive endurance. On the one hand, this was Judge Addie's maid, but on the other, she was quite daft. Poor Addie.

"Tea in the afternoon is very comforting. There is cream if you wish. How can I help you, Miss Atterby?"

"I've read little in the news of Ms. Williamsburgh's death. Word is that it was of a natural cause." She hesitated, watching him closely. "I am sure it couldn't have been natural Chief Detective. Am I wrong?"

He smiled, "The coroner's report emphatically concludes that it was death by natural causes. What do you know that suggests otherwise? We've closed the case, Miss Atterby."

"Chief Inspector, I fear this is not as simple a matter as it appears. It's all very complex." Lilly felt his indifference. "Murder is the most evil of sins and I am sure that Merryweather Williamsburgh is more than a simple 'case,' as you put it."

"I see, Miss Atterby. Please tell me the facts as you see them." His smile still fixed, "You say that you didn't see the body of Ms. Williamsburgh when you went to her hotel room? And you…"

"That's correct, Chief Detective. A few things were not as they should have been. Have you finished your investigation?"

"An investigation? No, as I said, the coroner says that she died of natural causes. As far as the reports go, and the interviews with the staff at the inn, it appears that Ms. Williamsburgh died during the night between four and six in the morning of heart failure."

"But, Chief Detective, as I said, a few things just don't add up. I am sure that Ms. Merryweather Williamsburgh did not die naturally. I believe that she was murdered!"

The Chief Detective flinched and couldn't hide a grin: "There is no evidence to report otherwise. I'm sorry Miss Atterby." He looked at his watch.

Lilly squared her shoulders. "Warm tea, hours after her death. Bed perfectly made with sheets folded carefully under her folded arms. Makeup naturally done. Hair brushed as though it were purposefully arranged. Why such detail? One question, Chief Detective. How often have you or your detectives ever encountered anything like this? Can we look at photographs?"

"There were no photographs because of the apparent cause of death. I'll have my staff check this over at the morgue, Miss Atterby.

You can be sure that if we see anything suspicious, we'll take care of it. That's for sure. We'll let the coroner make the decision."

"Yes, Chief Detective, let me continue a bit more. Though a few things do not add up, a few very important ones do. Who asked Alcuette Mortuary to get her body from the coroner; who told the coroner to release it to Mr. Alcuette? If you will check, you will find that it was Mr. Happy Alcuette himself. Unusual? Perhaps not. Then again, you might ask the coroner's examiner if he has ever collected remains that had been meticulously coiffured. Then ask a more serious question: why was Ussie Willow, the housekeeper who found the body, not questioned?" Lilly paused, took a slow sip of tea, "Shall I go on Chief Detective?"

Hearing no response, Lilly took another long sip. "Yes, Chief Detective, as I said, I am sure that Ms. Merryweather Williamsburgh did not die of natural causes. I believe she met with foul play."

Detective Westerly felt her insistence as almost a personal affront. "Now, Miss Atterby, it's almost shift change time. We appreciate all that you've told us." He half grunted, to make light of his feelings, "Judge Tutter often says that her Miss Lilly lets little escape her." He stood, put his hand forward to help her up, "Miss Atterby, you are indeed most observant and quite the detective yourself. I need more of your kind of energy and deduction on the force. You've been a great help. Thank you so much for coming by."

"Oh, Chief Detective, I thank you for the tea. You are very kind to listen to an old woman's suspicions. I too must hurry on. Have a safe day." Lilly left the room almost too quickly to be polite; but then, it's always best to turn the other cheek, even when being called self-serving.

*

Meanwhile, and far from the playing fields of Tutterville, the divisive and very self-serving fingers of Bebe Pipo were about to open new windows into the University of Science. Heycus.

Mayellen Newton snuggled to keep warm, no matter what; she loved cold spring mornings on the porch. The barren west shore of Lake Champlain was out of sight, but in her mind's eye she could see the sun blazing on its depths, relentless, and spinning patches of early morning fog all the way up to Rouses Point. Frances, called Fig since he was born, was her only child and what a man he was. He'd bought them this house, provided a comfortable income and, aside from assuring her comfort, the sign he'd planted on the front lawn on day one said it all: *Gone Fishin' – Don't wait tooo long*!

May sipped and stretched. The letter in her lap read *Personal, only for F. Newton* in bold print letters. Must be important, she thought, Fig don't get much mail that's 'Personal.' Funny how the sound of the wind off the lake and the growl of his Harley motor made it sound like he was flying home on the wind. She squinted and saw her son appear down-road and like the wind, in seconds, he swept up their drive.

"Hey Miss-Rosey-Ellen, caught some breakfast special for you. Come on in and give me a hand!" A quick kiss and he tossed his bike helmet on the other chair.

She poured his cup, "Got a letter for ya, came yesterday, and says *Personal*, looks important."

"If it looks important, you better read it while I clean these bass."

Mayellen sniffed the envelope and then sliced a kitchen knife under the flap. "The return address says, 'Hosea County University of Science' and let's see…" she opened the single page. "What on earth? Oh, for the love of Lord Harry. There's a check here! It's made out to you – look!"

"Let me see. My Lord, it's ten thousand dollars! What's the letter say? Let me see. It's from a Mr. Bebe Pipo. Hmmm." He read the brief letter quickly. "He wants you and me to visit him in Tutterville, at his home. Has a long-term deal about coaching basketball. Says that the check is to cover expenses. We have to be there next Friday. '*P.S., Call the following number to confirm. Arrangements have been made for both you and your mother, Mrs. Newton.*'"

"Well, by the Lord Harry! Fig. What are we gonna do?"

"Go, of course. Unless you have other plans?"

Meanwhile, across the country, another family had received a similar letter. "John, this letter is from a Mr. Pipo; there's a check here for ten thousand dollars made out to you! Ten thousand dollars! This Mr. Pipo, do you know him? Ten thousand dollars. Obviously this is some kinda scam – what's the gimmick? Can it be real? He wants the kids and me to go with you, to fly to Hosea County and stay at his home. I'm not sure I like that idea, bringing the kids into a strange home, even for a few days. This is a scam!" Carrie Stilton was never shy for words, "Read it again, John!"

"I've never heard of him, but Heycus is a very fine school; takes kids from pre-school all the way up. Great school. This has to be a job interview. Wow!"

*

Bebe Pipo stood on the tarmac; the bird was due in a few minutes. All he could think of was their amazing freshman, Mr. Hunter. Chief Detective Westerly had never seen anything like the kid. He was a flawless athlete.

Pipo began to pace, fists clenched. He always recognized a good thing when he saw it, and this one was better than most. The plan he was about to put into motion was intricate and complicated. Oh, how he loved a grand scheme! And this was about to become one of his biggest.

The almost silent whisper of the unmarked jet swept across the horizon and touched on Tutterville's private airpark just a few miles south of the Fair Grounds. Two sleek limos pulled to his side as the bird taxied toward him. When it pulled to a stop, its passengers stepped from the airplane onto a brilliant red carpet.

Hand outstretched and with a flurry of introductions, "Mrs. Newton, I am so glad you came with your son, Fig!

"You are young William Stilton, are you not? And, you have to be Miss Sarah Stilton, and you are," he paused and grasped her hand, "Mrs. Stilton? How do you do... Fig, John, nice to meet you both. Welcome to Tutterville.

"Let me introduce my secretary, Peter Windsor, and the lady who makes my house a home, Florence Marie. They will answer all your questions on the way to the university. Ladies and children, Florence will be with you in this car." He opened a door. "And gentlemen, with me in the other, please."

The first limo sped off to the north; John, Fig and Bebe followed a few hundred yards behind. "Your check was a surprise Mr. Pipo, what's it for?"

Before John could agree, Bebe answered, "Please, the money is my foot in the door of your lives. You may need it to pay for your lawyers. My basketball staff and I will do our best to get you both to move here to our university, permanently. We'll give you whatever you want for your houses. You each have a ten-year contract with the university, as well as rent-free homes on campus until you settle anywhere in the Tuttervilles. As for salary, you can almost name your price. Almost!

"The clincher will happen when you see our freshman basketball player, young Mr. Hunter. He's the best player on the planet! And, he's a freshman! You'll see both of yourselves in him. We want him and our teams to have the best coaches and most of all, good moral men who will help them make good choices as they mature, especially our very young Mr. Parker Hunter. You gentlemen have the history of greatness. That is a virtue I want our students to understand.

"We selected the best in the country to coach us. The clincher was a character trait that great men appear to lose when greatness is at point-game, and that's integrity. You are not only the best players from the recent past, but we love your morals. Our university has to keep its unique and flawless reputation. When all is said and agreed upon, if you accept, you will see why a good lawyer is necessary; but that's for later.

"Hotel reservations have been made should you prefer them to my garden cottages. Your quarters are a ball's throw from the pool and the main house. They're comfortable, very private, and each has a cook and housekeeper. I hope you and your families prefer my cottages. There's also an agenda for our meetings in each library.

We begin with dinner at seven tonight, children too, of course. Take a few hours to relax."

The weekend arrived just in time for Bebe to set his plan in motion. Fig Newton and John Stilton had signed on; albeit, neither would accept their ten thousand dollars until they understood that it was a part of their contract. The next step was to convince the Hunter family that their son Parker would be safe and in good hands. Lunch would be on the patio.

Sunday came very quickly and thanks to secretary Peter, each of the guests felt very much at home... Morale was really high! Splashing bits of sun sparkled like silver wisps across the pool. Spring storms passed through, the morning was fresh and almost a fantasy in perfect hues of color. All was cool, rain-bright and new. The terrace awning added a translucent pink and pale green haze to the crystal festooned luncheon table.

Peter Windsor offered Parker more chopped boiled eggs. "Looks to me, Park, like spinach salad and lamb chops make a good brunch for a ballplayer?"

"Yeah, real good." His wide, lopsided grin pulled one eye into a near wink, "Mom says I'm an endless eater!" He grinned, a bit embarrassed.

Bebe laughed at the boy's trademark smile; Mr. and Mrs. Hunter were not as comfortable as their son. He leaned toward the more skeptical of the two parents. "Mrs. Hunter, I speak for the whole university, as well as the Board of Directors, as I thank you and your family for joining our university. I have a feeling that these luncheons won't be infrequent. If you agree, everything we do is to benefit Park, his future and, of course, the university."

Mrs. Hunter's smile was not friendly, "Where does your 'we' come into our son's life, Chancellor Pipo?"

Bebe became all business. "We are told by our athletic scouts that your son is a unique and very talented basketball player. You and he chose this university. He wants to play ball here and we want that too. Why? Because he is one of a kind. Our coaches have never seen anyone like him before."

"You," he looked to Park, "can place yourself nationally at the top of your sport; that means, you have access to a great future. Not only is your ball playing great, but so are your GPA and SAT scores. With a lot of humility and very hard work, you can nail your future. That, Mrs. Hunter, is why I put the 'we' in there."

Taking his mother's cue, Parker interrupted. "Give me more on the 'we' part, Mr. Pipo," he'd replaced his grin with eyes that betrayed almost too much maturity.

"You are the driver, Park. This is your school, this is your family, and it is your life. As with every student, this entire university and its staff are here to serve our students. Because you are who you are, Park, we have placed a safety net for your protection."

Mr. Hunter was almost impressed. "Ha, now the catch, Chancellor Pipo? Nothing is free, right?"

"Mr. Hunter. Please! I promise you can trust us. Our university rides on the shoulders of its graduates and we are very proud of this. Our reputation is unquestioned. We lose everything with even the slightest scandal. I cannot afford to lead you or your son down any merry path; as I said, this is now your son's school to use to his benefit. The safety net?

"As Park's reputation grows, despicable people will press him to miss a hoop or two or do everything they can to lure him to a more affluent school for personal gain. I believe Park's integrity and honor will help him avoid the former, as for the latter, that's a family matter. For our part, we must help you, Park, refine your playing skills and hone your talent to its optimum. And that, dear boy, is our long-term, every day, 'we' enterprise."

He continued, "Park, who are John Stilton and Fig Newton?"

"Ah, just about the most famous basketball players there are! John Stilton was going pro before he got hurt, and Fig is the most famous retired ball coach there is."

"Should you and your parents agree, Park, we will sign them to be your personal coaches. Coach Newton has agreed to join the university as our Athletic Director and Head Coach, and Mr. Stilton has accepted the job as full-time basketball coach for our high school, a part of this university. As important, he will work as your personal trainer. Where Coach Newton will lead the team, Coach Stilton will be your technical advisor."

It was quite apparent that Bebe Pipo had just trumped the Hunter family's fears. Park's mouth hung open in stunned surprise.

"Peter, more cheesecake for Mrs. Hunter."

CHAPTER 6

THE SILVER SLIPPER

The access road to Tutterville Falls Park narrows dangerously just before it sweeps into the parking area at the base of the falls. On the best of nights cars won't take the risk, even the most ardent of secret lovers. This night was particularly dangerous. Dark, rain, and a cold mist intensified the darkest moments of the descent to the park. Carefully peering through the wipers, Hap Alcuette inched toward the only car he could see. It was parked safely away from the swollen falls. As he stopped, its driver's door opened and a huddled figure quickly slipped in beside him. "Hap, thank you for coming, oh," she pressed closer to get warm, "you feel so nice." She leaned over his shoulder and pressed her lips to his cheek.

Hap didn't return her kiss. "Why do I feel that something unpleasant is about to happen? I still can't believe Merryweather is dead. She was so full of life. It's all so impossible!"

Ussie reached to his forehead and brushed a curl aside. The fact he was annoyed made what had to be done easier. The year of planning was at an end; tomorrow, lawyers would give her everything she's ever wanted, and sweet, unwitting Hap had done her real well. "You really swept Merry off her feet that weekend I first introduced you. Then it was just you two."

"Things happen, Ussie. It was like you handed me off to her."

"I did. She was so utterly lonely for company and you didn't seem to mind. I'm sure she died quite happy."

"Really, Ussie, you make it sound so cold. What's on your mind, you were a bit emoted when you called? I can only stay a few minutes."

She smiled, "You were so nice to tidy her up, I ah, thought it so sweet the way you fixed her hair and touched up her face. You are so sensitive and so wonderful." Pulling away… "You… ah, you don't seem to be your usual romantic self tonight."

Ignoring her again, she moved closer. "Someone called this afternoon about a viewing. There isn't going to be a viewing. I don't even have the body, it's at the morgue," his voice terse. "Why would anyone ask? How could anyone connect my mortuary with Merry?"

Ussie's smile became exaggerated, "Who called?" She gamed carefully for detailed, loose ends. "Must've been the newspapers looking for an obit piece. You're worried about that?"

"It wasn't the press. Was like a family member." He squinted into the night. "You must be worried too, or else why are we meeting in this awful forsaken place? She was your friend, too. Only you knew about us." Hap coughed and felt a chill of apprehension.

Ussie moved closer. "I found her on the floor. I had to see if she was dead. I was scared. How often do you find someone dead like that? I could only think to call you. There is nothing to worry about my dear, dear Hap. Merryweather would have wanted no one else to come." She cuddled more, careful to watch his every reaction. He was right, something unpleasant was about to happen; she pressed to embrace him, not for the reason he thought.

"Ussie, I have to go. My wife doesn't know I've left the house, and she won't if I get back soon enough."

The darkened mist cocooned his car. He checked the park for any sign of another car. "I don't know if we should meet again, Ussie."

She pulled herself closer and as quickly, with the saddest smile she could manage, reached again to move the curl. She did it with her other hand, a gloved finger, "I'll always be here for you dearest Hap, goodbye my sweet one." As she spoke, Happy Alcuette suddenly convulsed and fell across the steering wheel. He was dead. She knew it would take but a few seconds. Hap was the last of her loose ends.

*

The fairgrounds had come to life long before dawn. The morning air was strangely damp, as though Tutterville Falls itself had made its way south along with the river. Doc Hendricks pulled into the space reserved for Emergency Aid vehicles. This year's fair was a big one. Emergency access to each of the fair's pavilions was a priority for both medical vehicles and the thousands of expected visitors.

Today's meeting was all about straightforward access to each pavilion and most important, emergency crowd control. Harry smiled to see others pull in for the same meeting: police, medics, pavilion hosts and most important, the Circus Director who, as he parked, stepped from her pink, candy-striped Jeep, just next to him.

Portly and fortyish, she hoisted herself out. No fashion plate, she wore her trademark faded cap which matched her very worn leather breaches, both of which blended well with her worn muck boots. Only one woman in the country wore that getup. Harry gave a scout salute, "Ms. Hattie Blake, I presume?"

His smile was as bright as any kid who dreams of circuses and lions and tigers and such things that wouldn't let them grow up. "Hattie, you are looking at me, your biggest fan! I'm Harry Hendricks, call me Harry!" He stretched out a hand and grasped a hardy shake.

"Harry, the pleasure is mine. I've been to a lot of county fairs and even seen a few dog fights in my time, but I've yet to see any place as gorgeous and well planned out as these fairgrounds." Her megaphone-like laugh was as keen and wholesome as her eyes were green. Harry was immediately swept off his feet!

After lots of hot coffee and well into the afternoon, the caravan of planners pulled into the Fox Glove Inn. Amidst standing applause, Grace and Millie McCalley led Doc, Hattie and the crowd to the dining room and the Inn's famous Tutterville Country Buffet.

Gracie couldn't hold back, "Hattie, you have no idea how happy we are that you're staying with us. If Millie here were twenty years younger, she'd run away with your circus. She is an unmitigated circus freak!"

"Well, we aren't much on freaks, but this could be a match made in heaven. We just lost our tightrope lady bicyclist, and you, Gracie, look in perfect shape to start training. In our trade, it's usually the accuser who's the guilty one. Ha, ha, haw haw! You're off the hook, Millie." Hattie Blake's laugh was a lovely bellow, so infectious, that the whole place attacked the buffet at once.

Over the noise a hand reached forward and touched Millie's shoulder. "Ms. McCalley, there's a Chief Detective at the desk.

Wants to see you and Gracie."

Gracie hurried to the front desk. "Mont! Have you had lunch? The circus is here for lunch. Join us?"

"Thanks, can't stay. I'd like to see one of your housekeepers, Ussie Willow. Is she around?"

"As a matter of fact, no. She took her check and left us yesterday just before noon; one of the cars took her to the airport." Gracie shrugged and glanced at Millie, who smiled in agreement and added, "She lived in one of the maid's rooms, downstairs."

"Can we take a look?"

Meanwhile, at the brunch, Doc Hendricks finally had a moment with Hattie. "Our program committee was thinking, Hattie, that we'd add an extra flare to the opening parade. Can we put the King and Queen smack dab in the middle of it?"

Hattie's grin was just as infectious as her laugh. "That's an easy one Harry, we can do more than that. We can make them the centerpiece! A horse-drawn float, lots of flags, old fashioned-like. We have some great show horses and lots of banners. We'll make a few demo-models and let the committee decide."

"Yeah, something like that. This could become a precedent setter." Doc Hendricks was lost in Hattie's green eyes.

*

The news of the death of Albert Williamsburgh headlined news media for days. His closest friend, 'Princess' Anna as he called her, was by his coffin in almost every photo. Forlorn, brokenhearted and grief stricken, the Principessa had remained silent until she learned of the death of his aunt, Merryweather. Anna Maria called a press conference, and in the presence of a selected few and the Italian Ambassador to Canada, made a brief statement:

"We find it very hard to speak. The loss of Albert is the greatest tragedy of my life." For a moment she hesitated, and with poise and an obvious draw on immense inner courage, continued.

"Albert and I were married in Rome in a Papal chapel on the eve of his death..." She sat down, completely overtaken. Looking at the Ambassador she said, "Since my husband no longer has family in this country, I will take him home with me to Italy." Looking into the camera she continued. "My husband was a virtuous man. We have been private friends for many years. Our honeymoon in Ortisei was the first night we've ever known together. Please pray with me that he has left me with child." With this last word, Anna Maria collapsed into the arms of the Ambassador. The cameras went black.

All media, international especially, was no more stunned than the people of Italy, let alone Canada.

*

A figure clothed in a long black ermine fur sat in the First Class Lounge; she was no longer the unseen Ortisei killer-shadow in blue. Now she was Ursula. Suddenly, the beautiful face of Principessa do Emmanuel flashed onto the TV screen across the room. She watched horrified! What's this? Married? The princess spoke of marriage? Transfixed, she watched as the newscaster flashed immediately to her palace in Rome. The Italian media was all over the marriage of the Principessa to Albert Williamsburgh. As Ursula watched, layer upon layer of options flooded her thoughts: Albert's heirs, the princess? Options began to clash with questions. Who could inherit the Williamsburgh family fortune? Ussie! Merryweather and Albert are dead.

Now, how will the new widow change all this? Body upon body, upon body. No, no, no – dangerous! Suspicion must never be aroused. The perfect solution will always come. Everything, after all, is a puzzle, and any 'thing' by definition could be resolved or changed. It is only a matter of time.

As Ursula was thinking, the edges of a solution began taking shape. She smiled and folded her coat on a lounge, just as the smartest looking waiter sped to her side with another drink. It was way too soon to return to Canada...

*

While the fair was in its opening days, greed and anarchy made her singular way to the Ottawa International Airport. Energized but terribly tired at the same time, Ussie Willow pressed the overhead button for the stewardess. "May I have some tea please, and a blanket? We land in Ottawa at noon, yes?"

As she approached customs, a flush of fear laced through her heart. In a few moments Ussie Willow would cease to be, and only Ursula Rhue would exist. The customs officer looked to verify her passport, hesitated for what seemed an eternity, then stamped it. Ursula strode quickly toward the exit, a new and very emancipated woman. Then, as if to contradict her very freedom, the name Williamsburgh flashed on an overhead television screen. She stopped dead in her tracks and listened while the media mourned the death of her cousin Albert. She bit her lip to restrain the pleasure that leapt to her face. Ursula shivered with joy. Albert dead!

Now indeed, everything was hers. The last of them was dead. With the world in her bag, Ursula swept through the exit to her waiting car. A change into proper clothes, meet with her lawyers, and then on to her bank...

*

Addie opened her AT-A-GLANCE, blew on her coffee and sat on the bigger of the two wingback chairs by her desk. Settled, she placed her cell phone centered on the tall pipe-stand that served now as an end table. The morning's appointments had been blocked for a very important call... a most important call. As if on cue, her cell chimed – only Lilly, Joanna, Doc or one unlisted caller could be on the phone – it was the last of the four. "Hi Maggie! Good morning." A bright woman's voice greeted her as only good friends do.

"Addie, you well these days? We miss you dearest darling; when you coming to town?"

"I miss you too. How are Grayson and the kids?"

"They are all perfect and so am I!" She laughed familiarly. "I have just two seconds before the boss leaves. His answer is a big yes!"

"Oh Maggie, you did it! You are incredible. This will make the fair the greatest it's ever been. Kiss the boss twice and tell Bonnie I love her. Both are coming, right?"

"Absolutely. It's all secret until they arrive. Right?"

"Oh Maggie, thank you. How do I return this favor?"

"Favor? It ain't no favor, honey. You and your family have always been there for us; besides, we have to get together one way or another. Gotta run. Love you, Your Honor! Bye…"

Addie hung up, clapped her hands and pressed for an intern.

"Yes, Judge?"

"Call Lilly and tell her I am taking her, Hadley, and Doc Hendricks to the Fox Glove for dinner tonight. Make a reservation for 7:30 and oh, call Doctor Hendricks and tell him to pick all of us up at my house at seven, if he's available. I've just hooked THE Grand Marshall Family for the parade!"

The national media was everywhere. Local radio and TV stations had that intimate, we-know-what-you-wanna-see familiarity that riveted the attention of the locals. Each network had its own crew nestled into the most prominent intersections of the parade route. Crowds had been gathering for the last two days.

The morning was simply perfect. Fluffy clouds and gentle breezes brought the best of spring weather from the valley to the northwest, down through the county, and then, with fresh-scented force, swept the hundreds of billowing flags into a flurry, like the heartbeat of a giant metropolis. Newspapers reported the crowds to be the biggest to ever open the annual Hosea County Fair. Not only were the parade routes crowded shoulder to shoulder, but also special stands for the aged and infirmed made continuous balcony-high seating available along the Hosea-Tutter Parkway, right into the center of the fairground park.

Due to its central place in the county, Tutterville City was the gathering place for every visitor. Hotels and B&Bs had been booked for months; balloon and vendor suppliers were earning a fine year's paycheck!

At high noon, the mounted County Police force led the parade in a glittering show of fine horsemanship, with flags that represented the Nation and State, followed by the flags of the Tuttervilles. Next, with sirens and bagpipes at their best, came the Hosea County and Tutterville Cities' Police Departments vested in their traditional crimson red parade jackets and navy/red striped trousers. Floats and school bands, more floats, and giant cartoon balloons were interspersed with civic banners and proud strutting drum majors.

Next, veterans and families of the fallen were greeted with applause, cheers and eye-watering waves from the grateful crowd.

Word had not leaked until some thirty minutes into the parade that a special Grand Marshall Family was going to be announced at the last minute. The news alerted all the media so quickly that cameras and lesser reporters rushed to the Airpark, just in case.

Then it broke like wild fire. Air Force One was going to land close to one o'clock. The Airpark reporters went wild with excitement. Cameras searched the sky while links with the nation's capital confirmed the rumor to be true. The media went absolutely aghast. The President of the United States and the First Family were to join Judge Tutter on her specially designed float. While all this panic was playing out, the crowds were too busy to hear anything because smack in the middle of the parade was the best band of all – Hattie Blake's Grand Circus Band. Dressed in their finery they outmatched and outstepped the imagination of everyone present. Behind her candy-striped Jeep was a massive seashell, brilliant in the mid-afternoon sun.

Glistening in gold and mother of pearl and seated in its center on a thrown-style dais sat the King and Queen of the Fair,

Mr. and Mrs. Justin Checkhaus. Standing behind them were their children and fourteen grandchildren. Elvira, Her Royal Majesty the Queen, was dressed in a soft yellow colored suit, lovely and elegant, while His Royal Majesty, King Justin, sat in a blue suit and royal blue silk tie. The two made everything as regal as any King and Queen could, sensational and striking, they reflected the home-heart of the County. The crowds went wild! And in return, the Royal Family waved elegantly with smiles and laughter that suited everyone very well, very well indeed. As the Royal Family passed, whispers became amazed wonder.

The President of the United States was on his way into Tutterville City! With that, the second half of the parade brought every kid and almost all adults into the street. The circus parade spread for five blocks behind the Royal Family and, last but not least, was the 300-piece University Band, more high-stepping than any of the others. Drum majorettes and cheerleaders surrounded the huge fifty-foot Float of Roses driven by the Secret Service, because seated in the midst of the float were Doc Hendricks with Judge Adelaide Adamson Tutter at his side, and a few feet in front of them, the President and First Lady of the United States of America – The Grand Marshall Family. Flags waved everywhere, shouts and cheers of deafening accolade spread through the streets, and more solemn were the tears and salutes that followed the President and First Lady. No one had ever seen a more impressive sight!

Near four o'clock, Air Force One left for Florida and the crowds followed the parade into the fairgrounds. At seven, the food courts closed in time for the opening fanfare. The shows began as the Grand Circus Band blared its welcoming trumpets on signal for the exhibition halls to open their grand gates.

As the clock struck eight, the King and Queen stepped from their dais. The Cardinal Archbishop of Tutterville City presided over the Royal Coronation, and the Grand Ball began. For the next hour, all food and beverages in the food courts were free, as the judges graded food cookoff samples and then voted for the best-in-show recipes. The winners in each food category were to receive their blue ribbons from none other than visiting international Four Star Chef, Charles K. Roast.

And so, with fanfare and great good cheer, the fair was underway. The fair's Grand Ball ended at midnight.

Soon after, Doc Harry pulled into Judge Tutter's drive. "Well, Addie, tonight proves again that my forte is the two-step – it's my best shot!" Then, with a grin forced with anticipation, "I thought these twelve years would never reach an end. You'll call, Addie?"

"Of course, yes, you know that I will… and I happen to love your so-called two-step. I thought we did just fine. I see Lilly is already home. I'm sure she has tea ready and I know that she has baked an orange cake. Care to come in for a while?"

*

Ursula Rhue, dressed in morning black, entered the Williamsburgh family bank with the final part of her plan ready to set in place. The final phase was to take complete control of her wealth, separate herself from any Williamsburgh influence, and to destroy the enemy completely, simply with the wave of her checkbook. Her black satin hat accented the dark makeup that helped sadden her gaze as she spoke. The impression she made was one of elegant empathy on the one hand, and firm control of her demands on the other. Her lawyers and new bankers sensed the beginnings of power that always came with new wealth.

They answered her questioned concerns for the welfare of the Principessa and, with a maternal smile, the welfare of any child she might bear as result of her Williamsburgh marriage,

The Chairman of the Board smiled. "As accurate as can be determined at present, it appears, Ms. Rhue, that Albert Williamsburgh's child, should one exist, would inherit the Williamsburgh estate. However, since you are at present the last living relative, you will be his or her regent, so to speak, and have complete control until the child reaches the age of twenty-five. Obviously, if no child exists, you are, in absolute, heiress to the estate."

A few hours later, puffed with a newfound touch of arrogance, she watched with relish as the trusted guardian of the Williamsburgh Family Estates fought for his livelihood:

"Ms. Rhue, I am certain our bank can continue to serve you as we have for generations of the Williamsburgh family. At least wait for a few months, give yourself time to evaluate the ramifications of this massive transfer."

"My decision is my business. All the family holdings, everything, all financial matters and properties, as well as their management is to be, by close of this business day, transferred to the Union International Bank. Your last task for my family and, ah, I alone am this family, is to ensure that 25 million dollars is deposited into my new personal Union checking account, as I said, by end of today."

As the Director watched her leave his office, his frown became a dry smile. He pressed the silver button on his left. A crisp metallic voice told him he was online. "Call Q and Dianna. I will see them tonight at the Randolph, eight o'clock." He swiveled his chair to face the wall. At once the wall panel whisked silently open. A laser visual swept his eyes and the panel slipped closed behind him; he barely felt the swift descent that brought him to his Operations Suite, more than twenty floors below ground level. The door opened. The command suite hesitated for a moment, then as quickly, burst to life.

Four laser-keyed rooms led away from the command dais: a cafeteria with a gym and its three-lane speed pool; a four-bed dormitory with an exit/entrance ascending to a vault in the bank above; a suite for the Alliance Director; and a systems room that spider-webbed beneath the complex to serve the command center. Stepping through the identification screen, the Director walked toward his command desk. Immediately, the walls, ceiling and floor illumined to a soft onyx-black glow that cast the room into soft daylight. In the center of the room were metallic-glass steps leading down to the raised command dais of similar glass-like clarity. As he sat, screens slid to eye level while panoramic giant panels appeared on the walls before him. The complex was a laser and fiber optic environment.

Within milliseconds the life-sized panels came to life. As the Director pointed to his left, two uniformed agents entered from the dormitory; both in their seventies, they sat in similar chairs to his, on either side. They were trim and dressed in silken-like jumpsuits, tan colored Alliance uniforms that were standard protective against electronic or object intrusion. They wore the rank of senior class commanders.

"Good morning, Director," each greeted him as they sat.

"Good morning Jorganna, Jason. It's time to get to work." As he spoke, he tapped the command tab on his screen; moments later the Country Security Intelligence Service (CSIS) Director of Operation's face shimmered lifelike before him. "Good morning, Victor. You should have received my earlier transmission."

"Good morning, Alliance Director, yes I have. The CSIS Director is reviewing it as we speak. Ms. Rhue appears to be an unknown heir. We thought the dynasty was at an end with the untimely death of Merryweather Williamsburgh and her nephew, Albert. She appears to have come from nowhere!"

"No, she is a distant cousin, no question about that, at the moment she is the legal heir."

"Is she able to end your funding?"

The Director leaned into the screen: "Why did I know, Victor, that would be your first concern. Our Trust legal staff says no; however, times change, as you know. Our operational funding depends in very small part on the Williamsburgh Trust; we do have other resources. No Federal or Provincial funds; it is our independence that allows us to be autonomous and to operate outside your system. This way, the Cabinet Chair or higher authority can, without accountability, employ us. I alone, Victor, am responsible; only I take the hits. My underlying task is to do all I am able to do for you and the government, within the law of the lands."

Victor interrupted, "I just received a note for you from the Director, CSIS. I've downloaded it into your discreet dropbox, for your record. In essence he says that you are to handle this matter as you think necessary. He also gives you control of all of our assets if you are in need. And, he sends his best wishes."

"Nice, Victor. Remind him that I'll meet him at 11 PM on Sunday. We'll keep in close touch as this business unfolds."

"Yes, that's 11 PM; see you soon, Director."

The Director of the Alliance's screen slipped silently into his desktop. Looking to either side, "Well team, what do you have for me so far?" Settling into his chair he put his feet up comfortably. The command center wall panels were ablaze with information. The onyx-black walls shed their soft daylight into every inch of the Center. Jason and Jorganna looked crisp and ready. "Children," he said slowly, "it's time to get to work."

Jason was ready. "Ms. Rhue's best photo shot is on screen one. On screen two we have her coming through customs this last time. She looks a bit pale. On screen three we have her at Tutterville departure, changing flights at Detroit International. Last, we have her leaving the airport – her car."

"Nice, Jason, looks like that is where we'll begin while we do the background into her history. What do you have, Jorganna?"

"I've floated her profile over the ethernet; we have four matches. I have her on screen four departing JFK for Naples, Italy, Sunday a week ago, and at customs in Naples after landing. She rented a car and disappeared for two days. On the next screen, we show her at Naples again, then at JFK, and her return flight to Tutterville Airpark.

"The Naples car rental agent says that she returned with 770 kilometers on the car. A radius of 350km around Naples includes some interesting places. I get the feeling that there is more than one Ursula Rhue. Don't know why, except she seems everywhere at once! Joanna, almost all of your intuitive feelings become facts. Until we know differently, let's keep it a fact!"

"Good. Let's time all of this for the record, post everything after the conversation I just had with Victor. Prepare identical chips for Q and Dianna, include all the information and details we have, especially her phone voice, the sound of her digital-mobile voice, and full body 360 digitals of her in action. The chips are both to destruct if anyone other than Dianna or Q so much as touch them."

"Any data on her history yet?"

Jorganna nodded affirmatively. "She's very private and out of sight except when she works behind the scenes for prominent anti-war politicos. Even during those occasions, she is very invisible. Until a few years ago she rarely traveled; now, she's a veritable world traveler! Peculiarly, her closest travel companion is a woman named Dianna – no last name at present."

"Well now," The Director began absently tapping his desk, "another Dianna! Looks like she could pass in a pinch for our Dianna... Ussie and her 'friend' certainly would not fund an organization like ours; most likely, they'd want to shut us down, I think. Hmmm, I wonder how much the outside world knows of us. Children. We may very well have a leak among those who know our business. Is all this bank activity today of hers merely a coincidence? I think not! Children, we could well have a mole here at home. Both of you look into our own laundry. Interesting!

"Put everyone we can spare on this woman's background check. Go into the policy-influencing structure of her political associates. Infiltrate with Q-level implants; we have to get all we can on her, and sooner than later. No one needs to know why, children, it's all about background.

"Get Victor back on the phone and tell him all you've told me. Tell him we accept his offer of a few of his operatives to join us." The Director hesitated, "Rescind that! No, no! On second thought, don't call Victor. His place is a sieve! We will have to hunt for moles within his domain. As they say, leaks mostly come from high places.

"Better still, Jackie is staffed to help. She is far from the Cabinet Committee on National Security and her operatives are almost as good as ours. Along with the background check on Rhue, they can ferret any moles at the Cabinet level and here, for that matter. Tell her I need only information. We do not want to flush the bird or give away our hand. She'll understand.

"For a start Jason, enter hedge.row for the list of our employees. Only I can access hedge.row.bag. I'll take care of that list later today with Jackie's HR person.

"What time are you two relieved today?"

"Two this afternoon. The chips will be upstairs by noon."

"That won't be necessary, Jason. I'll be back here at noon for a swim. We can have lunch. Spinach salad for me."

Within moments the Director was twenty floors above, back at his desk overlooking the city. He pressed the silver button, "Please bring me all of the GPS links that are being used to track Q and Dianna."

*

The Hosea County Fair was well into its third day when the Police Desk pressed the Chief's intercom, "Yes, Sargent."

"Chief, I have a Chief of Police from Canada on the phone. His name is Chief Thomas Kilmein. Your line three."

"Good morning, Chief Kilmein. This is Chief Joanna Cutter. It is truly a pleasure to meet you."

"Thank you Chief, likewise. I'm calling on a bit of business. The remains of Ms. Merryweather Williamsburgh, one of the most prominent women in our country, arrived here a few hours ago. Her accompanying documentation reports that she died of heart failure; she was released from customs this morning. Have you closed her case based upon these findings?"

Joanna pressed Chief Detective Westerly's remote phone. "At this time, I believe so, Chief Kilmein. Let me bring Chief Detective Mont Westerly in, we'll make this a conference call. And please call me Joanna. He will be here in a few moments. Okay with you?"

"My name's Tom, Joanna, how're things in Hosea County these days?"

"Very busy. We happen to be in the middle of our annual County Fair. All's quiet; I think the citizens are too busy enjoying the holidays. Mont has just come in, let me put us on speaker. Detective Mont Westerly, this is Chief Tom Kilmein, from Canada."

"Good morning sir! Wish you were here to enjoy our fair."

"Good morning to you, Chief Detective, we understand that you are the investigating officer in the case of the death of Merryweather Williamsburgh? Her remains have just arrived."

"Yes, Chief, our County Coroner's examination reports her death as heart failure. He signed the Death Certificate noting that to be the case."

"We have his report; however, Ms. Williamsburgh was one of

our most wealthy citizens. Our court system and her family lawyers will require tertiary certification. And, I add, an accompanying physician at the hearing. Her family will cover any expense, Chief Detective. Was there any thought, or any rumor, or word of the unusual, or of foul play?"

Joanna and Mont's eyes locked and mouthed the same words at the same time. "Miss Lilly."

"What was that?" Chief Kilmein asked.

"Yes, Tom. We have our own prominent citizen who plays detective now and then. She was the only voice to raise a question. Ah…" Joanna shrugged with a nod to her chief detective, "We'll bring her in again to hear what she has to say. I'll get a transcript to you once she signs a release."

"Excellent, Joanna, Chief Detective. I'll wait for your call with her comments and the signatures supporting the Coroner. Have a great day and enjoy your fair."

"Best to you, Tom, talk with you soon."

"Well, Mont, I'll call Judge Tutter and ask if we can meet with her and Miss Lilly." Mont's eyes rolled, he shrugged and stretched out in his chair.

"It begins…" he groaned.

*

The ship's log from the sailing schooner Silver Slipper, New Year's Day, 1900, was torn from its ledger and safely secured in a strong-box, all its own. The log also included a contract written in the hand of Randolph Abbott Bedford and signed by him and his five guests. The contract was a simple charter that formed signatories into a common alliance of service to the nation. Called the Alliance, it was dedicated to serving the highest levels of government where other organizations could not, and to always work within the laws of the land. The six signatories have direct descendant heirs involved to this day – Merryweather Williamsburgh's great-great-grandfather, Albert Williamsburgh was one of the six, and the first Alliance Director.

Randolph House was Randolph Bedford's home and place of business. At the signing of the Alliance, he gave the property as the command center to the Alliance; ever since, it has served as the social and business center for its director.

To the public and to all but a very select few, Randolph House is a private business establishment used for executive conferences, and to serve as a focal point for civic charities and apolitical conferences. Its actual purpose is to serve the families and selected friends of the original signatories of the Alliance. Each staff member is attached as an employee to a specific member. For example, the Director's resident staff includes his butler who also oversees the service staff, the chef, the gentleman's housekeeper (with bodyguards), the drivers, and security. Each an integral link to the Alliance Command Center. In appearance, his personal staff, actually Alliance employees, ensure his command and control is never uninterrupted. Security is synchronized with the command center's every need.

Posh? The house and its members and guests are digitally supervised. Everything of importance is with digital-assist! The inner foyer doors open only as a result of scan approval. Members do what is natural and desirable to each. No matter the moral appetite, no matter the need, members rule absolutely.

A few minutes before 8:00 PM, the Director settled into his tailored, soft, leather dining seat. His unusual smile betrayed something different tonight; it dimpled at the sweet thought of impending danger. It was the feel of real action at home rather than abroad. The Director was on a mission of what would be survival! No turning back, the game was on.

Not a moment before or after eight, Dianna and Q stepped into the room. It is impossible to describe either of them except that Dianna caught the breath of most every man in the room. Q, on the other hand, was casual and athletic, the two a picture-perfect match. They pulled their chairs away and sat before the Director.

Most would say that the goddess was named for Dianna, her voice, throaty and soft-cold, could only be hers. "Director, I live for these moments. With you and Q, a woman is nothing but complete. Why must it always be a working dinner?"

Q could only smile. "Why is it that you never say that when we're alone?"

Leaning forward, "Children, before we begin dining, I have instruction for you both. Q and Dianna are your names for this exercise, but when you report in together or use the dropbox, your collective name is DQ.

"The envelope by your water glass contains destructible digital copy. In it is our descriptive format chip with virtual pictures taken in my office this morning. The woman, Ursula Rhue, I sense to be very dangerous. We will refer to her from now as Medusa, her code name. I want to know everything about her identity, her past, her intentions and especially her endgame which ultimately could include closure of this Alliance. Her confidant is a woman named Dianna.

"Should she be a pure and dumb innocent, I will give her every apology. There is no budget, no limits; use any secure government agency here or any place in need. Be slick, be silent and fast; in other words, work as you always do. As in the past, I am home plate for you. We will meet exactly two weeks from today at this Greenwich time, within one mile of wherever she will be.

"Please enjoy your dinner, children. She is dangerous. Almost as dangerous as you, Dianna!" They chuckled. Dianna had not taken her eyes from the Director, while Q searched her body language for any indication of what she was thinking. "From what I saw of her this morning, she is vindictive, without conscience, like a dangerous child, cruel. She is more than likely psychotic. That means, as you know, that she uses living things for her benefit. There is no empathy, just cold calculation. Should she lose with stakes too high, she will self-destruct, especially if she finds herself out of control." He raised his glass, "A toast to good hunting children. Deliver her to me. Oh, and Dianna, we are very interested in her political associations and activities especially here at home and the places she frequents. As I said, her confidant and, we think, her intimate friend, is also called Dianna!"

The Director smiled. "I am not sure I like where this investigation is going. For this reason, you are perfect for this piece of work. And Q, your chip will tell you more of her moral disposition. Because of this, she easily maneuvers an unsuspecting accomplice to do her worst work. I am sure that, should she see you, she would do all to move you into her plans."

As he raised his glass, his work phone buzzed in his jacket pocket, "Good evening Chief Kilmein. Nice to hear your voice…

You say that you have the Tutterville's amended Coroner's report? Can you have it brought to me here at Randolph House right away?"

"Well, children. We have an on-the-scene addendum to the Williamsburgh death file. By the way, Williamsburgh is pronounced Williamsboro, as in Edinburgh, Scotland. It appears that Tutterville's Police Department is one of the first we must visit. A Miss Lillian Atterby, a housekeeper, may have solved a significant part of our puzzle."

CHAPTER 7

RANDOLPH HOUSE

Anyone who lives in mountain foothills has experienced the tremendous power that thunderstorms can unleash. Once rolling thunder hits a mountainside and is drawn down into an open pass like the one that empties into the Tutterville cities, the titanic crash of thunder is indefinably deafening! It was this type of flash of thunder that sounded directly overhead as Miss Lilly placed the tea tray on the table next to Judge Tutter's chair. It was ear shattering and settled the house even further into its old and solid rock foundations. The pleasant part of such a storm can be the fresh scent of spring as it spends itself in torrents of water with unbridled force against windows and storm shutters.

A bit shaken by the sudden explosion, Addie continued to pour tea into each cup. Lilly served their Canadian guest first, then Chief Joanna Cutter and then, with a smile that hinted of intimidation, gave a cup to Chief Detective Westerly who did his best to hide his exasperation at her meddling annoyances.

Nodding toward Dianna, Judge Addie cooled her cup with a short breath, took a cautious sip, and then addressed Lilly. "We've sent two affirmations to the Coroner's report for Dianna's colleagues in Canada's Alliance. As one of the Alliance's inspectors, Dianna is here to bring home any dissenting views on the case. Apparently, Ms. Williamsburgh's death has drawn a lot of attention at home.

125

Chief Detective Westerly says that you, Lilly, suspect foul play."

Lilly walked pensively toward the mantle as a flash of lightning preceded another roll of thunder. "I seem to be rehashing old clues," she said absently. "There are three major contradictions that wouldn't fit, and each one of them involves the hotel housekeeper, Ussie Willow, who, and this is the third of the three contradictions, happens to fit the identity of Ursula Rhue.

"Just before last Thanksgiving, I went to the City Zoo's Botanical Garden. You know," she took a sip of her tea, too cool now, "that's when the Garden curators usually trim their rare and gorgeous plants, to graft or replant. And they have such rare and beautiful plants. Well, let me tell you, it is the best time of the year to just happen to be visiting if one would like some leftover clippings." Lilly smiled and pointed to a few plants on one of the more visible sideboards.

"Before they throw clippings out, I usually get first dibs on the discarded plantings I like."

"That's so nice," interjected Dianna. "My grandmother exchanges clippings from every home in her neighborhood."

"Of course, dear. Is there a more prudent thing to do?" Lilly smiled as though justified with her frame of thought. Chief Detective Westerly held back an enormous yawn. Lilly sipped again and caressed a new bud on her flowering Brugmansia suaveolens.

"This sweet and lovely flower isn't so sweet or as lovely as it appears. It is also known as nightshade and is of the potato family. It is actually quite poisonous. But not the poison that killed Ms. Williamsburgh and poor Happy Alcuette. No, that was quite a different poison, one more dangerous and an instant killer!"

Chief Detective Westerly bolted upright. "You've never mentioned this before Lilly. What's going on? What does the Botanical Garden have to do with anything?" His voice escalated impatiently.

Judge Addie waved a hush finger toward him. "Go on Lilly. Please. Dianna and I, we all find this very interesting."

Everyone went from Chief Westerly, to Addie, to Lilly, quite like a tennis match. "My dear Chief Detective, this is all my fault. When we spoke last, the pieces had not yet fallen into place. Now, with the death of Mr. Alcuette, I believe they have." Lilly poured a bit more tea, "The Botanical Garden happens to be contiguous to the zoo's Reptile Gardens, and in that garden, Chief Detective, you will find the murder weapon." Lilly smiled and sipped again, this time the pleasant taste of hot tea was very soothing.

Dianna stood. "Really, Lilly, I'm spellbound. You are a cool one, I have to say."

Lilly continued, "The second contradiction was solved with the death of poor Happy. I am sure that he was simply a necessary pawn in the hand of evil. I am also sure that he had no idea of his complicity in Ms. Williamsburgh's death, even as he himself died."

Lilly went on, quite absorbed in another clash of thunder, and began to pace absently, as in deep thought. "You must recall the housekeeper's comment to me, about when she discovered the body. She said that it was well-groomed, with natural looking makeup, and with her hands folded nicely atop her coverlet. Yes. Her exact words. I am sure she, whom we called Ussie at the time, gave the second contradiction its truth. Who would groom a corpse? Certainly not the dead woman herself. According to the hotel staff, Ussie was the only one to have discovered her death. Then, who would have the wherewithal to apply blush, comb and adjust hair, fold the body's hands so neatly, and finally, and most rationally, adjust and close the body's mouth?"

The room was stunned into silence, "Good Lord!" was all Chief Detective Westerly could muster. "Good Lord!"

Another long sip. "Yes, that was it, the makeup. The coroner's report mentions nothing of the makeup or the paste or device in her mouth, or whatever Happy Alcuette, or Hap, as he was called, used to clamp the body's mouth closed. At death, one's mouth is always quite agape, and because there is no face muscle for support, the mouth becomes completely flaccid. Perhaps the coroner's staff, not thinking, overlooked the device or paste because that's how things are done before the viewing. Poor dears.

"Happy Alcuette was a mortician, and of course, the perfect person for Ussie to call after she had killed Ms. Williamsburgh. Ussie Willow had a well thought out, and premeditated plan. There are more than a few funeral directors and morticians in the area. I am presuming she finally found one who was not beyond a simple seduction, or two. I think that's how Happy was lured into this very intricate and evil plan. That, of course, explains the warm cup of green tea on the bedside table, and its missing teabag." Lilly took a long breath… then smiled at the Chief Detective. She continued.

"Recall the tea bag question? I knew there had to be a very good reason for not finding it on the room's tea tray or in the wastebasket. Why would there be warm tea in the victim's room?

"Simply this. Since the death of Ms. Williamsburg was reported as heart failure and not foul play, no fingerprints were taken. Were there to have been fingerprints on the cup, they would have to have belonged to Mr. Happy Alcuette.

"Just after we last met, Chief Detective, I visited the hotel kitchen and found the reason there was no teabag in the bedroom. A gentleman, described much like Mr. Alcuette, made his own tea using a hotel cup. He discarded the teabag in the hotel kitchen where he'd made it. The staff houseboy recalls him quite vividly, and remembered him as, "attractive." The kitchen was at the height of morning activity, preparing breakfast for the inn's famous breakfast buffet. Mr. Alcuette was very out of place and was therefore quite obvious. This proves that poor Happy was not aware of any murder, he simply thought as you did, Chief Detective, that a heart attack or the like had taken Ms. Williamsburgh's life."

Dianna was first to speak after a rather long pause of surprise. "Lilly, I am completely caught up." She stood to leave, "That was a very comprehensive wrap-up. But, it's all very circumstantial. Any report I'd take to Canada would need to have prima facie evidence. Lilly, circumstantial isn't enough. When I get home, and we pull all this together, I'll call to coordinate your findings and ours, and those of Chief Cutter and Detective Westerly. I promise to keep you in the loop, Lilly."

"It would be premature to leave now, Dianna," Lilly, alarmed by Dianna's unrealistic reaction and abrupt body language – and Lilly knew body language. "The first of the three major contradictions is, I believe, what you are looking for and are here to find."

Dianna's stark reaction to what Lilly had just said accented the last of the storm's lightning that coincidently lit the room as Lilly continued. "Sorry to again contradict the finding that Happy

Alcuette also died of heart failure. No, he too was a victim. This is why the evidence becomes more than circumstantial, Dianna.

"Yesterday, when I heard of his 'accidental' death, a sudden flash of recall brought him back to memory. I had seen him before. He was in the company of no one other than Ussie Willow, aka Rhue. Where? Oh, near the Botanical Garden. It was on the same day I went for the clippings. He is, or rather was, a strikingly handsome man, 'attractive' as the houseboy recalled. A face and bearing one isn't likely to forget. They made a very attractive couple. I noticed that while he was looking at the exhibits, she was warmly chatting with a curator in the Reptile Garden, some distance away. Far enough away that poor Happy did not have the opportunity to see the murder weapon!"

"The murder weapon, Lilly?" Judge Addie asked incredulously.

"Yes, one of the deadliest poisons in the world! Before I say anything further, can we meet at the Botanical Garden tomorrow, at 10 in the morning? A demonstration, I think, will help."

*

The eastern slopes held the line of thunderstorms in place throughout the night. As the weather dissipated with dawn, early summer winds drove soft and silvery mists through Tutterville City, erasing traces of moisture and damp. The boulevard leading to the zoo glistened in a ribbon of platinum hues.

The zoo's lattice steel gates slid apart just as the police van approached. It was a good two hours before the public would arrive.

The Zoo Director opened the sliding passenger door and helped Lilly step down as Judge Addie and Chief Cutter opened theirs.

"Good morning, Chief, Judge, Miss Atterby; the rest of your party is having coffee in the Botanical Solarium. It's this way." He led them to the Atrium.

The Tutterville Living Zoo was enormous, a showcase not only for animals in free-range animal habit, but for animals that preferred indoor environments. It also contained a world-class Sea World, a Botanical Garden, and a university-sponsored Reptile Exhibitions Concourse.

The Atrium housed a multi-purpose visitor's center neatly divided into ticket booths: visitor assistance, souvenir shops, and its centerpiece, the University Culinary Institute Food Court.

Dr. Hendricks and Detective Westerly were about to order coffee when the Chief's party approached. "Is Dianna with you?" Mont asked, noting her absence with surprise.

Chief Cutter pressed her mobile unit, "Officer Green, do you have Dianna with you?"

"No, Chief, the desk says she checked out a little after four this morning and took a cab to the Airpark. One of our guys just reported a woman of her description left an hour ago for Detroit. I've checked her room, looks like it's never been used. Want me to check it out?"

"No, Billy, thanks. You can get back to duty. Thanks again. By the way, nice patrol work yesterday, City Circle. Nice work!"

Chief Cutter was more than angry. "Mont," she waved her phone at him, "what's going on, did she say anything to you about leaving? She really, I mean really, must be convinced that all we have on the Williamsburgh case is circumstantial. I have a sense that something else is going on right now – a puzzle within a puzzle.

They have the two signatures on the coroner's report citing death from natural causes, but now we're hot on what actually is otherwise! Let's finish here and get to the office, I have to call Canada…"

"Why am I not surprised?" Lilly interrupted, her face screwed in dismay. "All the evidence fits nicely; yet yesterday, she insisted that all we had was circumstantial evidence. I told her that the murder weapon is here in the zoo, along with an eyewitness. My intuition tells me you are correct, Joanna. There are layers to this murder which we don't yet see. Interesting! Someone has another agenda, or agendas. I think Dianna knows more than we might ever know."

Detective Westerly stood, "Well, Miss Atterby, it's time to show us your murder weapon."

Lilly beckoned to an attendant. "Chief, this is Mr. Rachman, the Reptile House Manager, the gentleman I spoke with a few days ago. He recalls Ms. Willow, whom we now know as Ursula Rhue, but he more clearly remembers Mr. Alcuette."

Mr. Rachman gripped Lilly's hand, "I have to see a picture to be sure she's the one. She's a persuasive one for sure! Her gentleman friend wanted nothing to do with snakes. He insisted I take a hundred bucks as a contribution to the zoo if I'd give his girlfriend a special tour. She was real excited, like a kid."

Lilly led him on, "What interested her most?"

"The darts, like I told you before. They have their own glassed-in exhibit." He pointed toward the exhibit, "Follow me."

The glass exhibit was moist and misty, a jungle habitat meticulous in detail. The frogs, brilliant yellow and bright red watched as they approached.

Lilly pointed to the service door, "Better still, can you show us how the exhibit is maintained? Is the door locked?"

"No," the manager answered, "but of course, once we're inside, each exhibit's access door is secured. It's a very dangerous place – double-locked doors for some, like the darts. Some of these animals are fatal to the touch."

The service area was a broad corridor with doors on each side; the exhibit cages for viewers on one side, and opposite side doors to related maintenance closets.

"Once we're inside the dart frog's atrium, we need a special key to enter their habitat." He opened the door. "As you see, it's a special dressing room, and directly across from us is the only entrance into this particular exhibit.

"The atrium has to be antiseptic and spotless. On these special racks we hang vinyl one-piece jumpsuits with protective headgear. Each atrium has its own stainless steel hose rack fixed over the room's central drain system. The slight slope of the floor permits liquid to flow right to the drain."

Only Lilly appeared to be comfortable as they stood together in the frogs' atrium.

Lilly observed, "Why the suits and hose?"

"Miss, these frogs are a few of the deadliest reptiles in the world. We have to hose down before and after we go in. You have two seconds to live if you just touch one. A designated vet and I are the only ones with a key."

"May Detective Westerly and I look at the lock on that door more closely?" Lilly moved forward.

"Before you do, please wear these latex gloves, Miss."

Lilly looked closely at the lock system. "Fairly ordinary,

Detective? A credit card might do the trick?"

Westerly smiled, "If you look carefully, there are some very light scratches on the inner bolt. Anyone forget their key lately, Mr., ah, Mr. Rachman, is it?"

"Never! There are always two of us here."

Lilly removed her gloves. "Mr. Rachman, it appears someone gently forced the latch. Were I to have the opportunity, could I reach in with, ah, say, with something like a barbecue skewer, wipe it along the back of that particularly beautiful red dart frog and, ah, have a good sample of poison to take away?"

"A good blowgun dart hunter would have preferred taking the sample from the yellow dart's belly. Deadlier, Miss. Just a touch will do... don't need penetration. To answer your question, yes, and the sample would be effective for at least a year..."

Chief Cutter studied Doc Hendricks face, "Can a new autopsy decide this?"

Judge Tutter settled her papers neatly into her carry-folder, left her bench, and took the few steps to the heavy door that protected her chambers from the usually crowded courtroom. She closed the door, pressed its lock and slipped from her robes; it had been the busiest day since the fair ended. Lilly's performance at the zoo earlier was an extraordinary analysis of the Williamsburgh deaths. Absolutely well thought out. And she's made perfect sense. Her Lilly, her housekeeper-detective. What a day.

The chamber was a rather large office and meeting room. Except for the fireplace wall and the wall directly behind her desk, bookcases stretched from the floor to a wall balcony, and then to the paneled ceiling. Two enormously comfortable leather chairs faced each other between shuttered windows; the brass pulls for each defined the bottom of each window, just inches above the floor. Usually the shutters were concealed in the walls behind the bookcases. Because of the heavy rains, the shutters were partially exposed.

She sat in the larger chair closest to her desk. It was warm and comfortable. Except for the lamps and chandelier, the room had gone unchanged since the first judge's wife had decorated it almost one hundred and some thirty years ago. As far as Addie was concerned, nothing would be changed. It was mellow, patinated with the years, and its walls knew the secrets and history of Hosea County since day one. Next to the phone table (the old pipe and tobacco stand) was a curiously ornate spittoon. It now served as a small but very adequate wastebasket.

Addie caressed the phone, her head back in thought, her body more than a little tense – now is the time to call him. The time is now, she thought, so quickly come, yet we've waited for years for this moment.

With a deliberate touch she pressed the speaker button, then dialed Harry Hendricks. As his phone rang, she placed the receiver to her ear.

"Doc Hendricks."

"Harry, good afternoon, busy?"

"If I were, Addie, I'd drop everything just to be with you. You know that. I pray it's about you and me..."

"Yes, it is. Can I take you to dinner tonight at Billies, say, at eight?"

She could almost hear Harry take in a long and deep breath. "Yeah, Addie, can't we do it now? Eight is a long way off."

"Gotta close the court and get my briefs ready for the morning. Seven-thirty?"

"I'm gonna dress up, just in case the judge hands out a life sentence!"

Addie laughed. "At seven-thirty. Bye."

Billies is a steakhouse with a simple menu: strip steaks, burgers and salads. Every side, no matter what, is ten bucks an order! So, Billies serves steaks. Harry waited for Addie by the door. Small talk later, they sat in a corner booth, private and comfortable with one another.

Harry's smile was intimate and longing. He couldn't take his eyes from her, measuring every word, every move. The waiter interrupted, "The usual steak, split, one salad split, and double fries? And to drink?"

Both nodded yes. "And," added Harry, "a bottle of Dom Perignon. It's a kinda anniversary."

"It's twelve years today, Harry," Addie touched his hand, her eyes searching his.

"I know. We did the right thing. It's been so, so very hard. We had to grow. School. Career. Getting established. We've done what we set out to do! You're a lawyer and judge, I'm a doctor. Twelve years, and here we are. I can't tell you how hard it's been for me. No one can ever, ever take your place in my heart, Addie."

"I know that, Harry. It's been harder for me than you know. I can't count the times I wanted to call. But even now I don't want to leave my work."

"That's the last thing I want, too. My life is to make you happy. Can't we get married? Can we?" his voice impassioned and insistent. "We can keep our careers and work together. I know we can." He pressed her hand; he had that soft smile that always calmed her.

Addie hesitated; she felt the warmth of his hand pressing hers, her memories a kaleidoscope of images passing by. Impassioned post-grads, they had set a plan into motion to finish school, to get established on their own, and then to discover life as real adults. Twelve years would be a good stretch of time, twelve years from career-day-one. They both had the same idealistic resolve, and as the years passed, there was no intimacy, only casual dating, busy at work, divining happiness into how they would spend their lives.

She reached for his hand and pulled it to her lips. "Oh yes, my sweet darling! I've ached so long for this moment, and it's come just as we'd planned. Our plans. Our decisions. Please, please my dearest, ask me that question just once more. Please."

Harry's eyes were wet and overwhelmed. He pulled a box from his pocket, opened it, and held it for her to see. "I've been saving this for you, for more than twelve years."

Addie was aghast! "What is it? Oh Harry! It's beautiful. Oh Harry..."

"It's your engagement ring." He held it out for her finger. "My sweet and beautiful Adelaide Tutter, woman of my dreams. Will you marry me?"

Addie slipped her finger into the ring, "Oh yes, oh yes Harold Hendricks! How many children like you can we have?"

Harry laughed. "As many, as many as you wish. Oh Addie," he reached across the table and they held a kiss that was as sweet a kiss as God has ever promised lovers. A voice pulled them apart.

"Your champagne?" The waiter shrugged, completely captivated by the lover's kiss he'd interrupted, repeated, "You want your champagne now?" As he placed their glasses down Addie asked, "Is Billie here?"

"Yes ma'am, he is personally doin' your steak. Something none of us has ever seen him do before. The chef is very upset!"

Harry's grin was a glimpse into his heart, "Tell Billie that if he isn't at this table within a minute, Judge Tutter will make his life miserable."

"Yes sir!" They both laughed.

"Oh Harry. At this moment I can say that I have never been as happy. In my dreams, I have never been this happy, and we're just beginning. Everything is different, the whole world is different!" Just then, Billie slipped into the booth beside Addie.

"What's the celebration all about, you two?"

Harry beamed, "Billie, meet the future Mrs. Hendricks. You are the first to know."

"Dearest God, I've waited for this for years! Addie, you have no idea how much pain this guy has been in. I don't know who he talks most about, you or that '32 Jag coupe he keeps working on."

"As my best man, Billie you'd better plan to close this place down for a very big wedding feast!"

"What do you think of my ring?" Addie held her hand toward him. "It will never leave this finger."

Billie held her hand to the light, "By the Lord Harry. This is absolutely gorgeous. What is it?"

"Remember our vacation after I finished my bars? You wanted

Australia and I wanted South America? The green stone is three carats. I found it in Guatemala. It was in a jewelry shop next to the museum. The guy cut it into this oval shape. Said he thought it was jade. When I brought it home, I had it appraised. It is jadeite. I've had it locked in a vault ever since! The four stones on each side are from Argyle, in Australia, remember their red diamonds? I bought a few chips and did the setting. It all proves that an amateur makes out when he doesn't know what he's doing!"

"Unbelievable Harry. It's gorgeous. You could buy half the county with that! It out-trumps any diamond ring I've ever seen this size."

Lilly had paced the floor for hours. It was after three in the morning when she recognized Doc Hendricks' car pulling into the drive. They opened the door together.

Before Lilly said a word, Addie pushed her hand forward. "What do you think of this?"

If Harry had not been there, Lilly would have collapsed on the spot. "It's a. It's a. It's an engagement ring!?" Harry held Addie tight.

"Yes, Billie's going to be Harry's best man, and you, Lilly will be my maid of honor."

"Oh Addie – oh Harry," she began to weep, steadying herself. "When everybody saw the two of you together on that parade float, we all knew this was going to happen. Oh, look at that ring. It's beautiful! Is it engraved?"

"Yes, Harry has thought of everything. It says 'Addie&Harry Forever.' I'll never fall asleep tonight. Please let's talk. There's some sherry, just what's needed!"

Harry exchanged his sherry for a whiskey and when Lilly had exhausted her natural search for detail, she settled forward, face screwed into an exaggerated frown and asked the question she'd feared to ask since her ward, Addie, took her first step. She needed to appear unconcerned, to look curious, anything to hide the feeling of fear that clutched her very heart.

"When," she swallowed the smallest sip of sherry, "when will you turn this old place over to the county, you know, as an historic family library?" No matter the answer, her life would now cease to have its present meaning, everything must now change.

"We are afraid the county will have a long time waiting. Tell her, Harry, what we've been thinking."

"Around Easter, you will have a bigger family on your hands, so we're sure you'll want to take on some help." Lilly froze, not daring to signal anything but the most agreeable and positive expression.

"Addie wants to add on a small wing that would connect her rooms to a larger suite, about the size of a new bedroom, with a nursery, if God wills. And you, Lilly, have to design that, as well as make room for an office for my research, and maybe a small workout room. Billie's brother is an architect and he is supposed to get the ball rolling as soon as tomorrow. What do you think?"

Addie glanced at Harry – she sensed Lilly's well-hidden concern. After all, Lilly had raised her as a mother and she could read Lilly like a book. Harry's news had taken Lilly's breath away. As usual, Lilly had turned everything over to God because He was always at hand. And, so He was!

After moments, Lilly could no longer hold back her emotions, she began to weep, a deep and silent weeping that released more than she realized.

"Oh, Lilly. Oh dear."

It took a few moments for Lilly to compose herself. Finally sitting back, she shrugged and smiled almost sheepishly. "My brother and I have been making very different plans for me. We thought that one day when you married, you might move, and the county would take possession of this house as a museum, as an historical place. When that would happen, we thought a nice apartment down from the courthouse would be just right for him and me."

"Lilly Atterby!" Addie was shocked. "My good Lord, Lilly, I had no idea that, that... the thought never crossed my mind that a day would come when we were not together. An apartment? Oh Lilly, would you want to be on your own? You must think me very selfish. You would be self-sufficient anywhere. I just have never imagined us apart. Is Hadley having any difficulty living alone?"

"Dear, Hadley is an institution. He and his friends are well beyond my league. Hadley is a very happy man. It isn't that I have ever wanted to move away. It makes sense that the man you would marry might want to live elsewhere."

"Not this man, Lilly. Family is family. You and Addie are just that, family, and I believe with all my heart that I belong to your family," Harry smiled.

Both Addie and Lilly gave him a hug.

Lilly's smile was proof enough that all was as it should be. She took Addie's hand. "Since you took your first step, Addie, I knew this time would come. I was never sure how I'd see it. You have made this the happiest day, not only for yourselves, but also for me. No, you very dear family, I will never need 'help' as you suggest, Harry. I don't care how many children you bring home. A nursery? I can't wait! There is a great deal of work to do and I am so proud and happy." With that, more tears, but quite obviously, happy ones.

"Oh, and another thing, wouldn't I fit in the category of grandmother of the bride? I know it's none of my business, but wouldn't Joanna be the better maid of honor?" The three smiled, quite content with the turn of events.

"That said, I am going to cook breakfast. After all, the three of us have to talk with the architect and you two must get to His Eminence for wedding planning. Oh, this is sooo exciting. Maybe I should have a sip of whiskey too, Harry!"

Addie gave Lilly another hug, "Now a few things add up Lilly. I thought that I had you figured out. After all of these years..."

*

The Director silently watched Q bring stats to life on the command consoles. A formidable agent, he thought, there's just one way to skin this cat, as they say, the end must be justified by its mean-equation. Q gave no sign of emotion, only professional calculation, and with a coldness that pleased the Director. My successor? He wondered.

At Q's command, Jorganna and Jason spilled Dianna and Medusa's profiles onto the great monitors. Q looked as calm and cold as he would before any kill. Completely in control, he was resigned to accept the greatest, if not the most personal, tragedy in his career. In fact, he was about to condemn to death the woman he'd come to trust with implicit conviction.

"In a nutshell, Director," his voice flat calm and detached, "as you see, the beautiful Dianna is our mole. Her trips to Italy coincide with Ursula Rhue's trip from Tutterville under guise as Ussie Willow. Once in the Alps, Ussie fingered Albert Williamsburgh while he was skiing on the slopes. They ignored the Principessa as just another of his friends, and both returned home, Willow to Tutterville and Dianna here, after, of course, Ussie'd killed Albert Williamsburgh.

"The next slide is their passport photos on return; once home, they go about their business. Ussie the killer, and Dianna the mole. We have no record of them ever being together except on Willow's return to Canada, and it was in a taxi just after she left your bank offices.

"This is Dianna at work. Had you not GPSed us at Randolph House, we would have missed this very quick meeting.

"The taxi driver is Dianna. Watch her hand a package to Medusa. There she goes. The package contains a new passport, traveling Euros, and a one-way first-class ticket to Cuenca, Spain, where they've rented a villa. Literally, Dianna is helping Medusa escape to nowhere! As you directed, I've reserved a suite for the three of us at the Cuenca Parador Nacional – four miles from Medusa's villa."

"Perfect, Q. When did you first suspect her?"

"The Tutterville action was too messy and way above Medusa's league. She was a careless puppet – her strings got a bit too tangled. Imagine, Director, Dianna an almost perfect double-agent, brought to check by a judge's housekeeper."

"Yes Q, and now we have to deal with two very difficult

national problems, quietly and efficiently." He smiled at this extraordinary, loyal agent. "You know what must now happen? Dianna is as dangerous and as calculating as you are. But, she doesn't play chess." His smile had become cynical. "We do... she will play this thing out. She is dangerous and must, I am sure, think she can't take a chance that we may be on to her. Yes, we will meet in Cuenca as planned."

Turning his attention to Jason, the Director asked the final crucial question, "I presume, Jason, that either you or Jorganna have something working on Albert's wife. Is she pregnant?"

Jason spoke first. "When she announced that she was his wife, Jorganna looked into the Principessa's entourage and found no medic or physician." He nodded to his assistant Jorganna, to complete the scenario.

"One of our Rome Italian-speaking nurses was dispatched to the Italian Ambassador and was in time to conveniently ask to assist the Principessa. That was the woman you saw helping the ambassador carry the Principessa to a seat when she collapsed. Apparently, the prayers of the world helped because she is carrying Albert's child."

The Director sat with a resolute frown, "So, when Medusa hears of this, that woman and her child will be put out of the way."

Joanna continued, "Yes, however, our nurse just left for Rome as part of the entourage. The Principessa is quite safe, at least until after Medusa's visit to Spain."

Jason continued, "With your permission Director, we can have our Italian offices warn her family, as well as the Italian police."

"Good, Jason, do that immediately..."

CHAPTER 8

CUENCA & SWEET CARLOS

A new moon washed Hosea County into different evening hues. The air was clean, the sky bright, and the night stars brilliant enough to grab from the sky. Addie Tutter felt as free and happy as the air that rippled into the roofless top of Doc Hendricks' Jeep. She looked at Harry. She loved the frown of concentration that furrowed his brow as he maneuvered through traffic. He's so perfect, she thought, so strong, so very masculine! She gazed at his profile, drinking in this man who was completely and wonderfully hers.

Harry caught her gaze, "Know how much I love you?"

Addie nodded yes, "And I love you so, so much. Did we waste our twelve years? Sometimes I think that had we struggled together, we'd have children by now and things would be very different. It hurt to wait. It was a struggle for me." She pressed into his shoulder. "We made a promise and we kept it."

"Darling, regrets are the devil's playground. The best to come for us started the moment you said yes!" Harry winked and grinned. He meant every word. "His Eminence is quite a guy. I think he looks at you as his daughter. When you said we'd like a date at Easter time he was very happy to accommodate!"

Addie laughed, pulling herself closer to him. "Yes, the Sunday after Easter in the late afternoon."

Harry turned the Jeep onto a cross-town road, the shortcut

to Addie's house. As he began the turn, the flashing red lights of a car in distress made him turn wide. Reaching for his medical kit, he pulled to the curb in front of the car.

"That's a woman waving." He came to a stop.

"Can we help out?" He called.

"Oh, thank you for stopping! Our car just stalled, and it won't start!" She called back.

Addie and Harry hurried to the car. He pressed his police phone to his lips. "Hi, this is Doc Hendricks, I have a stalled car with a family at this fix, can you send a car?"

"Roger that, Doc, one's already on the way," came a quick reply.

He approached the car, "Hello, I'm Doc Hendricks and this is Judge Tutter. Everything okay? I've called a police car. It's on the way."

"Hi, I'm Isz Hunter. It just stalled right here in the middle of the intersection. My husband's on his way."

"Hey! Judge Tutter! It's me, Park!" A young voice called from the car.

"Park Hunter! The best basketball player in town." Addie grinned in surprise.

"This is my Mom, Isz and my brother Will."

Isz Parker took her hand, "How do you do, Judge. I know you, Doctor Hendricks – you did such a spectacular job putting that fair together." Her laugh was sweet and soft, "You should do it for us every year. It was a gigantic success!"

"Why, thank you very much!" Doc replied, "once is enough though, I have to say. Nice to see you again Park. This is your brother

Will? Nice to meet you, son." Will nodded, silent.

Isz Parker leaned toward him. "Willie, say hello to Judge Tutter and the doctor."

"Ta Ta Ta atter, Tutter, hi, Judge. Ha ha hello, da da doctor."

Isz's smile was loving and not at all one of concern, "Park was just like Will until he turned twelve. I mean, the same way of speaking. We guess that William has another year or so to go before his voice clears up."

Addie's eyes went wide! Her teeth grasped her lower lip. She could hardly say a word. Finally, almost in a rasp, "Are, are you saying, Mrs. Hunter, that his speech impediment is hereditary?"

"Why, yes. Oops! Here is the police car…"

Addie was silent all the way home. Finally, comfortable in the 'Great Chair,' she felt shock growing deeper by the moment, rooted in utter dismay. Red faced and almost shaking, her heart beating almost too rapidly, she shook her head quickly, attempting to regain control. She looked at Lilly and Harry.

"Will? That boy? He has our family stutter! It's like hearing myself twenty years ago. Over and over again."

Lilly brought some tea. "Has to be a coincidence dear, and it's an extraordinary one to say the least."

"I don't think it's a coincidence. His mother said that Parker had the same impediment until a few years ago; it's a family thing. Just like ours."

Lilly took a breath to cool her tea, "If it is, Addie, it might be tooo big a coincidence;" she shrugged, "if there is a link between you and them, DNA will solve that question instantly!"

Harry smiled. "Does the name Hunter have any relevance to

your family tree, Addie?"

Addie's eyes misted. She looked into Harry's soft and emoted face; a smile of recollection and dim memory broadened into a romantic grin. "I recall great-grandfather's stories of his family in Virginia, how after great-granduncle Hosea's death, he couldn't go home and face the family. He blamed himself for his brother's death, and especially the broken dreams of Hosea's fiancé Sally *Hunter*. They were to be married the Christmas of that very year.

"Parker Hunter. This is crazy!" Addie reached across the chair to Harry.

Suddenly, Lilly stood, waving to everyone to stop talking. An incredulous thought made her wave her hand again. As quick as that, she had what could be the answer to everything.

Lilly cleared her throat with anticipation. "Addie!! Isn't there an old oilskin packet in your safe at the courthouse?"

"Why, yesss, it's to be opened some time in the twenties, or something like that! It's in great-grandfather's second will. To be opened some 200 years after his death. No one has any idea what's in it."

"Yes!" interjected Lilly, "and doesn't the letter with it read that it is to be opened on that date, *or earlier*, if 'a direct heir deems dire need'?"

"Dear Lilly. You recall as much, if not more of this family than I do. How can we live without you? If tomorrow doesn't tell us anything, DNA will. Without you Lilly, where would we be?"

*

The blue skies of arid, central eastern Spain barely transformed the stark hillsides of the city of Cuenca. The presence of its famous fortress-like hotel, Parador Nacional, dominated everything within miles. Once an enormous convent/monastery, it now attracts wealth and those seeking elegance. Small windows betray little of its tradition and luxury. Perched cliff-like and well above the village streets, the Parador is stark and solitary in its amber-aged walls, accenting the privacy its guests seek.

As planned, the time had come to meet near Medusa – the Director, Q, and Dianna, for their ultimate decision regarding Medusa, Ussie Rhue. Too much was happening to even imagine that Rhue wasn't a big player in all that was going on.

A bunch of surprising pieces were beginning to take shape in Dianna's three-dimensional mind!

Multinational banks – one plan – global – all coordinated – sudden premeditated deaths of great wealth heirs – poison – lotza mulla! (Thank the Lord for Lilly, now that's an IQ.) Rhue! She's deeply involved. Should the Agency, including the Director and Q, see the puzzle as she did, there might be a leak big enough for Ussie Rhue and her gang to disappear into hiding until a safe time! Awareness of the biggest clue of all would really blow the whole thing away. If that should leak – WOW, all my work would be changed. This was so big a clue, that very powerful forces were purposely keeping it silent – at what cost, or what bribery, and how deep into their plan had they moved? How could the lid be kept closed when billions of international currencies moved silently to each of seven global banking systems? Hmmm... Dianna smiled. *Seven banks and Ussie. Let's call this the Candidate of Seven and Rhue! The Stock Market is my crystal ball! Why? Because it can read like a book. Because,* she believed, *the flow of currency foretold more than the state of a nation's wellness, but also the wealth of huge multi-national banks and corporations. As a student of finance in school, one soon noticed that before a financial crash, a severe market fluctuation (positive or negative) or the transfer of large sums of money from one bank to another connoted disaster for either party, or a payoff for something. Like myself,* she thought. *Knowing the time to buy and sell was the success of my own big bucks!*

During recent months and too coincident with Ussie's treachery, she'd observed a new and interesting huge change in global transfers of money. At first there were a few moves of significant volume – and no one sounded an alarm. A few days later there were more transactions with different currencies. No alarms, yet very private transfers of large sums, as well as metal currency. The first few were from Calcutta to Switzerland, the others to five global banking systems around the world. It was such a vast amount, yet done secretly, as if by sleight of hand… so very discreet and quick; yet, no alarms. Coordinated? Apparently so and yet, why never before and suddenly now?! Then, a few weeks ago, an enormous correction occurred from Canada to a Swiss bank – a canceled transaction of one hundred and fifty billion Canadian dollars. The transaction went down in the blink of an eye – Dianna had it on tape. It did happen? The time frame coincided with Ussie's appearance in Canada. Global crisscrossing transactions. But, not with Alpine countries. Why?

Something could very well be afoot. Too much murder and too much money! Worldwide. A clumsy endeavor, or at worst, an international maniacal plan for world dominance?

Was it the awakening of a master plan to eventually change the politics of the west? Is Medusa's wealth key? The shadowy fingers of the person or persons she had long ago labeled 'Candidate! Now Candidate of Seven!' Austria... What about Austria? Aloud, Dianna laughed: "My dearest, sweetest, darling, most-sexy Carlos will tell me that when he awakens me with a deep and sweet kiss!"

She knew beyond doubt that her suspected conspiracy was valid, and that Medusa, Ussie, was a master co-conspirator... Ussie had to be neutralized!

And so, in a most secure and private lab, she and Carlos had developed the death frog's deadly poison into a diluted drug that would neutralize the Director and Q while she and Carlos took care of Ussie.

*

Late that evening they arrived in Cuenca, the *darkest hour* had come. Dianna, dressed as black as the night, slipped from her bedroom in the Royal Suite. Its tapestried walls hushed the room, lavish in alabaster, silk and gold; the quiet noise covered her secretive movement along the balcony that opened from the suite's three bedrooms. The posada was at its darkest this part of the night.

She listened to be sure the Director and Q were asleep; they'd had a long day. Good wine and tales of Medusa's flight from Canada to her hillside villa a few kilometers nearby had finally lulled the three to deep yawns.

Dianna paused, cat-like and silent against the wall. She listened for their heavy breathing. The Director slept silent, unlike Q's purr-like snore that she recalled from late nights past. The three bedrooms opened onto the balcony; hers was the center. As she expected, their doors were open and draped only by dark-colored silk gauze. It was time. First the Director, then Q, and then before dawn to the villa, and to Medusa and Carlos. Medusa had to die, the others had to sleep while she disappeared to uncover the Candidates' nest – for were she to build her case with the Director, word would certainly leak and the Candidates would live for another day.

Her black outfit covered all but her eyes. She waited silently until a good breeze moved the Director's draped doorway. Heavily gloved, she slipped a small wooden cask from her side pocket, opened it, and looked inside for the needle-pin protruding from a single, rubber glove-like finger – she slipped it snugly on her left forefinger, smiled, and took a soft and deep breath; so far all had gone well. Now, she whispered to herself, one small touch each, and both will fall into a deep sleep, and that will be the beginning of the change of everything!

Just as the crescent moon slipped into sight, a gentle breeze separated the drapes enough for Dianna to slip into the bedroom, and as quietly, to the Director's bedside. Gently, she pressed the fingered needlepoint into the Director's scalp. It was done! As she moved away, the envelope of silence suddenly *vanished*! She froze! Mesmerized in prickly fear! It was another presence, close, but in the room. The Director's distinctive sigh froze her in mid-step; as suddenly, light filled the room.

The Director's voice was cold and detached, "Dianna, you played the evening well. It was interesting being the hunted for a change. You are very thorough. By the way, that's a dummy under the sheet. Your touch would have been quite fatal. Ah!" Beckoning to the door, "Q! Please come in."

Q stood just inside the window, "You were right as usual, Director. She went for you first."

Dianna's mask hid all but disbelief in her eyes. She smiled at Q and then at the Director, and as quickly took a short, deep breath. Reaching to her cheek, she tapped it with her fingertip. In a moment, she fell to the floor, apparently quite dead!

"And now Q, on to Medusa."

Q pulled the rubber fingertip from Dianna's hand and slipped it into its cask; the evil needle-pin sheathed once again.

A profound sadness darkened his face… his voice deep with emotion. *"And now… death, the night yet must be your shield; one last time the dart will speak."* Quickly, he draped Dianna over his shoulder.

Minutes later, their black Ferrari Enzo slipped through the Posada gates and sped toward Ursula Rhue's villa; the black night to supposedly forever seal the lives of Dianna and her friend, the very evil Ursula.

*

Another black, less elegant car was parked hidden in the best man's garage. It would be there until the end of the wedding reception, ready for a fast getaway with its bride and groom.

Addie, Lilly, Isz Parker, Joanna, and Doc Hendricks' mother Beth, sat comfortably in the great Tutter House living room. It was late Friday eve, the wedding just two days away. They'd long since finished tying the loose ends of their pre-wedding meeting. All attention was on Lilly as she proudly described the new additions to the house, especially the nursery. Looking at the bride, her smile betrayed her love, "Addie, I can't wait for the future, your babies and Isz's cousins!"

"Don't rush it, Lilly," Isz laughed, "everything is so new for us. The big news goes public this Sunday in the Center Section of The Tutterville News Times. A front-page story, too!"

Addie laughed, "That picture of you and I, Isz, *Reunited Lost Cousins*, will be the talk of the Tuttervilles for weeks. If it weren't for Lilly's suggestion to open great-great-grandfather Tutters' second will, none of this would have happened for another 12 years, and even then...."

Beth interrupted, "That was truly an extraordinary thing you did, Addie. Your decision to share what you already have, and then to give all of your great-great-granduncle Hosea's hidden treasure to the Hunter family. All this will become a centerpiece of Tutter history forever!"

"By right," Addie continued, "all of it belongs to your family, Isz. We can't deny that great-granduncle Hosea would not have meant otherwise." Addie meant every word. "At last, I think, great-granduncle Hosea has taken care of his family. Imagine how much great-aunt Sally suffered. I don't think she was consolable. The Tutters, Hunters and Parkers have become an extraordinary family, all because of those two."

Isz, moist-eyed and resolute, "Can you imagine Sally moving to New York when she discovered she was pregnant? She and Hosea were too young. She lived to nurse their son for just a few days before she slipped away. Little Parker Hosea Hunter went back to Virginia and grew up sailing and farming, a Hunter-Tutter boy. How that child must have been loved!"

Doc Hendricks mother, Beth shook her head, "The whole story is like a fairy tale. I'd love to know the particulars! I heard a little of it when I came in. Is it too long a story for tonight? How the gold was recovered?"

"Of course not, Beth, but it's really Lilly's story to tell. If it weren't for Lilly, none of this would have happened for another 12 years. Thank the Lord, Lilly, that you remembered great-great-grandfather Tutter's second will. Tell Beth, Lilly."

"Well," Lilly began, "the second sealed will was in the Courthouse safe. I remembered seeing it some years ago. It was to be opened before August of 2022 only by a direct heir, and only in the event that a dire emergency existed. Of course, with Will's stutter being hereditary just as Addie's was, Addie wanted it read. The will was succinct and quite clear:

> *Beneath my dear and most loved brother Hosea's coffin is a sealed crypt, carved from stone. His name is engraved on its door. A copy of this will lies within a Bible, just inside the crypt.*
>
> *I divided all of the gold we mined — one-third I take with me; Hosea's gold is with him in his crypt. Sally Hunter was to be my brother's wife. This gold is for her descendants, for her direct heirs, and no one else!*
>
> *I am responsible for my dear brother Hosea's death! I love him so, so very much.*
>
> *This century is a difficult one with few to trust, and so I have delayed making known this treasure, prayerfully*

hoping that a new generation will honor this will, as my dear Hosea's bequest.

Signed: Adam Tutter, Jr. — Hosea's Brother

This 4th day in August 1822

Isz filled the silence. "My husband's great-great-grandmother Sally Hunter died just after her baby was born. Imagine how much they loved each other."

The phone brought them back into focus. Addie went to her desk. "Hello? Yes, just a moment. Joanna, it's Chief Detective Westerly for you."

"Mont, what's going on…? Chief Kilmein? Of course, patch him in. Good evening, Chief. Nice to hear your voice too. Oh… oh, how sad. Yes, things do have a way of working themselves out. Yes. As a matter of fact, Lilly is right here… oh… how amazing! Thank you. You have a safe and peaceful weekend as well. Yes… Good night, Chief. We'll talk on Monday. I'd like to close that case forever! Good night."

Putting the receiver in place, Joanna turned to Lilly. The smile she wore brought the room to the edge of curious disbelief. "As this city's Chief of Police, Lilly Atterby, I have to say this is truly a first. I think we need to pass some champagne around." Lilly stood. Joanna raised her hand. "Not for you to do, Lilly. Addie will serve it!"

Joanna had to sit. "The Canadian Chief says that if it were not for your diligent work Lilly, Merryweather Williamsburgh's murder would not have been discovered and Ussie Willow, Rhue as she is now known, would be a wealthy and quite prosperous woman. As it is, both Ussie and our friend, Dianna, were discovered dead this morning by the Cuenca, Spain, police. Dead of natural causes – I wonder about that!"

"Good Lord!" Lilly sprung to her feet. "Natural causes? The Spanish police?"

"Chief Kilmein reports they were found in a villa. The circumstances imply that they were, how shall I say, more than friends? He's to call me on Monday with the details." Joanna went to Lilly's side.

"Lilly, the Chief claims that they both planned to harm national security." Joanna straightened her shoulders to police-like attention. "And you, Lilly Atterby, are to be awarded their National Citizen's Award for Diligence and Bravery!"

With that declaration, the cheers and yells of five wedding planners moved the old Tutter homestead at least five inches further from its foundation.

*

Had anyone predicted that this wedding weekend would exhaust every form of media within 500 miles of all the Tutterville cities, as well as draw national media, they would have underestimated the event by half! The big headlines: "Bottomless Wealth in the Old Tutter Tomb!" "Our Own Hunter Family and The Tuts of Tutterville!" "The Last of the Old Tutter Family to Marry Today!" "Canada's Citizen Award to Lilly Atterby!" "Judge Addie's Wedding Dress and THE Honeymoon!"

The bride's carriage and her cortège were minutes away. The

groom and his best man Billie, along with Father Russ DiPasqual and Cardinal von Hertzog, sat comfortably in the cathedral sacristy lounge watching Addie's wedding cortège move slowly along the crowd-packed boulevard leading to the cathedral. The voice-overs went from one network to the next, "… the Chief of Police, Joanna Cutter, is the Maid of Honor. Her mounted police escort numbers over 200 horsemen, brilliant in gold and crimson uniform jackets – spectacular!"

"The Bride's dress is ivory! Reports are that it was her great-grandmother's…"

"Unquestionably, the Hunter family has a big role here today. Mr. and Mrs. Hunter and their two sons look gorgeous in their open landau – already they're referred to as the royals of Hosea County. What a story that is folks; a few months ago, middle class, and today, mega millionaires!"

"The third woman in the bride's landau is Lillian Atterby. She was the Judge's childhood nurse and her confidant ever since. She's acting as the bride's mother, and oh, she is one very sharp lady – her Canadian Service Award is a scratch on the surface. Nothing escapes that gal's uncanny logic!

"We can see the bride! Oh… She's beautiful! The last to carry the Tutter name… Soon it will be Her Honor, Judge Adelaide Adamson Tutter Hendricks… the family says they've been in love since they were teens. How romantic is that!"

Father DiPasqual knocked, "Your Eminence, looks like it's time. This way Doctor Hendricks. The bride's carriage is just about here."

Moments later the satin slippered bride stepped onto the

crimson carpet that led to the altar. Breathless, Harry reached for Billie's arm, "Billie, do you believe this is happening? That woman is to be my wife! Lord, Billie, how can this be?!"

*

Silvery blue water caressed the hull of the Lover's Waltz. The shallows south of Turks were warm and almost still. Addie and Doc sat tanned and dozing in their deckchair. The boat's butler coughed softly, "Ahemm. Doctor and Mrs. Hendricks, dinner is served…"

Addie raised her glass to her husband. "To us, for always."

"For always," Harry replied…

Chapter 9

The Metamorphosis of Dianna

Dianna awakened, slow pain forced her eyes to open – but they would not... she was buried far from the world in an abyss, beyond her grasp. Dazed, her heart barely skipped, as though opposing each breath. She pressed harder to see, to hear, to recognize the urgent call that would not come to memory. Danger, danger! Dianna gasped for air. Each push to open her lungs brought more and more memory rushing in to fuel her fear. David flashed as a blur, a haunted child... screaming for her to save him. Albert atop, as on a pony, laughing with a maniacal crescendo in pace with Satan. Filled with fear Dianna grasped for her falling children... The next breath came deep from exhausted lungs. She was fleeing from the bottom of the deepest of pits, dark, wet and yet... Just for a flash, she was fearsomely comfortable. She swam up, up, no air. "Oh God," she screamed! A vice-like, powerful grip locked her in place, keeping her from leaving the abyss. Grasping at anything, she flailed her arms to reach the surface. Desperate to come awake! Fists slamming flesh – fists bashing and clawing at flesh – flesh struggling to pull her away... and a silvery, shimmering voice, "Awaaake my ladee, awaaakee, we arrrreee herrrrree..." The Spanish-accented voice pushed her memory clear of vice grips while her legs involuntarily intertwined with cold, dead flesh. Screaming again, she was muffled so forcefully that she could neither bite nor breathe. Losing consciousness, the hand released her.

"Come with me, my lady," the voice repeated, "we must flee before policia people come!"

Dianna fell from the bed, half conscious. She shrugged, her mind cleared, bringing her into the present.

"Carlos..." she whispered.

"Yes, my lady. All is as you have contracted." Carlos, a brawling brute of a man, helped her to her feet then reached to the dark floor and lifted the nude body of a woman onto the bed. With practiced precision he put it alongside the other body so as to make the appearance of two women who'd fallen asleep in their intimacy. "This is what you wished, my lady, I am sure, my lady? The Ursula one fainted when she saw the corpse I'd placed in her bed; I muffled her breathing until she was gone and placed them in bed, as you instructed."

Dianna looked at the sleeping tableau – Ussie Rhue and a woman who looked very much like herself. "Ussie. Oh, Ussie..." She reached for the silent body sprawled naked across the bed and repulsed. More than just recognition flooded her memory; everything at once came clearly into complete focus. She had survived. The Director and Q had reacted to the better scenario, as she'd expected. They thought her dead! No. Everything had gone precisely as she'd planned. Now she was free and only Carlos knew she was alive. When I drive from here, she thought, all must change. I will never be the same Dianna. The edges of fear gripped her with a sensation she's never before experienced. Carlos' voice broke into her conscious.

"My lady, your clothes are in your car; it is parked close by. Let us hurry. The policia have been called."

Carlos pulled her up, lifting her weight so that she could walk in her still drowsy state. He easily lifted her through the open portico, along the arched garden walkway, and onto the patio path that led to an old and unkempt garden, then beyond into a forested glen, and thence into the night's darkness. It took a few more minutes until they reached an unpaved road. A car was parked at its edge.

Pulling from his grip, she opened the door and sat for support. The car was an old, small Fiat tucked well into the roadside bush. Carlos pulled a small suitcase from the back seat. "No one can see us here, my lady. All is safe now. We must drive away as soon as the policia drive from the cottage. We will see the car headlights through the trees."

Dianna studied Carlos as he spoke. Brute, and so attractive. She thought of Q. The side effects of the drug and the thought of Q, the excitement of success, whatever the reason, flushed through her senses; she became thoroughly aroused. Carlos saw her catch her breath as he placed the suitcase on the ground. "May I help you dress, my lady?" His smile gave way to a glance that weakened Dianna knees... their kiss and embrace was long and furious.

At last, breathless, they stood, leaning against the car. Dianna's flushed face became serious. "Seville will complete the first part of our contract," she held his gaze, "Seville must be done as we've devised. No changes. No time to waste. When you see that I've parked and left the car, when all is clear, quickly get into it and release the hood. You will find my new name in the fuse box. Once you read it, you are to forget previous names I've used.

"Wherever I go in the city, remain close but out of sight. When you see that I have left Seville, drive to Lisboa, Portugal, and then find Bella at the Hotel Fortaleza Guincho in Cascais. The hotel is a few kilometers northwest, on the coast. She works at the desk, night shift. She will recognize you when you tell her my name. After Guincho, go immediately to the Casino Estoril. We will meet there." Dianna leaned against Carlos as if to emphasize all she'd said. "Do you have any questions, Carlos?"

"None, my lady. Everything is as you have described before."

Dianna pressed closer to see if he would be ready a second time... he was. "Oh... perfect, Carlos... When you check your bank again, you will find I have doubled your fee." Carlos grinned. He held her closer, "My lady, the world is yours. No mortal man will find a better employer." His laugh was cut off as she pressed him against the car...

Not too much later, he nudged the Fiat into the roundabout and exited onto N-420. He pulled to the side of the road and parked; it was a few minutes before midnight. "In an hour or so, my lady, you will reach highway E-901/A3 toward Valencia. From there the signs will direct you to Seville. With the usual traffic, it is 350 kilometers, about a six hour drive." He opened his door as Dianna left hers to take the driver's seat.

"You have done well, Carlos." She reached up to hold his arms and pulled him into another long, and hungry embrace. "You have helped me many times. I know that only you, as ever before, will have my back in Seville for seven days. Remember, no contact between us unless it is urgent. You will leave the city after I do. Soon we will meet again." She settled herself into the driver's seat.

"You are a good contract, my lady. I will always be here for you... whenever you call me."

"It is you, Carlos, who makes the contract good." Dianna smiled, "Tonight, you sealed it two times in a very special and pleasant way. Keep safe and always be careful, you have never left a trail that could be unraveled; do it now. Goodbye." And she sped away, leaving him alone in the dark quiet of Cuenca.

*

Dianna accelerated to the speed limit and drove absently for a few minutes and then, sleepily, she grasped the wheel with both hands and leaning forward, fell into an unexpected reverie. Almost hypnotic, she looked into the stars that filled her windshield. In moments, self-absorption transformed her reverie to sadness. Memories from long ago crowded her conscious mind. Innocent memories of childhood, but as quickly as each formed, it was overcome by adult, fearsome, and almost self-loathing images. Borderline frantic, she swept her fears aside, her rational conscious replacing them with feelings of pride. For the Ussie equation, she had always been on the heroes' side of justice, the side that fought for good. She and Q worked as a team, always with a professional distance that blanketed emotion. How long had she loved him? Forever. She knew that he felt deeply for her as well. She could not shake him from her thoughts. The intimate moments earlier with Carlos were really with Q. Where Carlos was an athletic and bulky man, Q was as elegant as a fencer but with the power to break the neck of a Carlos in seconds. Q was lithe, quick, tough as steel and almost too good looking. He could pass himself off as a peer to anyone – from laborer to prince. Now, he is mine and a tough one he will be. She smiled. He thinks he knows me... he doesn't, but I know him! I can calculate the factors of risk better than he can.

Dianna understood the cost of her risks. The country's security meant that the end of this great adventure had to justify its means. Most in her business only saw insidious evil for what it appeared to be, and not so much for its root. As with all puzzles, the picture was amiss if one of the pieces was misplaced, misunderstood or faked. Dianna's forte was to see the overlooked, the hidden piece, and trace it to its source before anyone else could; thus, before the agency knew, she would literally have executed that 'hidden piece,' thus neutralizing the enemy's threat. Unbeknownst to everyone, especially the Director and Q, she had long ago assigned herself the task of 'fixing loose ends.'

With the security of the west in question, Dianna had to usurp evil as it presented itself in its nescience – but carefully! The evil could escape for another day and not be unmasked.

The name Dianna was known in agencies around the world. She'd stood for justice; that is, until shred-like inklings of the darkest evil had led her to Ursula, the loose link so intimately attached to so dreadful a cause. The puzzle-like pieces always matched-set, and that is how she kept on track!

Ussie had to be managed until she, Dianna, could process the link between Ussie and the darkness that threatened the very way of life for the west, perhaps the world! For now, she had named that darkness the 'Candidate of Seven.' She had no idea the source of this name, except that in her mind it footnoted a singular, master manipulator. So, she'd filed it in the hidden, impenetrable compartment of her mind. It was as good a name as any, for the darkness was an entity, and its cognitive energy may well be beyond her own.

Ussie was connected to it, some way, somehow, and the Candidate was now in his germinal stage, the stage that by definition had to devour victims, money and secrecy.

The darkness had so lured Ussie into its strategy, that she may have become a most willing tool. And, there was much to be gained, for Ursula Rhue, as a distant cousin, lived contiguously to the vast Williamsburgh fortunes.

Dianna sensed the fragmented evidence that had intoxicated Ussie. The only way for her, Dianna, to discover more, was to join Ussie in her conspiracy... to become a traitor. That she had done. Now, on the outside and disgraced, she was free to interact with evil. There was just one slim chance to one day both justify herself, and to thwart 'the Candidate of Seven;' this was now, her only path... or to die in disgrace, trying...

She smiled to herself; should the Candidate know of me and my disgrace, he too must believe I am dead. If I play my plan well, he or it will not suspect me as a challenge until I am ready for him. A thought almost made her laugh aloud. There was the insane chance that he, or it, might come to me for help! I wonder if he owns Carlos... No, he doesn't. Of that, she was quite correct. And Bella, too.

The road signs indicated that Seville lay ahead in the darkness. Looking at the stars again she thought of the disgrace she would soon face unless her plan worked. She whispered aloud, somewhat more tired, "My life is always at the call of someone else." Tears formed and began to fall. She pushed them aside roughly and laughed aloud. "It is over! No more. Now I am completely alone!" Eyes dried, she settled back. Q will one day be mine, she had to believe it! And we will have a life filled with grace and loveliness. He will find me. But he must not… not too soon. The evil one must be destroyed for the cancer that it is. The 'Candidate' will be stricken… The finality of that thought and the fullness of its meaning sealed her as a sole conspirator. She was truly alone!

An hour or so before Seville, as though involuntarily stricken, her heart seemed to surge again. She leaned forward to look again at the stars; instead, the morning moon beaconed with the most intense clarity. In its fullness, a white brilliance swept the skies, blinding the stars. Dianna, a little dazed with exhaustion, breathed a deep sigh and the whisperings of a prayer-like dream began to form on her lips. Her eyes became moist again. How can I do all this alone? The prayer went to God, whom she knew would hear. I can, I can do this. She almost shouted aloud: "With so much evil to undo, only God – you, God – must be on our side!"

Sitting back, Dianna searched for the calm she would need to complete what had to be done; no, what must be done, before she could prove her innocence and find happiness.

The remainder of the drive gave her time to recall and validate what she had to do. She thought of Ussie and Ussie's clumsy impulsiveness. Ussie'd lost everything because of her greed. Grandiosity stood in her way. Ussie's plan to assassinate the Williamsburgh heirs was clinically perfect. As the last remaining and distant heir, Ussie Rhue would inherit their vast fortunes. Dianna watched Ussie plot each step to gain her fortune. The 'Candidate' was using her to cut Williamsburgh funding to the Director.

The prize offered her must have been blinding.

All Ussie's plans had crumbled to nothing and she, the silent Dianna to the scheme, watched while Lilly, the grand-master-intellect (at least a Mensa), a simple housekeeper, do her work. Now, that is a woman! Dianna smiled. Even before Ussie began her merciless rampage of murder, Lilly suspicioned the plots, one after the other, each buried in layers of intricate schemes. Within a few days of simple analysis, that woman had completely unraveled Ussie's plan, and had even exposed them to the Director! Dianna had to leave town before she herself was discovered!

Lilly, hmmm… Dianna wondered; her IQ was probably near her own, probably near 160. Extraordinary, she was not afraid to expose her intellect. She'd put Ussie's strategy together from recollection and fragmentary clues: a casual recall of Ussie visiting the Tutterville Zoo. Dianna laughed: the corpse in the hotel with its mouth closed, a warm cup of tea by the bedside, poison-carrying frogs, a promiscuous undertaker. Dianna shook her head. That poor fellow was probably the only innocent bystander! Everyone had to die to make Ussie rich… Lilly, the master detective, how she would love to know her, to be her friend. How good it would be to live with someone with reasoning and cognitive power similar to her own. In her mind's eye she recalled the images of Lilly fondling her plants, pacing before that huge fireplace, and deducting the evidence as she analyzed the crime in perfect sequence. Print dress, auburn hair pulled back, five feet two inches and exactly 110 pounds, 74-ish… brilliant. Q was there. He too had been amazed listening to her. He could never have suppressed a smile as she had to do.

Since a child, she had always faked her intelligence with

everybody, especially at school and most certainly with the Director and Q. Their IQs ranged fairly high. It would have made life different had they known her intellectual identity; else, how could she remain ahead of their planning and logical sequencing. How could she so easily "fix-the-loose-ends." Her future had to keep her well ahead of everyone. To do this she hid her intellectual identity.

Thanks to Lilly, Q and the Director now knew her as a deceased double agent. She had conveniently had to 'die' a few hours ago in an old Cuenca cottage! She and her 'lover.' Ussie… She wondered how the police would report the double deaths – Carlos would let me know.

She caught her breath as she recalled the tragic look on their faces as she held her finger to her face, poised to prick herself with the deadly poison. Her hurt at the thought was a stabbing pain of grief – her friends, their faces drawn in disbelief. She couldn't be captured; they had to believe her dead! In fact, her plan was to make them believe she had to kill them; what a shock they must have felt when she fell, apparently dead, as they watched in horror!

Well, Ussie's death was imminent. That had to happen. Ussie had to die that night. Dianna had surmised, and correctly so, that the Director would place her own body with Ussie's for the police to find. Two crazed and psychotic killers.

Dianna took a breath, and so they had set an ambush to catch her, the traitor, Dianna; and it had worked, except that she had exchanged the deadly poison for one that would feign death, one that would render her death-like as she fell to the floor, unconscious.

Dianna drove through the early dawn into Seville's cities industrial east side. Now she was to set into play a new scheme, one that could finally take her to Q and to freedom – but that was long away and with awesome personal cost!

Just before noon, she pressed the bell to Dr. Romero Lunes' office. A clipped voice: "Si?"

"This is Athena, I have an appointment with Dr. Lunes."

"Yes, one moment." Silence. "Please return to your car. There is an envelope in the glove compartment with an address. Goodbye."

As Dianna approached her car, a small smatter of mud on the windshield lifted her spirits – she was not alone. Carlos had taken her new code name from the fuse box: Athena. She slid into the driver's seat, popped the glove compartment and retrieved Dr. Lunes' envelope. The GPS directed her to the very heart of Seville, to a prominent medical building where the affluent would expect not only privacy, but any treatment suited to their financial means. An elegant and hooded Dianna was greeted with familiar poise and led to Lunes' more than well-appointed suite.

He rose to greet her; she sat without being invited. Lunes was the image of middle-age success. His coiffure and dress were Italian; his smile gentle and charismatic. From the moment she saw him, she kept her eyes on his while assessing the powerful hidden body language he tried to hide.

"Miss Athena," he took her hand and gently brushed it with his lips, "you come to us highly referred." Dianna caught just a bare edge of an accent. It had the sweet depth of moneyed Munich, and with it, she recalled a dangerous memory. Though the face was strange, the accent was not. He had once been a highly paid double agent in the not too distant past. Peripherally, they had worked together.

While he obviously knows me, she thought, he gives no sign that I recognize him. She answered cautiously:

"My friends highly recommend you, Doctor. Privacy and location come at great price." Lunes' smile did not change. "Tell me what to expect." As she spoke, she wondered how many criminal and agent's faces he's altered, and probably blackmailed as well.

"Not only privacy and location, Miss Athena. My staff and I have made dreams come true, and from what I see from here, you are already a dream." He smiled more deeply, watching as though cat-and-mouse. "Let me relate your instructions, and you correct where needed. Before I begin, ah, a drink, a coffee or tea? A small lunch is prepared, if you wish."

"Nothing, thank you. Please continue, Doctor."

Lunes began. "Most important, the surgery is designed to be undone. When you wish. Considering your age and years before it is attempted, it can easily be reversed using the photography we will give you.

"We have studied images you sent to us and we see no major facial changes, and from what I see, this will not be a major change for you.

"We will implant to broaden your cheeks and broaden your jaw just enough for balance. You will not look as you do now. Your symmetry is youthful and beautiful; the surgery will give you an aged but lovely appearance." He walked to a broad-screen monitor, her face flashed into its center. "As you entered our outer office, a camera caught this photo; my computer has taken your image and conformed it to a post-surgery image." A second image of an aged Dianna-ish face flashed next to her own. "We hope it suits what you are looking to see?"

Dianna gave no indication of surprise. "It is excellent, Doctor. How much time do I have before restoration surgery is done?"

"No later than seven years."

"Now, Doctor, what is to be done next?"

"From this room you will be taken to a small suite where you are to shower and shave as instructed. Our staff nurse, Marcella, will be with you to assist. Everything you will need is provided. I suggest a small fruit salad after you shower and nothing more until after the surgery. The surgery will happen tonight at 11 PM. After six days, if all is satisfactory and there is no sign of infection, you will be free to leave."

Dianna watched his face muscles as he spoke. The veins on the back of his hands were thin lines and not the full veins of a relaxed professional. He is nervous, she surmised. Should he find that I know him, he could have motives contrary to my safety. Well, she thought, if he is a professional, it will be necessary for me to be seen leaving this building. After that, I wonder… Carlos.

*

Dianna turned and swirled before the circular full-length mirror. The image that flashed back was of a middle-aged matron, dressed in black from shoes to shawl. She looked every inch a widow. Her broad healed, laced shoes helped her walk become much less feminine and gave her the look of a woman setting out to work. She pronounced her birth name with pedestrian authority, "Marjorie Margaret Harrington – Maggie Harrington." Dianna appraised it all with an almost sacred approval. Now, she mused, the work is to begin. A new identity is not just a new face and a black dress; the work is to be a Maggie, a strong, independent Canadian woman. She touched her face. Yes, she thought, all this is the beginning of my future; what would Q think? She laughed, almost aloud, yet a shudder of utter loneliness shook her to the core. It could all be irrevocable. She breathed slowly, smiling at her image, "Mirror, mirror, on the wall..." She studied herself for at least a minute, then she carefully opened her door to the hall. It was well before dawn. Barefoot, she walked quickly to the elevator, directly in front of Lunes' suite. Pressing 'up,' she waited a moment and then entered the lift. No one had seen her.

On the top floor she looked for an unmarked closet door and found it conveniently adjacent to the elevator. She tried the door. It didn't open. She slipped her vanity fingernail file against the inside latch and pushed it aside. It worked. She pushed the door open. As expected, the security alarm system was eye level, just inside the closet. She smiled. Lunes was saving money; his security devices were wired into the building's system – what absolute luck! Apparently he doesn't plan to be here long. She looked for the fourth floor circuit. Taking a wire she'd cut from her bathroom hairdryer, she attached it to the lead-in wire and bypassed it to the fifth, isolating Lunes' circuitry. Carefully, she clipped his circuit with her vanity scissor. Silence!

Minutes later, back on the fourth floor, she jimmied the door to Lunes' suite. Again, more luck: all the building locks were by the same manufacturer. Her nail file worked as before. She opened his door; all was as she recalled – behind his desk was the only other door. Again, the latch slipped as she pushed it back. She entered.

Wonderful silence! The inner room was windowless, with another door that must have led to his surgery.

In the room were a conference table, chairs, and another desk. A solid steel file-safe stood adjacent to it, in hands reach. How obvious, she thought, and leaned her ear comfortably against the combination dial. Breaking and entering, safe-cracking – both flawless skills she'd never lose. She smiled, comfortably searching for the telltale feel and clicks that would open the safe. With the fourth slow spin, it was open. She pulled the top file drawer out. The sound of a nearby flush froze her fingers! No time for delay... she opened the top drawer labeled *Recents*. A file labeled *Athena* was not there. Where could it be? Quickly, she closed the file drawer and opened the drawer *A-D*. Footsteps! No matter what, she would strike to kill should the doorknob move. It didn't. She looked into the drawer. Unsurprised, the front folder was labeled *Dianna/Athena*.

She pulled the file to see if it was complete: medical write-up, CDs that had to be of the surgery and her interview with Lunes, and photographs. She smiled, closed the drawer and locked the safe. The suite was silent. Lunes must have either been a lousy agent, or he was on the move; in any case, she was in danger. She returned to her room, slipped into her bathrobe, tussled her hair, and rang for Marcella. It was just breaking dawn.

Marcella knocked and opened the door. "How are you this morning, Athena? Are you ready to leave us today?"

Dianna yawned as though just awakening. "I really don't want to leave. You have spoiled me completely, Marcella. I promise I'll finish my bath and be ready for breakfast at exactly eight o'clock. Is that alright?"

"Of course, Athena. Will you need anything before that?"

"No. I'll see you then."

As the door closed, Dianna slipped into her shoes, placed the file *Dianna/Athena* inside her blouse, waited a few minutes, and then opened her door. Silence. She was alone. At the elevator, she pressed 'down' and within a minute was on the street, an innocuous, middle-aged woman, presumably on her way to work. She signaled a cab and was pushed out of sight into the back seat.

Lunes. He's made everything too easy for me to get away. He knows I've left the building; he does not know I have my file!

The Fiat was where she'd left it, but just a bit off-center within the parking lane. She smiled... Carlos! The mileage was the same. Carlos had moved the car off-center, a sign that it was safe to drive. Were the car where she'd left it, Carlos would be dead, and the car booby trapped.

Carlos had left the car safe.

"My Carlos," she breathed aloud, "now the proof." She turned the ignition, Dianna heard only the low purr of the Fiat. She laughed softly and backed away. Carlos would do to Lunes, but in spades, what Lunes had planned for her! At end of day, Lunes would start his car. Dianna wondered what would happen!

The Fiat turned north, then west, then on to Lisbon.

CHAPTER 10

HOTEL FORTALEZA DO GUINCHO

Rain had come down in sheets ever since last night. It's a wonder, Lilly thought, the house just didn't float away. Mercy. She settled more deeply into the 'Great Chair.' Aside from her rooms down the east hall, this was her favorite spot… crackly fire just about out, tea in the cozy and lunch finished, hmmm… snuggling more comfortably into the 'Great Chair.' Addie is in a mood today. By the Lord Harry, if it weren't for Doc looking after her. Seven months to go; a December baby, mercy. Lilly's smile was as big as one comes.

"Miss Lilly, you smilin' like a Cheshire cat. What you thinkin' 'bout?"

"I'm thinking about the baby, and Addie, and Doc and you, of course. Where would we be without all the work you do to keep this great house just spic-and-span? Would you like another tea, Margaret?"

"In a few minutes, when I get…" The phone interrupted, "the foldin' done, thanks, Miss Lilly."

"Hello. The Tutter and Hendricks Home… Why, hello! Chief Kilmein. How nice to hear your voice! It's been quite a few months… Yes, yes… I recall… You mentioned he would visit us with Dianna. He didn't come…

"I'm so glad to hear that. You have, then, spoken to Chief Cutter? Yes, that would be best. Judge Addie and Doctor Hendricks should be here in a few hours. Perhaps it's best for you and Chief Cutter to settle on a time... I certainly will be here whenever you like... Will you be with Mr. ah? Q, you said? Oh. To see me...? You are so kind... Yes, there were some loose ends; in fact, there still are!

"A hotel is unnecessary. We insist you both stay with us... No, not a concern... Certainly, why thank you, Chief Kilmein... Good afternoon." Lilly cradled the phone. Were her earlier smile demonstrative of blissful dreams, it was replaced with that of a woman vindicated and smug! "So," she said aloud to no one in particular, "Dianna isn't coming... but, Mr. Q is."

*

Meanwhile, many miles to the northeast, Q and Chief of Police Tom Kilmein boarded a helicopter for the international airport... "We left Spain just before the police arrived; two bodies were found: Ussie's and another woman. Dianna's wasn't. It's missing! Who took it, why, and for what purpose. This looks well-planned and timed. I keep thinking, too well-planned. Something is very wrong!"

"All I see, Q, is that the Director believed it best for the Rhue woman not to be returned home. I think his decision was a good one. That woman was a psychotic."

"We know; however, someone else got to Rhue before we did!"

"What?"

"Yeah. We were in the bedroom seconds after we arrived at her cottage. She could not have heard us. When we got into the bedroom, we found her dead! Someone got to her before us. The unanswered question, Chief, who did it? Everyone in the agency is accounted for. No family we know of; she was killed, and not by an amateur."

"Also, someone with a motive."

"It wasn't Dianna, Chief. Dianna poisoned herself, and we carried her there to the Rhue cottage – I carried her myself and placed her beside Rhue. But the police didn't find Dianna, only Rhue and an unidentified woman. No Dianna anywhere! That's why we have to get to that housekeeper, Miss Lilly. Someone else killed Ussie Rhue. Who and why, Chief? There are sub-layers to all this that we cannot see. Were I a betting man, I'd say Dianna knew more than we do."

"Yes, like another force with its own agenda. How did Dianna, die? Be specific. Could it be that she really was aware of another angle to this case? Dianna was one of the best agents we've ever had. How could she be gone without some angle, or some ulterior motive? I somehow do not see that woman killing herself – she was too savvy, too beyond all that."

"True, but disgrace is nothing any one of us can live with; she was caught double dealing. Simple as that! I checked her pulse. I checked her vitals. No, Chief." Q shook his head in obvious grief… "It took all the evidence and more to nail her guilt. She was on the way to kill both the Director and me. We figured it out. She was more tangled in this than we thought. Damn, the most perfect woman I've ever known. The only woman I'd ever want to live with!"

*

The unmarked Canadian jet entered Tutterville airspace a little before noon. In minutes it was on the ground and parked adjacent to Chief Joanna Cutter's car. Tutterville tower was instructed to record the flight as private, civilian. Two guards emerged first, then Chief Kilmein and Q.

Joanna's greeting was both hospitable and curious. "We've been waiting with bated breath, gentlemen; mystery murders in Tutterville are quite frequent these days. So very nice, Tom, to see you again."

"Me too, Joanna. I must begin with big thanks for all your help. That Rhue case is messy business and for some of us, more mystery than you'd guess. Let me introduce you to Q."

Joanna put out her hand, "Mr. Q, or just Q?" Her smile engaged a quizzical response.

"Just Q, thanks. It's been a long time since my last name has been important; I use it only when I pick up my paychecks." He grinned. Looking for Joanna's comeback.

"Perhaps, after a few hoops tomorrow, we can discuss the 'last' names you've most recently used! You play ball?"

"I do."

"Lately, Tutterville has become a focus for people with a variety of last names." Joanna liked the banter and encouraged it with another handshake. Turning to Chief Kilmein, "A few people are waiting for us at Judge Addie's home. It's an hour's drive north."

Q could not take his eyes from Joanna. "Yes, we play. Hoops tomorrow? Great. Tell us about Miss Lilly? Is it Ms. Lilly or Mrs. Lilly?"

"Simply Lilly. As for tomorrow morning, we'd love to have you play some ball with us. If you want, you can drive in with Judge Addie and Doc Hendricks at 5:30 in the morning for some basketball. We usually work out well before work."

Kilmein answered for both of them, "Hoops at 5:30 AM, perfect. When will we meet with the Judge and Lilly?"

Q interrupted, he had to press Joanna, "Is it usual to put up a few bucks per hoop?"

"We draw for a team; if it's between you and me, I'd love to drop a few bucks. I drive pretty hard!

"Right now, we are on our way to the Tutter home for lunch and a bit of business. I have to be at my department by 4:00 PM for the shift change."

The trip into the city was comfortable; it was the beginning of new friendships.

Lilly looked across the table at Q and preempted the others. "Ah Mr. Q... what is it like being called Mr. 'Other'? Is diversity your livelihood? Are you one of many? You are strikingly handsome. I am happy you are not embarrassed with my questions. Are you? Old ladies are allowed to ask questions, Q. I agree, I like just Q. Please, call me Lilly?"

As she spoke, she glanced at the others around the table, Addie, Doc, Joanna, and Detective Mont Westerly. They all seemed pleased that she was taking the lead – even her antagonist, Detective Monty, as she liked to call him.

"My impression is that you and Dianna were an operative team. Are you free to discuss her?"

Q replied, "Dianna and I often worked together. We understand that she recently died while on a mission. She was a remarkable woman."

"Really, Q? I believe she is brighter than any of us believe. She plays a game with many different layers. Then, you did have a positive identity on her death?" Q nodded, yes. "She left us with too many 'obvious' contradictions. She knew beyond a doubt that we had all the evidence needed against Ursula Rhue, or Ussie Willow as she was called. Dianna knew we had the murder weapon."

Q gave no impression of being annoyed. He exchanged glances with Chief Kilmein. Critiquing Dianna was not what he'd come here to do. Kilmein interrupted in her defense. "Dianna gave us a tidy report after returning from Tutterville. The murder weapon wasn't in your hands, she reported." Q still remained passive.

Lilly interrupted fiercely, "That is not true! She left this room before the conversation was concluded. She did not remain to discuss the weapon. Why, Chief? My question has but one answer. If you have another, we ask you to speak up!

"She did not spend the night in her room but left surreptitiously on the first airplane the next morning. She knew we had conclusive evidence… and I have a report from two guards at our zoo that they had seen what could have been an intruder. All they report is shadows, nothing positive. And so, the reptile cage we visited had been jimmied again, from the looks of it. More than once! The reptile cage with the most poisonous frogs on the planet; one touch of their secretion kills animal life instantly, a nerve poison. So, your Dianna spent her last night here following someone else's business. More than just her own. Were it just hers, she needn't have visited us in the first place. It is my conclusion that Ursula Rhue and Dianna were employed. By whom, gentlemen?"

A very long pause, Lilly sat back in her chair. "Nothing about frog poison in her report, Chief, Q?"

Chief Detective was precariously balanced on the back legs of his chair. "Gawd! Lilly," he slammed forward, hand on the table.

"We do not use the Lord's name in our house, Chief Detective…"

"Sorry, Miss Lilly."

Lilly continued, the attention of the table completely hers. "Were her, or their, employer the Justice Department, Chief Kilmein, you would presumably know or be investigating her or them. Were it your Agency, Q, the same. Your silence implies that the 'employer' is unknown. In any case, perhaps it's important to consider my proposition a valid one, that is, of course, until proven otherwise."

Chief Kilmein tapped his fingers together and pensively returned Lilly's smile. "Q and I, and our government did not fully accept Dianna's report; we did, however, rely on Chief Cutter's coroner's report from you, Doctor Hendricks. We used it to settle questions about the Williamsburgh estates. As I said, we thank you for your help.

"You, Lilly, have brought a totally different problem to light. What more can you tell us about Dianna, and especially anything she may have had to do with Rhue?"

"I thought you would like to know more, Chief." Lilly looked to Addie. "If you and Doc agree, and Addie, if you are up to it, I've made arrangements to meet before dinner with the zoo keepers who reported seeing a 'shadow' in the night. I also want to show Q and Chief Kilmein the frog exhibit. As for dinner, I've already called Billie and he has agreed to cater his special salad and steaks at seven o'clock. Is that alright, my dear ones?"

Addie looked at Lilly with amazement. "You've thought of all that? Yes. Of course. Your energy never ceases to amaze us! And, ah, we should dine well after the department's shift change. Is seven o'clock good for you Joanna, Chief Detective?" Both nodded yes.

On the way to the van, Q held Lilly's jacket for her. "Layers, you say. Yes, layers. There were qualities about Dianna about which only a few know."

"Oh?" Lilly queried, "I think I know what you are about to tell me."

Q responded, "She kept her history, and especially her IQ, very secret. She slipped up, too rarely, and it was because she wanted to. I don't know how many languages she spoke; I do know that she was surprised by very little."

Lilly smiled. Layers, she thought. The higher the cognition, the more intricate the layers... layers that hide layers... secrets. And, Lilly wondered more. Who was her real employer, who would that be? I warrant, perhaps a consortium in need of a future...

After the zoo and at dinner, the focus centered on the power of the frog's secretions and even more, on the presence of the dark shadow in the night at the zoo. Dianna's signature? Never seen, she always went where she wanted to be. Q sat silent during most of the evening. Layers – he could not put the thought of layers aside. Now and then he caught Joanna's glance, about as often as she caught his. She leaned toward him. "Two bucks a hoop in the morning?"

"Ho, ho." The table laughed. "Q looks like he might do some real damage, Joanna! We'll see."

*

The university gym was abuzz with shooters, but this was a very different morning. Everybody knew the Chief, but who in hell was the guy? Whoever he was, he was keeping hoop for hoop with a Tutterville legend! They'd been at it nonstop for almost an hour and were as fresh as when they'd began. Onlookers were going nowhere…

It was close to quitting time when Q realized Joanna was holding back. She was one hoop behind and her breathing was very easy. She's measuring me, he thought. That sweet, pretty woman is playing me. I'd better start breathing heavy. I'm gonna steal this lady's money! As if reading his thoughts, Joanna slipped under and inside, stole the ball and tossed it half across the court. It slipped clean through the hoop without even the sound of a swish as the buzzer blew, time up! Joanna had tied the game…

Someone shouted, "Fifteen minutes more? This is too perfect!?" No one disagreed. Two teams and Q played against Joanna.

Q intercepted her first pass and bent low to dribble fast; then, with a quick fade-like turn to the left, he felt the sudden lunge of a guard foul-slamming him from his left. Q saw the guard crumble to the floor as a white jersey tripped into him. Doc reached to pull the guard to his feet, but he didn't move. He was out. He put his hand to his neck. No pulse. Eyes were open wide. The guard was dead! Both teams stood panting, stunned at what had just happened. Chiefs Cutter and Kilmein dropped to the floor beside Doc, all three dripping sweat. Doc looked from Joanna to Chief Kilmein. "This man is dead, in fact, he has just been murdered!

"Please, give us room, everyone. Call an ambulance. This man was dead before he hit the floor! Everybody who isn't necessary, please leave the court. My bag's in the car, can you bring it to me, someone?"

Joanna had taken control as soon as she saw the guard fall. "Deputy Chief Westerly, you make sure that nobody leaves this campus. Shut the gates! Now! You stay with him, Detective Hart, and wait for EMS. Everyone else, please wait for me by the exit door."

Doc Hendricks looked at Joanna and pointed to the open palm of the dead guard, "Do you see that small pin-looking thing protruding from his hand? Yes, there," he nodded, "that's poison! Stay away from this body. This man's been poisoned with a dart, just as the others were!"

Joanna was on her hand-held, "Desk! Get the duty SWAT team to the university gym immediately and have the secondary team on call. We have a code, and the killer is within a quarter mile of me. Nobody leaves without a clearance – the university gates are closed, NOW! That's NOW, desk. Move it! Officers, get suited up. We have business!" She looked up just as the man she was hoping to see would appear. "Mr. Pipo! I am very glad that you are here this morning, as usual."

Chancellor Bebe Pipo was moving quickly toward them. It was his daily amusement to watch the PD's morning workout. "Yes, Chief Cutter. I was watching you all play. It was one hell of a show! Who's that fellow who's almost run you into the ground? We need him here!" Catching sight of the fallen officer, he caught his breath. "That's Officer Greenman. What's happened here?" Bebe Pipo tried to get closer.

"Yes, Chancellor, it is. Did you observe anything unusual while you were watching us?"

"Not a thing, Joanna, except, I think, a woman. Hum, yes. I think it might have been a woman, or a young boy… was, ah… sitting near the center door just over there, gone now. Didn't recognize who. I thought it was one of the staff, or a student."

Joanna shrugged, disappointed. "At this time of day, the campus is packed with kids and anyone who's anyone. The crime lab people will be here in a few minutes; have them cover every inch of this gym.

"In the meantime I'd ask both you, Chief Kilmein, and you, Q to get into my SWAT car and be escorted to Judge Addie's home. And you, Addie and Doc – I will have a few motor bikes lead and follow you home.

"If you don't mind, Chief, Q, can you both stay with us at least until tomorrow? We'll have a patrol car parked by your jet in a few minutes. Two officers will be detailed to you until you leave for home, and Judge Addie's house is under surveillance."

Q nodded in agreement. "We'd like to see how this develops. Thanks, we'll stay to see how things go." Chief Kilmein, meanwhile, was examining the body along with Doc Hendricks, affirming Q's comments to Joanna.

*

The dinner table was cleared, Q stood between Lilly and Joanna. Looking to Joanna, he asked, "Tell me, Joanna, about the victim. Was he on any detail assigned to escort or accompany Dianna? Did he ever come within talking range of her?"

Lilly also glanced toward Joanna, "Or Ussie Willow, known

as Ursula Rhue? If you answer "no" to either of us, I agree with what Q is about to conclude, and that is, Officer Greenman was an unintended target. I believe that you, Q, were the target!

"Q says that before Officer Greenman collapsed to the floor he slammed, as you put it, into you as you took the ball. I believe your back, Q, was the target. The game was fast, if I know Addie and Joanna; Officer Greenman probably thrust his hand into the air for interference; unfortunately, his hand got in the way and caught the dart. Someone believes you know too much, Q. As I said yesterday at lunch, there are layers upon layers of plans here. It's you who should be dead, Mr. Q.

"Whoever planned your murder is still very much out and about."

Addie looked first at Joanna and then Tom Kilmein. "He left no weapon behind. How will we ever find him?"

"Oh, my dear, we will find him, and he is not a he, he is a she! Chief Detective Westerly can explain what's going on in the city as we speak," Lilly nodded to Mont Westerly.

"Just a few minutes after Greenman died, Miss Lilly called me." He looked at Lilly, who nodded in agreement.

Lilly continued, "Addie called me immediately with the news of what had happened; she repeated what Bebe'd said. Of course, it had to have been a woman. What was the first thing Bebe said? That he thought it was a woman. I am sure he actually saw a woman. Bebe Pipo's unconscious would suggest to him that it was a woman, since he most certainly enjoys the frequent company of his women friends." Lilly hesitated and cleared her throat, obviously wishing not to imply anything difficult. "His instinct is quite reliable in these, ahem, these matters. That is why I suggested Detective Westerly look for a woman."

"I am. And as usual, Miss Lilly is two steps ahead! The security guard at the east campus saw a woman drive from his gate just as the alert was called. Our security cameras picked her up. Thanks to Lilly, her picture is plastered in front of every ticket stand at the airport, train and bus stations, every hotel desk, car rental office, and every cop car in town and highway patrol vehicle. She ain't goin' nowhere." Westerly looked at the stunned faces around the table and pointed to Lilly.

"Joanna's police force is the best, just as is yours, Chief Kilmein." Lilly looked confidently at Westerly. "And I understand that she is also on local and national TV? It would be wise were you to put it on the air in Canada, Chief Kilmein. Her employer will not like the publicity. Messy. I've always believed in old adages, Chief, 'Fear is the arch-enemy of curiosity,' and that works in reverse as well. Her curious employer will be forced to tighten up his game. When that happens, another adage comes in to play, 'The best defense is a good offense.'" She looked at Q. "You know too much, Q. Whoever wants you out of the picture would prefer you to die on someone else's turf; it takes the focus from his court."

"Yes, but unlike your safety, Lilly, our frames of reference are very broad. Everyone knows I know too much. I've learned to be very careful."

"I am sure you have, Q; at the same time, your 'friends' are always watching and those brightest will see your patterns – even the best draw habit patterns in their lives."

"You are quite a woman, Lilly. You've played this whole thing from that chair you're sitting in. All from fragments of information…"

Lilly waved him to stop, "Please, Q. Observation is…"

Q interrupted her, "That's true, Lilly, observation *is* deduction's forte. Critical curiosity and flash-fast deduction, you have rare gifts. Fear, anger, and stress are one's great enemy. Each of them reduces cognition almost proportionally. It takes monumental training to neutralize all three. I hope the Tutterville treasury reimburses you!"

Everyone laughed as Chief Joanna held up a hand.

Lilly's reaction was very noncommittal. "You are a joy to be with, Q," and turning to the Canadian Chief she added, "of course this mystery, as you aptly call it Chief Kilmein, I believe is an orchestrated agenda well beyond your government's knowledge. I truly believe Q is in immediate danger. I suggest no heroics for him. Perhaps you should send him away, somewhere very secret, until you unravel this very big mystery just a bit more!"

Of all those in the room, no one really noticed that Lilly had taken charge. The nature of her charm and simplicity of synthesis of fact made her an unnoticed leader. As Q had said, 'critical curiosity' was key; and Lilly's curiosity was just that, and not that of an intrusive gossip.

A phone rang. Detective Westerly answered his hand-held. "Yeah, go… yeah, when, where? Oh… is SWAT on the way? I'll be right there.

"Chief, fatality on Exit 14. Car crash, driver out of control, woman dead on impact. Same car and driver picked up earlier by the university gate cameras…"

*

Long years ago, Q had fallen in love with Guincho the moment he'd set foot in its enormous subterranean dungeon. Built by the Moors more than a millennia past, its huge granite silhouette thrust itself deep into the North Atlantic, as a guard post to protect Europe's most western shore.

Massive green waves, glittering aqua-green at their crest, battered the fort with such tremendous force that surf and wind blanketed its three sides. The sea made the fort impenetrable from the ocean. Inside, the fortress-hotel was utter luxury from dungeon to its tallest parapet. Q slowed his Porsche to a quick stop before its massive front entrance. Flipping a key to the valet, he strode slowly through the foyer and down the long, open hall to the desk, at the most southwestern corner of the lobby.

A crisp and very lovely concierge extended her hand before he could speak, "We have been expecting you, Mr. Quinhollande. Welcome to Guincho. You may call me, Bella. This way to your suite."

"You have been with us before?"

"Yes, I have. It's a most private and lovely place. Before we go to my suite, may I speak with tonight's chef, please? I want to eat the same dinner, every evening I'm here." Bella shot a message from her hand-held. Seconds passed, and a tall, very slender man approached from the elevator.

"I am Chef Joseph, Mr. Quinhollande. We look forward to cooking for you and your guests."

"Nice to meet you, Chef Joseph. Can you prepare three dinner courses for me? First course: Amêijoas á Bulhão Pato; second and main course: Linguado; and the third course, dessert: Arroz Doce Flambé, topped with a bit of Cherries Jubilee. Of course, Portuguese champagne. Possible, Chef?"

"Most possible, Mr. Quinhollande. May I say that your Portuguese is native? I have a very special cognac for the flambé! What time will you dine?"

"Always at nine. The same menu each evening when I am here for dinner. Thank you, Chef."

Turning to Bella, "Shall we go to my suite? You can send me a bottle of your best whiskey, lots of ice, always made from your delicious Água de Luso. I'll be down to the bar at seven."

The bar was small and intimate, mostly couples and a few singles. A good-sized party filled the center of the room. An empty, large red leather sofa looked like the only place to be and not look like he was joining anyone. As he sat, a waiter placed a whiskey with ice on his side table and a tray of tiny pie-shaped hors d'oeuvres comfortably within reach. "Sir," the waiter leaned closer, "the chef sends his compliments. Drinks for you, this evening, are on him."

"My very best to the chef, thank him for me, please."

Q searched the room for anything or one of note, as was his habit. Within a glance, a remarkably stunning woman caught his eye. Their eyes engaged, and hers did not turn away. She was very much a part of the group, her arm draped over her escort. After a long moment, she turned away but not without a second look. She was lovely, long legs and her black long dress hid very little; her auburn-ish hair pulled back into a jeweled Spanish comb. He found himself a little more than excited. This must happen, he thought. Easy enough. He pointed to his waiter. "I see," he started, "that group has nothing interesting to drink. Without telling them, please bring them each a glass of my dinner champagne, and for that lady, there," Q made sure the waiter had the correct person, "place half a Maraschino cherry... and the other half in mine. Can you do that? Immediately? No one is to know who sent it to them."

Q settled back into his couch to watch the reactions to what was about to happen. The first to receive a drink was the lady in black. Soon they were all talking about the half-cherry in her glass. As they talked, she more than suspected that the gift was from him. When he raised his glass to her, the connection was complete.

The restrooms were next to the small bar. Putting his drink aside, he casually walked to the men's room. Inside, he checked his appearance, then waited at least two minutes before opening the door. Before it was open a fraction, he was stunned almost to staggering – the scent of Dianna struck him with full force. When Dianna wore eau de toilette, the intoxicating aroma of Jean Patou's Parfum Joy enveloped him with her presence. He opened the door to see the woman he'd hoped would be there. She was, lavishly beautiful, smelling like the image of Dianna.

Before he could speak, she put a finger to his lips and whispered, "We should bring our cherries together, n'est-ce pas?" She whispered more softly, "That will happen if you leave your door unlocked at exactly two in the morning. I am sure both halves will fit together perfectly in the dark of night." Bringing her finger to her own lips, she kissed them, turned away, and he did not meet her again, until a few hours later, at 2:00 AM.

While Q ate, he looked but did not see her. At midnight he went to bed, his door unlocked.

As he went to his suite, Bella opened the door to a smaller room, directly above Q. "Athena, welcome to Guincho! And you,

Eva, you are beautiful. Mr. Quinhollande has not said anything, but it was apparent that he was looking for you all evening. He just left for his room."

Dianna, now Athena, nodded in agreement, "Thank you, Bella, everything you've done is exactly on time and working perfectly. Have you seen Carlos?"

"Yes, Athena. He is at the Hotel Estoril at this time and looks forward to seeing you tomorrow evening."

"Your perfume is effective, Eva. The scent caught him by surprise. I'm positive. It is my calling card when we are together, but more subtle."

"I wish I were meeting him at two, ladies. He is absolutely stunning! I've seen only one or two men in my life as attractive, and that's in the movies."

They laughed. Dianna brought them back to the task at hand. "Thank you, Eva. Now you must flee into the dawn, as the poets would say. We will keep in touch in the usual way. You are a superb actress. Carlos or I will contact you soon. I have arranged a lovely villa for you just outside of Rome. Carlos will give you the address tomorrow. Spend money, look prosperous, and be seen. Goodbye, I will see you in Rome." Both Eva and Bella left the room. Dianna was alone.

Dianna stood before the dresser mirror. A new and much older Dianna looked back, a worried Dianna, a squarish face, not too unattractive. All of these plans, she thought, layer upon layer. More than she knew, this evening was to change her life. This was a pivotal hour. Her whole purpose was to become pregnant! Replacing Eva, she would trick Q into conceiving a child, their child. A year or more, or perhaps a dozen, her task of exposing the 'Candidate' would completely clear her name, and they, God-willing, would be together. By then, it would be too late to conceive, so now, it is to be done. Should he later reject her, he will never know of his child. But their child will be mega rich, mega beautiful, and have the world to play in – that is, if God wills. Would God forgive her for tonight? Would he punish their child? She sat on her bed and wept. "At least I will have something of Q, no matter..." and she cried, arms wrapped tightly against the excitement she began to feel. Long before two, she was ready. Eva had left her flagon of Joy. She touched it to her neck and in other places she knew would please Q. At two, his door opened easily. She walked to his bed.

"Did you bring your cherry?" Q reached for her hand...

*

Dianna, now Maggie Harrington, had rented a suite in the St. Regis Hotel for three months. Her neighbor, a few blocks away, was Princess Anna Maria. Dianna'd just brought a few things from Ortisei – a small suitcase and a travel kit. Life up in the foothills of the Alps was simple: black outfits with solid walking shoes. Everything unpacked and put away, she took the last item from the travel kit, a small sack made of soft natural-color lambskin. From it, she took an ornate mother-of-pearl cask. Unlike the usual mother-of-pearl veneer, this cask looked as though it had been carved from an enormous, lush pearl. Putting it center on the dressing table, she pressed its invisible latch and watched, always amazed, as the top half of the cask slowly opened, mechanically geared with expensive precision. The cask was not empty. Dianna touched the bottom center with the tip of her left little finger, and instantly the bottom parted with the same precision as the lid. A tiny, folded paper lay center on a white rose petal – so real appearing was it that even to the touch, the petal confirmed its natural-like beauty. Dianna unfolded the paper, kissed it, and gently placed it open atop the opened cask. Her smile turned slowly to very happy tears.

Six months after leaving Q's bed, she had a home far from the realities of the world, in a town dedicated to sculpture and art – Ortisei, nestled in the foothills of the Alpine, Dolomite range. She'd been there before on business; now it was home. She found a two-story house on the edge of town that looked very much Alpine, with a storefront on the first floor. It took a few months for a 'special contractor' from nearby Austria to secure it against any intrusion. The contractor's specialty was to covertly transform a home into a safe haven for very special people, high-risk families that lived in fear of kidnappers, and even from the media. Dianna had used the same company to secure the homes of special clients for the government. It was a reliable and first-rate firm.

She knew the mechanics of what she wanted in a safe-house, especially the need for a suite built well below ground, with an exit tunnel that led to a safe egress site. The tunnel was the first thing completed since its initial use was to secretly rebuild and refurbish the entire house from inside.

After a while, her little specialty shop became a fashionable place for very special shoppers. Ortisei trade was almost entirely religious goods, statues, and religious sacramentals.

The pearl cask was her invention. She'd designed it with the help of a German watchmaker who, not so coincidentally, was a retired special agent. The cask was made to hold the rarest of relics or to hide a precious object beneath its secret floor. She had designed it to operate using light-source batteries. Everything self-contained and digitally opened by the owner's touch.

Dianna's most precious object now lay exposed on her dresser. It was a small photograph, folded just so, to fit on top of the rose petal – a prenatal photo of her and Q's almost six-month-old child. Kissing her finger, she pressed it to the picture, "My dearest, tiny little girl…"

*

"Hello, I am Mrs. Marjorie Harrington. May I speak with the Princess Valois do Emmanuel's secretary? I'm a very, very distant relative of her late husband, Albert Williamsburgh. The Princess and I met briefly when she was in Canada…"

CHAPTER 11

ALBERT AND ALEXANDRIA AND HOSEA

Two nights in a row and Addie could not sleep a wink. Not only was she big enough to be having twins, she had the appetite to prove it. Doc was keeping them both in shape and on weight. Right now a snack would be good, and even better, a double dish of ice cream, "But," she whispered aloud, "a sip of Lilly's winter brandy is what I need…"

Pushing herself from the 'Great Chair' was more difficult these days than it was to get into it. A bit of a struggle and she was up. Balance was the challenge. The sideboard was just close enough; in a moment, the aroma of sweet homemade brandy waffled the air. She took a tiny sip, settled her robe more comfortably and looked from the cindering fire to the massive Christmas tree Doc and the guys had set in place – tomorrow, the branches would be out and ready for trimming.

Addie pressed back at the violent thud that slammed her side. "Tutter! You have one week to go. Relax. Your Dad and I are as anxious as you. And, Granny Lilly is all ready for you. I think you'd better get used to calling her 'Granny!'" Addie felt for the little foot, waiting for another attack…

She closed her eyes. How beautiful everything is. Doc was asleep. The smell of the tree and the hearth's sweet scent of birch filled the entire house. Tomorrow, the Yule Log. Two days until Christmas. She took another sip. Lilly does everything so very well!

Going to bed would waken Doc. She settled more deeply and felt sleepy, her hands on her belly. Tutter usually relaxed when she did that. "Good boy. Shush… be quiet now."

"Whaddya mean 'shush,' Addie?" Hosea raised his voice. "Would you please tell me how you know it's a boy? You can see mother is a bit upset! Tut's a good name for a boy. Hardly not for a girl. Mother is convinced she is her granddaughter."

"What are you talking about? Of course it's a boy. If Doc says it's a boy, it is. Please, Hosea. It is a boy, and that's that."

"That's ridiculous. Addie, there are nine guys in this family and the odds are more than seven to one that you are having a girl. Sally's had a boy and so, you have to have a girl!"

"How do you know Sally's had a boy? You aren't even married." Addie saw Hosea flinch and regretted she'd pressed him so hard.

"For sure you are a Tutter, Addie. You are sooo stubborn. Just because Sally is visiting up north is no reason to be insulting."

"I am not being insulting, Hosea. Be nice for a change and bring me a cold glass of water? We were thinking of naming him Hosea, but we don't need an opinionated sass like you added to the family."

"I wouldn't let you name him Hosea, if it is a him, and I know it isn't a him. That's my name. Hosea Tutter, and woman, I am not a sass!"

"Well you absolutely are a sass. Hosea Sass. What kind of a name is Hosea Sass? All nine of you have perfectly fine names, and Tutter happens to be the family name. Don't you think it proper to name the baby Tutter?"

"Don't you ever stop? By the Lord Harry, Addie, it's a girl I tell

*you, and everyone is expecting you and Doc to name her after mother.
Or even, after Sally."*

"Be careful, Hosea, that's a big pitcher of water. Oh. Oh.
Hosea, it's all over my lap. Help me up! Oh! I'm all wet!"

Addie couldn't move. Hosea? The room was empty! She felt
her lap. Wet! Oh, Lord...

"Harry! Harry! Doc! Lilly! The baby. The baby!"

Doc was at her side before Addie said the word baby the second
time. "Water. That's good. Any pains, sweetheart?"

"No. It's time?"

"Yes. Breathe even and I'll get the car. Lilly! You look ready
to travel."

"I am. I'll get the van in front and you get Addie to the door.
Better you be with her in the back of the van than me... I have all
your stuff, Addie. Oh, and Harry, get some shoes on and a jacket
from the hall closet. I knew you'd be early, Addie. Land. The van's
nice and warm. See you in a minute."

"I'll carry you, Addie. Let me get our coats."

Doc's hand-held was alive before he got to the closet.
"It's Judge Addie's time, we're on the way to the hospital... Good...
okay. When I see your flashing lights, we'll pull in behind you.
Call the Chief, too, will you?"

Within two blocks, Doc Harry saw the patrol car. "Ladies, we
have an escort! Tell Tutter he's gonna meet a lot of people tonight!"

Addie grasped Harry's arm, "I thought I had a slight pain...
Do you know, Harry, Lilly, I was having the most wonderful dream
as my water broke? I dreamed I was arguing with great-great-
granduncle Hosea! He was angry that we were having a boy and

we were going to name him Tutter. He was really upset and insisted it is a girl. He sassed me back!"

"You were actually arguing with the guy this whole county is named after?" Harry laughed, "Where was the dream taking place?" He needed to keep the conversation light; to keep Addie's mind relaxed until they were at the hospital.

"I imagine it was in his home. I was sitting in the 'Great Chair.' The one we have. He was so positive that we are having a girl. He said another boy in the family was against all odds. I called him Hosea Sass. I haven't used the word sass since I was a girl. He was such a sass that I said we'd never call the baby Hosea!"

"Addie," Lilly began. "Hosea Tutter Hendricks. Oh, that's lovely…"

"Yeah," Doc added, "we thought about that. Hosea is perfect with me. Whatever Addie decides."

"You know, Harry, Lilly, do you think the dream was meant to be? Yes, Harry, let's call the baby Hosea. Hosea Tutter. I have a feeling he'll have the family stutter and we'll end up calling him Tut."

Harry's answer to that became a family memory, "As long as I am called Doc Harry Hendricks, our son will be called Hosea… And that, ladies, is that!"

Two days to the day, Hosea Harry Tutter Hendricks decided to be the next Tutterville citizen. Almost twelve pounds and three ounces, he was a big baby. Three days later, Hosea had his home and his family completely trained and under his total control. Granny Lilly slept in the nursery, just in case.

For the Tutterville towns, and the whole of Hosea County,

Hosea's baptism was as public an event as was his mother's wedding. Godfather Billie and godmother Joanna had to struggle with Lilly to pamper the new Prince of the Tuttervilles.

*

Thousands of miles away, young Hosea's future was intertwining with two other children whose stars were crossed with his...

From an external perspective one usually would not suspect that the cube-granite building, blocks from the American Embassy, was a centuries-old palace. Its wall surrounded all sides and only opened into a gardened drive sealed from the palacio. Fronting the driveway was a patinaed, huge, bronze doorway. Only a few had access to the drive. Dianna parked her Maserati adjacent to the palace's massive doors, in front of an attendant obviously awaiting her arrival. A man in black garb hurried to open her door. Mrs. Harrington?" She nodded. "We will tend to your car, please follow me."

The entrance was brilliantly lit under great chandeliers that led into a columned grand salon. Turquoise marble columns garlanded with eye-level gold laurel leaves accented the Grecian-esque furniture and statuary. Beyond, were arched crystal doorways that revealed comfortable seating areas, an elegant fountain and atrium that opened onto gardens and formal paths.

As she entered the foyer, Princess Anna Maria stepped from a small elevator side door. "Mrs. Harrington, I am Anna Maria. How are you? And, welcome."

Dianna clasped her hand. "How do you do, Princess. I recall seeing you on TV in Canada. I am so happy to meet you!"

"May I call you Maggie? Some friends lunching at the Regis heard you called 'Maggie.' It is such a lovely name. Please call me Anna Maria, especially since we may be cousins by marriage. When is you baby due?" Anna Maria politely touched her own stomach as she asked.

"Six weeks, my doctor tells me, And you?" Dianna touched her own stomach.

"Four weeks. Come, my grandmother is waiting for us in the garden. As is my very nosy solicitor and my secretary. Tea is ready."

"Oh, how shall I address her?"

"Just, my lady, will be fine. We are a very informal family – among family."

Introductions and a sip of tea later, "You are related to my late grandson-in-law?

Dianna began, "I think, my lady, that my great-grandaunt was related by marriage to a Williamsburgh. I recall as a little girl hearing it discussed. It was so long ago. I looked into the family tree and there she was, barely within the family circle. I claim no blood; however, I've an envelope in my purse," Dianna placed it on the table, "that explains my relationship."

"How nice for you, dear. You are Italian?"

"No, my lady, but I do have a country home here in the north, as well as my home in Canada. I am a widow, and I am more than financially secure. You have references and a copy of my bank affiliation."

"How is that you are a widow, Maggie," Anna Maria's smile was as sincere as her grandmothers' was curious.

"My husband was lost at sea in a storm off the coast of

Greenland. He and friends were sailing and that is all we have heard." Dianna touched an eye with a tissue. "Actually, can I come to the point? I have a proposition to offer. Nothing that includes recompense or money."

"Yes of course, Maggie. What is it?"

"In that envelope is my vita. I am a certified chef, a certified bodyguard, I speak several languages fluently – Italian, German, French, Spanish, and Chinese. As imperative, is the fact that three of your best security guards together could not hold me. Because of my portfolio I would like to become a full-time aide, nurse and tutor to a privileged family. Your family!"

Her ladyship pulled herself upright. "My dear woman, this is outrageous! We don't know who you are? We are well-staffed, and your suggestion is most out of the ordinary." Looking to the male servant posted nearby, "Please escort this woman out, Paul. Really!"

"Please, Grandmama. We needn't be so disturbed. Maggie will be here for some time. Won't you, Maggie?" Dianna nodded. "There is plenty of time to know our cousin. I insist, Grandmama. Any relation to my Albert would bring some happiness to my heart. Please, Grandmama."

Grandmama was not finished, "How large a salary would you request?"

"None, my lady. As I said earlier, I am independent of need and your solicitor is free to examine my finances. I would love to have my daughter to…" Dianna was interrupted by a noise she knew as well as her own voice.

"Everyone! Get down on the floor!" As she shouted the command, Princess Anna Maria fell across the sofa. As she did, her secretary and male servant rushed to help her. Another hissing thud and her ladyship screamed. A bullet had cut her cheek. Dianna had her on the floor within seconds, her hand on Anna Maria's neck. No pulse. The bullet had blown a half-inch hole in her forehead. The Princess was dead. And so was her secretary.

"You!" Dianna yelled to the servant. "Hot water and ice. NOW!" She pulled the tea towels and napkins to the floor. "I need a sharp blade, NOW! All of you, keep down. There is more than one shooter out there. Pull the sofa close to me. Don't get up! Stay down and pull the sofa close. The blade? Water?"

Dianna pressed a wet napkin to the old woman's neck, "Press firmly, my lady. It is a surface wound. Just hold down the bleeding for a few seconds and it will stop. Your granddaughter is dead."

"Oh my God! What is happening? Help us! Anna's baby! Oh my God, help us!"

"My lady, there are only moments to save the baby! I need your help. Please wet the napkins and pull the shawl from the chair next to you. Yes, the shawl and that large tea towel. Where is that blade?

"Thank you." Dianna had already taken Anna Marie's shoes and under clothes off. She quickly pulled up her dress to above her waist.

"What are you doing to my granddaughter! Oh..." she watched in wonder as Dianna pressed the blade to Anna's stomach. "Oh, my good and dear Virgin!"

"I've done this before, please be quiet everybody." Dianna deftly made an eight-inch vertical transverse incision through Anna's skin and into the wall of her abdomen and then a smaller incision in the wall of her uterus. There was no need to concern herself with the dead princess, so she roughly pulled flesh apart and reached in for the child and pulled the boy free. "A boy!" She whispered. She tied his umbilical cord, slapped his bottom a solid blow that filled the room with the wail of a very angry male child. As Dianna washed the child, more shots shattered glass and dropped another servant at the door. "My lady. I must get the child to safety. His life is in danger. Is there a private, hidden exit close?"

"Yes. Oh Lord! Save him! He is all I have!" She pointed to a tapestry by a bookcase.

"I will get a message to you when it is possible. Dianna held the child to her chest and squat-ran to the tapestry. In moments, she was in a passage. Well lit, she followed it for a good distance to a narrow, very heavy side door; it opened onto the side street. She saw no one. A taxi. Nothing! Her breathing easy, she walked as casually as she could from the door and into the street and stepped in front of a taxi as it swerved to a stop. The risk that the cab was safe was her only choice. "The Hotel Minerva, please." A circuitous route to her hotel was the only plan she could try. The shooters wouldn't suspect a woman with a child. Natural, she thought, act very natural. No rush, next – Carlos... a doctor...

Miraculously the little prince kept silent for the twelve minutes to the Minerva. The stress of the past half hour made her somewhat nauseous, akin to the first few weeks of her pregnancy. Anxiety made her clutch the child more closely. She watched the taxi turn away and strode into the hotel to a pay phone and inserted her card...

Three rings and she hung up. Dialing again, and three rings

later she hung up. The third time and three rings, Carlos' voice was crisp: "Ola." Dianna spoke slowly, "Athena needs a 'trusted'..." she pronounced it slowly, "pediatrician in her room at the hotel quickly. He must be a practicing surgeon registered in Rome. Thank you." Dianna hung up and went from a side door into a narrow Roman street. The next taxi she took to a side street, a few blocks from her hotel.

Within twenty minutes the prince was bathed, dried and nursing from his first bottle. As he slept, so did Dianna. A sudden searing pain thrust her into the air. As quickly as it started, it stopped and burst again, more severely. Dianna gasped in pain and fear. "Oh, God, please..." In answer to her prayer, a soft tap on the door focused her. "Yes?" She gasped.

"Carlos sent me."

Dianna struggled from the bed gripping her stomach. She opened the door. "Doctor?"

"Yes, you are Athena?" His accent, very Italian. Seeing her affirm him, "Carlos sent me. I am Verde, Doctor Verde."

"Thank you for coming." Dianna gasped quickly and pointed to Albert. "Please care for my son, Albert. I am an agent with Carlos and must remain under protective cover. I delivered him two hours ago in my train cabin. Look to him, then to me. Hurry."

Verde looked at her incredulously. "This is your baby, Athena? And you delivered him yourself? You are quite a woman. You have done well." He continued carefully checking the infant. "Until next feeding time, he will sleep well, here on the chaise."

"I barely recall leaving the train and calling Carlos from the taxi." Since the doctor's arrival, the pains had appreciably diminished.

"Albert is wonderfully healthy, and you?"

"Just a moment, Doctor." Turning to her pocket book she opened her checkbook and quickly wrote a check. "I am writing this check for you, Doctor Verde..."

"Carlos has already seen to my expenses."

"I know that; however, Carlos does not know all that I need. I am not a fugitive from the police. I am a fugitive from a certain government. Carlos and I sometimes work together, as now. I need not to pay for your silence, Doctor, Carlos sees to that. I must pay for your extended services as you think I will need in the future weeks. And, I will need nurses for a while. Your first name and middle names, Doctor?"

"Antonio Paulo Verde..."

"Do you have an iPhone with auto bank depositing?"

"Yes."

"Then deposit this check immediately and please help me!" She fell to the chaise beside Albert.

Verde gasped, "This check is for two hundred thousand Euros!"

"Deposit it, I say, now! In exchange, you are to have round-the-clock nurses in this room until we are safe and well. You are to visit us as you see necessary..." Dianna flinched in pain. "Please clear everyone you select, maids and nurses, with Carlos. He will see to their expenses. I know that I cannot buy your trust... but I must have your services until I am well. Only you and Carlos know that we are in this hotel room. You are to ensure that no one else knows. Can you help me? Secrecy is vital? My name is Athena, just Athena to those you send here.

"Albert and I, and this child I am about to deliver... We are in a code-blue danger. Use those words when next Carlos contacts you."

"The check cleared. I am at your service, as I am with Carlos..." Verde opened his case and continued to examine Dianna. "Your baby has a... oh, my, you are about to have a, I believe, a spontaneous preterm birth. Get into this bathrobe – we'll get you ready."

Dianna rolled on top of every pillow Verde could find, her legs gently apart.

"When you feel more pain, pant lightly and push. Everything is ready. I have placed the shower curtain beneath some sheets. The baby's heart is a little fast. I see no danger at present. Thank God you are in good physical shape. May I call the hotel nurse to assist?"

"No! Should this become... Oh!" Dianna pushed... "If this becomes an emergency my babies must be saved. Only if this becomes dangerous to me or the baby... Oh!"

"Your water is coming. Breathe with short pants. Push, push. This child is coming quickly!"

"Like her brother..." Dianna gasped and pushed.

"Ah." Verde smiled. "Albert has a baby sister... Good work, Athena. Relax... Breathe as evenly as you can..."

*

The windowless great door appeared as old as Rome itself. Sheer window curtains gracefully covered the narrow windows on either side of the door. The convent was not at all big, though quite tall with four second-floor windows open to the cooling breezes of the afternoon. She knocked a second time, more firmly. The door opened quietly. A nun with hair pulled back beneath a white, starched shawl, her eyes raised in question. "Si?"

"Good afternoon, Sister. I am Elizabeta do Emmanuel. I am to give whoever answers this door this envelope." Reaching into her purse, she extracted a small unopened, pale green envelope. The nun did not take the envelope.

"Yes, please come in. The visitor's room is just there," she pointed across the hall.

Elizabeta, her eighty-four-year-old chin up, breathed calmly. In moments she expected to see Albert, her three-week-old great-grandson. A few steps later, she tapped on the closed door and opened it. She caught her breath... There, on a large sofa sat that severe-looking woman who had brought such unbelievable tragedy with her. Unable to remain calm she gasped again at the sight before her – one child feeding at the breast, another asleep on the woman's lap. "Oh! I want my grandson!" Her voice breaking with grief. "Please... my baby child."

Dianna smiled. She put a finger to her lips and beckoned the old woman to sit beside her. She had to nod her head and point firmly before Elizabeta do Emmanuel came closer. "Your great-grandson has an enormous appetite. He is lunching again. I am sure that if he knew that his great-granny were so close, he would want you to sit with us." As she spoke, Albert smacked his lips and pulled away. Dianna smiled, again, "Please, hold him?"

Granny carefully reached for the child and carefully took him in her arms, then pressed his head to her lips. "Ah, my child, my sweet and only child… ah…" and she began to weep almost without control.

Dianna relaxed into her chair. "Hours after he and I were safely hidden, my baby girl came." She patted Alexandria's back. "I think, Grandmama, you should burp him. Yes, put him on your shoulder, like… yes, like that. Look, he already can hold his head up! Pat his back, not too gently."

"I am so confused and afraid. All I do is cry… The police are everywhere and when you left, guns kept firing at us. I don't know how I survived."

"You survived because your great-grandson needs you as much as you need him. He is in the gravest of danger, still. Albert is heir to the vast Williamsburgh family fortune held in banks in Canada, the United States and here in Rome. Not to mention your family estate…"

Becoming very alert, Elizabeta looked with contempt at Dianna. "Now that you have my grandson, you plan to help him control his money?" Her question was accompanied with an iron smile of disgust. She clutched her great-grandson closer; firm enough to make him start."

"Please be careful, my lady. It is because of me that Albert lives! I am sure that you did not have your solicitors examine my portfolio as I suggested. Once you do, you will see that I have no need of gold and silver." She watched the woman's disgust turn again to fear. "Do you have a small green envelope for me? May I have it?"

"It is in my clutch, take it."

"No, my lady, you take it and read it, please."

Holding the baby as close as she could, Elizabeta took the

envelope from her purse. "You open it. I cannot."

Dianna took a folded green letter from the envelope, opened it, and handed it to Elizabeta. "Please read it. I believe a goldsmith, working restoration in your palace, gave this to you and instructed you to come here. Yes?"

Elizabeta said nothing but kept caressing Albert. Dianna brought a smiling Alexandria to her breast.

"The man who gave you the envelope is my closest confidant. His name is Carlos. A name you must not repeat. He has secured this convent and we are safe. Please read the letter – it is very brief."

The Principessa Elizabeta's household is insecure. The Chef Marcus and his wife are in contact with the doorman who works for the 'Candidate' in Canada. The three of them will be taken care of by nightfall. The four of you must leave immediately for 'HOME' – the Principessa and Albert will never make it back to their palace. Agents are patrolling as police to arrest them. Your hotel is compromised, Athena. Napoli will be at the garden door immediately at 4:00. Be ready.

C...

Elizabeta look up from the letter. "What does this mean? I am to be arrested? Who dares such a thing!"

"My lady, Carlos will be driving us. You will recognize him immediately. He will drive us past your palace. I pray that I can convince you to come with me long before we get there. We have fifty minutes until four…"

"We are almost at the portal, Athena. You should awaken the Principessa." The morning sun illuminated the side of the van as Carlos parked. Napoli Water Company was written on every side. Carlos pulled to a stop and exited while Dianna pressed the small stone on her necklace. Without a sound, a large boulder slid from behind a shield of trees. Barely visible was a glass tube suspended by a cable that led into a tunnel.

"Come to the house back door as soon as you have taken care of the van, Carlos. Principessa Elizabeta, bring one of the children and follow me."

CHAPTER 12

CODE ALPHA IN PLAY

Peter Merlin stood relaxed before his dressing mirrors. He looked tight and trim. Pleased with what he saw, he posed for a moment, then began to explore his body for a blemish or any disagreeable mark that would cause concern. Not with a sense of ego, but more with a feel of pleasure in himself, he pressed against his stomach to enjoy its hardness. As was his way, he stepped up onto the mirrored platform to check his body more closely. He stroked the small scar just below his left nipple, then glanced at its matching mate above on his left cheek. "Albricht..." he whispered. The word punctuated the scar. He pinched his nipple to recall the slight numbness that forever attended the flesh around the wound... all these years, he thought, "Albricht." Rubbing his nipple more firmly, he felt his pleasure becoming more and more aroused. His smile-sneer had never changed during his fight with Albricht. It was natural for an aristocrat not to betray emotion in the public presence – equally for Albricht. No one would have noticed his eyes register pain.... For in that moment, he'd returned parry and thrust, keenly slicing Albrecht's right dimple into a clean and surgical cut. No plastrons or jackets, the fight began duel-fashion, spontaneously arrogant and akin to something sexual. Blood, nothing fatal, egos satisfied with blood. He had smiled as his thread-thin foil inscribed its gentleman's mark of chivalry. Their blood mingled generously as they bonded in seal of their play!

213

Now fully aroused, he pulled the cord that hung to his left and as he did, the paneled mirrors slid apart opening into a brightly lit shower room. He stepped down into a comfortably hot rainfall.

In a very aristocratic tone: "Good evening, Frankie," he splashed water onto his face, "a shave and then a good scrub; don't be nice, I'm in a mood..." Frankie was more than a personal valet. She was a priceless coach and one of three who never left him alone. Each could pass as a slight-framed double for himself. They worked in shifts, one or the other always within a protective distance. Not only as valet, they were athletes, linguists, aviators, and women with priceless recall that was accompanied by a speed-reading skill that almost surpassed his own.

Today's duty: Frankie had fenced with him a few minutes earlier and had pressed his workout until both were physically spent. Dressed in an almost invisible, gauze-thin jumper she lathered him from hair to toe and scrubbed him while he sighed in utter contentment. After a shave, she rinsed him and with a wave of her hand changed the water to cool, scented mineral water. The rain ended in a perfect drizzle.

Once toweled, she carefully trimmed his hair, powdered his comfort areas and dressed him. "Your guest is upstairs, Mr. Merlin."

Merlin turned away and strode toward the lounge lift. The Director was not expecting him nor had he any idea of what was about to begin... The initial step toward the Director's demise: first the illusive Q must have an accident – and this time, a successful kill; then the Director; and finally, the loose ends, one by one until the fatal circle is completed and the last thread remained – the old bitch Lilly in the States.

Merlin inhaled the soft scent that enveloped him, the barely traceable aroma of talc. He stepped from the elevator, "Mr. Merlin, good evening. The fencing master reports that your workout this evening was Olympic! He is impressed," the house butler bowed just so slightly, with no trace of a smile.

"Yah. Will you tell the chef that I'd like to begin dinner with a small salad, then Portuguese Linguado seasoned with just white pepper, watercress, and lemon on the side. Rare, be sure the fish is rare. It should look like a large Dover Sole."

Seeing the Director, Merlin left the lounge and walked comfortably to the Director's table. "May I offer you a drink, Mr. Bedford? My name is Martyn Merlin," he extended his hand. One was not offered in return. Merlin's eyes fixed on the Director, as one would in the presence of proper comportment. He continued, "Perhaps we can speak after dinner? Our families have to talk, and I am the designated sacrificial lamb. We have more than a little in common. As it happens, our long gone ancestors founded this club."

The Director stood and moved to adjust his handkerchief pocket – the motion was immediately recognized by security, which in turn connected the Director to the alert system in the Command Center. "*We're hot, sir,*" the metallic whisper in his earphone replied instantly.

"Mr. Merlin, yes, thank you for the offer. It would be my pleasure were you to join me. It's good to meet you."

"Thanks. You are Randolph Abbot Bedford the VI. My origin began, as did yours, long before the age of the schooner Silver Slipper. Our grandfathers, many decades removed, formed this Alliance on that schooner. I use the word 'ours' only obscurely since the United Kingdom's members of our family have never sought to be involved," he hesitated… "Until now."

A few miles away, a photo-recognition was beginning to download on the Command Center's prime monitor, "*There are two files coming up, Sir. The most recent ID is listed as from TXL airport, Berlin passport security, a couple, male and a female. Brother and sister, reported as twins. Merlin family…*"

"Mr. Bedford the Sixth, I know exactly who you are. And you know nothing of us. Ah! There is my guest. I'll no longer interrupt your dinner; I am sure you will want to continue this conversation soon?" Merlin patted the Director's arm and turned to leave. "Ah! Miss Jay. Our table is over there. Shall we dine?"

Without looking away, the Director continued, "Please have your guest join us. I insist."

"*Merlin's Scottish accent is fake. It hides a positive Austrian sound… Martyn Peter Rhue Merlin. That's your man, 99.99 percent positive. The woman with him at security – his sister, I presume – referred to him as 'Peter' while in the passport line.*"

The Director waited as Merlin held the chair for his guest. "Mr. Randolph Bedford, this is my assistant, Frankie Jay."

"Hello Miss Jay; Frankie is short for?"

"Frank, Mr. Randolph."

"Frankie is your pseudonym – as, ah… as when Mr. Merlin, here, interchanges Martyn for Peter? Very interesting." Looking at Merlin, "Variations on names, that reminds me, I recall your twin sister, but for the life of me, I can't think of her name," he said, pensively, touching his chin.

"*Bettavia. Her passport reads just one name. 'Bettavia.'*"

"Yes. Yes. Bettavia..." He seemed to stroke the name... "Interesting that these days she infrequently uses the family name..." As the Director spoke, the scar on Merlin's cheek pinkened ever so little; his expression however, did not change at all.

"We've heard interesting things about 'our' Command Center, Director. Perhaps you will give Frankie and me a tour?"

"Belinda Elizabeth Rhue Merlin, changed her name to Bettavia while in boarding school as soon as she reached 18. We have a very sketchy file on both of them. Looks like more is downloading..."

"Have you and Belinda moved to Canada? It's interesting that after all these generations you are interested in returning to the founder's charter house; I am sure you set the clock back when you introduced yourself to our staff."

"The staff seemed to be prepared, and in a seamless way. I am sure that Frankie here, made everything fall into place. Charming... a stately home, and yet, a fortress. I can see why you stay here; it is verrry, ah... secure. Ah... at last we eat!"

Dinner took its time. Frankie remained interested, but very silent throughout.

"Are you from Europe, Miss Jay? Your work with Martyn must call for a great deal of travel; do you have a life of your own?"

Frankie placed her fork on her dish as though finished. Her interest in his question brought a smile, "Mr. Merlin is a wonderful employer. I never know from day to day which language he prefers – we live for his schedule! It's exciting and very interesting. And yes, I do have a life of my own. I'm a personal trainer as well."

"The system has nothing on Frankie, Director, search is worldwide negative. She isn't Canadian. There is a Georgian texture in her voice –

crazy cockney gone Russian, gone Georgian."

"It's never good to question Frankie; no matter, her motives are always in my interest. Rather than worry about Frankie, I'd like to discuss your own iteration of Frankie. I gather that would be your asset, Mr. Q, who fills that role; such a pity that you lost the beautiful Dianna. But Q, he's your future, isn't he? Checkmate? Ha, ha, yah!" Martyn swirled his drink, watching the Director carefully. His body language gave nothing away.

"Checkmate, Mr. Merlin? What interest do you have in either Dianna or Q? I am sure they are both able to cope on their own. Your interest in them I presume brings you here?"

"Sir, we've placed Q on hold. He was about to leave Tutterville in the U.S. on a corporate jet, but when Martyn mentioned his name we thought it sounded sort of nefarious. We've put a hold on the plane until we are sure that it is clean! The ground crew is our asset. They need about fifteen minutes..."

"As you imply Martyn, our beautiful Dianna is unmatched. Much, I am sure, as is Frankie. Tell me about Frankie. I have a sense that she is more than an 'assistant,' an operative-assistant? Is our Q in danger, Martyn? Tonight? On the tarmac in Tutterville?"

Merlyn's face muscles involuntarily tightened. 'What does Bedford know?' He thought.

"Director, acid canister in the toilet! Clear your throat if you want to play Alpha, twice for Bravo."

"No. Ahemmm, sometime after takeoff. Martyn, please have a small port? It's from our farm in Porto, Portugal – a very rare vintage, '76." As he reached for the decanter, he accidentally tipped Frankie's water glass into her lap! "Oh, Frankie, I'm sooo sorry.

Let me get some help."

"No, thank you, I can…"

"Not at all, not at all, oh waitress, please help our guest to the lady's lounge. They'll fix your dress in seconds…"

As Frankie left the table, their waiter refreshed the water glasses and placed another napkin on Frankie's chair. Martyn took a sip of water and as quickly slumped forward into his dish. Alpha was now in play.

"It appears our guest can't hold his liquor." Looking at nearby guests, he continued in a barely audible whisper: "Take our guest to the elevator but instead of to his room, to the restroom in the lower lounge. When he comes to, take him to his room." He smiled as two of the staff helped Martyn to the elevator; the dining room guests saw no cause for alarm. The Director left the table and walked to the bar's elevator. In moments, he sat in the laterally moving elevator car. As quickly, the door opened again, and the staff slid Martyn into the car and slumped him across the side seat, very unconscious. With a soft air-hiss, the car door slid shut. It moved a few yards backward then, on a pivot axis, plunged swiftly far below the streets above. It took all of ten seconds before the car slipped to a stop; the door opened in a room alight with media screens flashing live across the curved far wall.

A woman and four staffers, meticulously dressed in the Directorate tan uniforms, instantly wrapped Merlin in a comm-proof silver sheet and placed him on a gurney. "We are now in full Plan Alpha." The Director checked his watch. "He is to be returned to his bedroom suite dressed exactly as he is now – the only difference is that he will have lost some twenty-four hours of his life. Be careful.

Before he is touched or exposed, give him a digital physical. I am sure he has GPS implants. Check him for everything, inside and out. We are about to gamble everything on this. Should anything appear unusual or suspect, stop and re-evaluate with me. We have to be flawlessly accurate. Before the MRI series, do a total body scan; we mustn't trigger or activate any comm-system or alarm. No one must ever detect that we've interrogated him. All that is to be known is that he was helped to his elevator and taken to his room.

"He will live today over again, everything he did today he'll repeat. Frankie is also about to go through the same interrogation. When they are fully cognitive, life will be like déjà vu for them both. They are to be awakened just as they enter the elevator for dinner, just as they did tonight. When he walks toward me for dinner, he will become fully aware and introduce himself as he did this evening.

"And, this is his wake-up scheme: his memory is to be cleansed of all that has happened to him here, and he is to be brought back to the moment he exited the dining room elevator this evening. For him, this evening will be happening all over again." Pausing, he looked for questions or comment. "Now, let's take him to Suite Alpha 1, and her to Alpha 2.

"You, Evelyn, take the lead with Frankie. I think she'll be a tough one. You know the routine: her memory banks are to coincide with Merlyn's and remember both she and Merlyn are to be fully awakened as Merlyn introduces her to me tomorrow evening at exactly eight o'clock." The Director smiled to his team. "Same table, same chair, table just as it was a few moments ago. Hopefully we will have a proper game to play with these two. Let me know if there is any delay. Oh, and tell Q that he is to be dining with me as

Mr. Merlin comes to my table tomorrow. Can't wait to see Merlin's double-take."

Both the Command Center and the staff around him responded together, *"Yes, Director,"* the Command Center added: *"The interrogation teams are ready sir, in Suites #1 and #2. To ensure compliance, Director, your instructions are recorded and will be subliminally replayed during the interrogation."*

It took some twenty minutes for the interrogators to remove Martyn's clothes, set them aside, identify the body powder he'd used while dressing, and complete the scan-physicals. The room was darkened, and a new and more calculating voice joined the others in the Director's head-receiver, *"The subject is as healthy as a man can be; however, he has three well-hidden implants. There is a flat, small bladder chamber, 3/8th-inch in diameter, looks like a GPS; there is a micro-receiver located in his right armpit, next to a chest muscle; and looks like a lovely data chip next to it. All of a latex composition, impossible to detect without using a body-view scan. Below his left ear, and lookie there, it is actually a pocket with what appears to be a suicide pill! Either self-activating or externally activated via satellite. This is usually carried by operators who must not be captured nor interrogated.*

"There is a second GPS located between his left una and radius at his wrist. Whoever is controlling him sees him right now as fast asleep from natural causes or booze, dreamless.

"He also has a micro TV camera in his right eye, activated by a micro switch in his eyebrow. At the moment, it is not operating. His controller must think he's asleep."

"Thank you, everyone, let's get to work, team; be very cautious, we don't want him compromised or activated!"

A white smocked young man leaned over the nude form of Martyn and kept repeating in a whisper until Martyn opened his eyes: "How shall I call you? Mr. Merlin...? How shall I call you? Mr. Merlin...? How shall I call you? Mr. Merlin...? How shall I call you? Mr..." Martyn's eyes opened slowly. "Call me Peter."

"Thank you, Peter," the interrogator replied, "We are happy that you are comfortable and asleep... Peter. You must be feeling very well, you appear so comfortable and relaxed. How comfortable are you, Peter? Why do you prefer to be called Peter instead of Martyn, Peter?

"I am very comfortable; I'm always called Peter when I'm at home with my family."

"You have a very pleasant home here, Peter. Where can we go to talk freely; where no one can overhear?"

"Right in there, the office. Father always uses this room for business."

"Your father is away for a few days. What is his name?"

"Yes, for a few days. He is called Prince Martyn Peter Rhue Merlin, or 'Prince.' He is our defacto leader of the Seven."

"At this moment, Peter, is your father the most important person in your life?"

"Oh, no."

"Who would that be? Please tell me."

"Yes, my sister. She has two names: Elizabeth and Indigo."

"Why two names?"

"Her real name, of course, and Indigo when we are to be in secret."

"Why does she have to be secret?"

"Because of the Seven."

"The Seven. Who are the Seven?"

"Our friends. Everything belongs to them. We like to joke that we are their hands and ears. They own more of ourselves than we do."

"What don't you have, what do they have?"

"Everything. Money."

"Who knows most about them, you or Elizabeth?"

"I do."

"Tell me about the Seven. How much do you know about them?"

"Their net worth is above three and a half trillion dollars each."

"Very wealthy people, Peter; what are their names?"

"Their names as a group are most secret. Separately, everyone knows their names. They are the wealthiest people in the world; but no one knows their actual wealth. Their code names are G1 through G7. Elizabeth and G7 are best friends, but actually Elizabeth and I are the real best of friends."

"Why is that, Peter."

"Because nobody trusts her more than I do, and she knows it."

"I can see that is the best of reasons. What is the purpose of the Seven, Peter?"

"To make steadfast their domination through manipulation of the world economy. This is the task of G7. G1 has the power to plan for international socialism and to finance worldwide elections toward that end; G2 has the power to establish a common government within international socialism and spread concepts of social justice; G3 has the power to set up a single monetary system; G4 has the power to degrade the major religions through relativism and disgrace, and subsequently help the 'faithful' see religion as irrelevant; G5 has the universal task to influence the world's youth through social education at all levels – it is imperative that youth believe in social justice, diversity at any cost, and political correctness from a strong liberal platform; and G6 has the power to eventually make public acceptance of governance and the security system of controls as determined by a democratic governance for and by the Group of Seven."

"In short, Peter, to dominate the world? G3 is most pivotal."

"They almost already do, just some loose ends."

"Someone has to be the grand master of the Seven. Do you know who that is?"

"Yes, she is dead. I think our father will be elected by the Seven."

"Was she G7? Who was she, and what was her name?"

"Ursula Rhue the Fifth, my mother. The Alliance's Master Dianna murdered her and her twin sister, our aunt; she was also called Ursula Rhue for self-identity purposes. I believe we have eliminated Master Dianna. We believe, at this time."

The interrogator hesitated. "This room is without windows, Peter. It looks like the perfect meeting room. How would one locate this residence?"

"Only by ADF beacon. When the Seven meet here, it must be absolutely safe for them; only security selected staff can be with us."

"How often do all of you meet?"

"Meetings are called only by one of the Seven, or my father."

"What is the ADF fix?"

"777.77 Its beacon location is centered directly in the helipad, 30 nautical miles southeast of Berchtesgaden."

"Is the helipad the entrance to your home, where we are now?"

"A camouflaged hangar door and a side entrance a few yards to the right are the only entrances."

"When it is imperative, can the Seven meet immediately? How is such a conference called? Is there a code system?"

"Until the imagery system... I feel so sleepy... I must lie down..."

"Of course, Peter. I have to be going soon as well. You can get some well-deserved rest. Sit back in your chair and rest a moment."

"We'll need about five minutes more; we're well within the drug's parameters. Just a bit more information and we can let him go..."

"Disconnect me from him for sixty seconds; let him rest."

"Yes, Director. All is in disconnect for sixty and counting..."

The Director looked around. "There is a nurse in the room, have her quickly bring me an antacid – *now*; must have been the port wine!"

"10 seconds and counting... 3, 2, 1, system's up..."

"As you were saying Peter: 'Imagery System.'"

"Yes... All will be holographic within a few weeks. We will never again meet in real-time. We believe that June 12 will be our final session before all goes electronic."

The Director interrupted: "We have what we need. Splendid work everyone. Let's close down if everyone agrees."

The interrogator: "You are very generous with your time, Peter. I must go, and you must rest." He then pulled the warming-environmental cloth across Merlin's body in a cocoon-like sleeve, sealing him in his unconscious state. "The subject is now all yours, Director."

"Session is ended, ladies and gentlemen; get the subject ready to go." Director Bedford stood. "Let's meet in the conference center. Who is on duty in the Center?"

CHAPTER 13

MASTER-DIANNA

Hosea Harry had at least a half hour before he'd awake. Lilly hummed softly enough that the baby would hear the soft sound of her voice and so, awaken sweetly. It was interesting, she thought, it had worked when she nursed his mother some thirty-five years ago; he was very much like her! Lilly smiled and whispered a prayer of thanks to the God who keeps her so happy. Harry and Addie had asked her to stay, as if they'd had to. Little Hosea was everyone's life… Truly perfect, so sweet. Oh God. She reverenced Him again as she often did, "Thank you Father…" Lilly loved mornings when everyone was still sleeping. She was up in time to water her plants, tend to Hosea Harry and begin breakfast. The soft, almost silent chime of the phone brought her to instant focus.

"Good morning. Tutter-Hendricks home."

"Good morning. Sorry to call this early… I pray that this is you, Lilly?"

"Why yes. Yes, it is. I know your voice…"

"Please don't say my name. I pray that Doctor Hendricks and the Judge are not nearby – can you talk freely, Lilly – please whisper if you can hear me."

Lilly help her breath a moment, "Yes, yes, where are you?"

"We will be together again in a short time. Do you know Director Bedford?"

"My land, yes of course! Are things happening again? You know what I mean. I knew things were not ended!"

"Until you recognize the proper time – and you will – please do not refer to me or this telephone call. To anyone! Can you agree?"

Lilly hesitated... Hosea was awaking. "Yes, what must I do?"

"Contact Q through Chief Kilmein. I hope that you are able to fly to be with Q today. When you meet him, immediately take him to the Director and tell them that 'the Group of Seven' must be intercepted immediately, in Austria. This is so vital Lilly, that you can repeat this message only to the Director in Q's presence. I repeat, this phone call did not happen..."

"I don't understand!"

"You must understand that if any of the 'Seven' escape, at least two innocent children will either die or forever remain in hiding."

"In hiding? Die?"

"Yes Lilly, and there is a very good possibility that all of you are in danger should a survivor of the 'Seven' want revenge. They are the most powerful Seven in the world; much is at stake... Tell the Director, in front of Q, that the oil from your zoo's golden dart frogs can be mixed into a gas that, once sprayed into a room of any size, all of the occupants will be made unconscious immediately, and the side effects will be to erase memory completely, and death within hours."

"My Lord! Why?"

"The Director will tell you. I must go. Please hurry to Q... and you must not reveal my identity to him. One day, I will do that myself. Please hurry, Lilly... Today, today!" And the phone went silent.

Pressing the direct-call button, Lilly was connected with Chief Kilmein. "Chief, this is Lilly. You must have a jet ready for me within a few minutes. I must be with the Director before noon your time... It seems that we are about to reach the end of Medusa... Who? Why Ursula Rhue, of course."

Lilly's jet touched down on a dirt strip just inside the city limits; moments later she was seated in the back of a nondescript limo facing Q and the Director.

"Ms. Atterby. I am very honored to meet one so distinguished and well-decorated. Without humor or any condescension, I have to say that you are an agency-wide hallmark. Q and I wish you were operationally assigned to 'our' agency!"

"Director, please... observation and deduction, anyone's forte. Thank you for your generous words. I must say that all this Rhue trouble is not yet resolved. Perhaps we should remain near the airplane until I've said what I've come to report. If you need me to remain, I will; if not, I would like to return right away."

"We can do that, Ms. Atterby..."

"Call me Lilly, please. I prefer Lilly. I really don't have much to say; rather, what I am asked to tell you is time-sensitive and urgent. It may require fast measures on your part."

"How can we help you, Lilly?" Q's smile was one of reminiscence; she could see great sadness in his eyes.

Lilly leaned toward him, "I believe, Q, that one day soon that sadness I see in your heart will go away.

"Let me get to business. Just before dawn this morning I received a phone call. I cannot reveal from whom at the moment; I promised that person I would not reveal the caller's name to anyone.

This is the message I was given, right to the word:

"'Contact Q through Chief Kilmein, as well as the Director. I hope that you are able to visit the three of them today. When you are with them, and I pray to God that it is today, please give them, and only them the following message, quote: 'The Group of Seven must be intercepted in Austria immediately. This is so vital, Lilly, that you can repeat this only to the Director and Chief in Q's presence. I repeat, this phone call did not happen... You must understand that if any of the Seven escape, at least two innocent children will either die, or forever remain in hiding. And there is a very good possibility that all of you are in danger... should a survivor of the Seven want revenge. They are the most powerful Seven in the world; much is at stake. Tell the Director, in front of Q, that the oil from Tutterville Zoo's golden dart frogs can be mixed into a gas, that once sprayed into a room of any size kills all of the occupants: first they become unconscious for many hours, accompanied with complete loss of memory, and death within hours.'"

The Director held up his hand in caution. "Who told you this, Lilly? Good Lord! We leak like a sieve! How did you get this information? From whom?"

"I recognized the voice and I believe all will be as she said."

"She? My God." The Director pressed the stone in his finger ring; a voice softly filled the limo.

"Yes, sir. We've copied everything."

"We are now in Alert Alpha +1. We are now all upgraded at this time to Plan Alpha +1. Please acknowledge for the entire Directorate that we are at +1 Alert status, and permanent until

I order otherwise. Please respond affirmative in Code: Alpha +1, immediate."

Silence.

"Alpha +1 Alert in place, Director."

"This is easy, ladies and gentlemen: get our chemists to develop a heavy fog-gas from the frog specimen-samples we have in the lab. The gas has to be sufficient enough in volume to neutralize the entire space the 'Group of Seven' will occupy in Austria. Oil samples from the South American golden dart frogs can be synthesized if more matter is necessary.

"Next, cancel Q's schedule for a few weeks." He looked at Q for a response. Getting just a smile, he continued: "He is to be on the mountain-top location in hiding from tomorrow dawn and be there until he has delivered his payload and confirmed its success. The chemists have some ten hours to develop the gas agent. When this is finished, we will determine the future of the so-called 'Seven.' Notify me and Q when the gas is a go." The car speakers went silent. He pressed the stone again.

"Yes, Director."

Nodding to Q and Lilly: "Place the Atterby-Tutterville home under full Alpha Alert surveillance until further notice. Send Chief Kilmein to visit Dr. and Mrs. Hendricks and brief them personally. No one is to enter that home without the express permission of Miss Lilly Atterby or myself. Do this now!" The Director smiled at Lilly.

Q had been silent until now. "Lilly, I am very concerned; all this is too personal. The phone call, the threat. I insist that you remain with the Director as a guest in our club until June 14…" He looked at the monitor to his left; "Still, it might be a better plan for your family to return here with Chief Kilmein, and all of you remain secure at the club. There, Miss Lilly, you can personally add to their safety and to their comfort."

"You took the words from my mouth, Q. This is the best plan, Lilly."

Lilly was stunned, "Are you serious Q, Director Bedford? I cannot see Dr. Hendricks accepting any of this. He is very capable…"

The Director appraised Lilly's thoughts. "I believe, Lilly, that your phone caller knew exactly what is about to happen! Dr. Hendricks must do as you suggest. You have to tell him that his son Hosea could be in grave danger."

Lilly gasped. The Director turned to Q. "Well my dear Q, it appears that our Dianna is in play again!"

*

The landing pad was invisible to the naked eye. Unless one stood on its surface or a few meters away, it could not be seen. Camouflage brush and low weeds covered its surface and gave the impression of a small mountain meadow. Any size helicopter could land in its center and with the correct frequency open the great hangar doors disguised as the mountain's face. The doors, made of trees and rocks, rolled back to form an opening large enough for a helicopter to taxi in with ease. Once inside the great doors silently closed, and on latching, light flooded the room revealing more than a hangar, but the palatial lobby to a grand house.

Q arrived after dark and set up a camp in deep woods, a few hundred yards away in the bush. His radio receiver was set to pick up broadcasts, sounds, and voices emerging from the small, private airport close to Salzburg. The target helicopter had arrived earlier in the day – one pilot, one crewman, no passengers. From the way the helicopter had been serviced, and the crew seated beneath its rotors, passengers had to be expected very soon – the flight from there to where Q stood would be seventeen minutes at best. Hopefully, there would be at least seven passengers aboard. "A relatively heavy bird," he whispered to himself.

Dressed in skintight fawn-colored brown, he would not be seen lying on his back, hidden in the tallish dusk-browned weeds, center edge of the landing place. While the bird hovered to begin its gentle pull-up to land, his plan was to spring onto the lower engine housing and fly crouched under the bird as it taxied into the hanger. Simple as that! Except his added weight had to be synchronized with the pilot's round-out. All this would have to happen within seconds as the helicopter momentarily hovered before landing.

Q hadn't long to wait. His earphone crackled into noise; the crew's conversation became serious: "*The family is on the squawk box, they're coming in separate vans. Let's get on board. They're arriving now…*"

Q watched the two men spring to their feet as four vehicles silently approached the helicopter; ten plus the crew boarded the chopper. Good, he thought, that weight would make it easier. He crawled to the landing pad through the high grass-brush; no one was anywhere to be seen. A fawn, spooked by something, sped away further into the dark forest. Q frowned, his weapon close. It would be deep dusk when they landed. He activated the small gas mask under his sock-mask and pulled it snugly into place, and then sprawled quickly to within inches of the landing pad, rolled on his back and pulled grass from the ground to cover as much of himself as he could. Minutes later, the huge bird floated swiftly above him, the wind almost blinding; the flare-out was perfect! Reaching up, he grasped the undercarriage in slow motion as it moved forward toward the invisible hangar doors. The bird touched down and slow-taxied toward the mountain wall. Within a few meters the fake foliage that covered the doors slid out of sight and the hangar doors silently parted. Once inside, they closed completely within seconds. Again, and as if in slow motion, he rolled to the dark side of the craft and crouched below the windows. Engine cut, a door opened. He pulled the pins on both grenades and watched putrid gray gas envelop the helicopter and begin to fill the hangar. Chatter on board turned silent. Counting to three, he opened the main cabin door. The gas had done its job. All were unconscious, slumped against one another. As far as he could see, ground crew had fallen where they'd stood – immediately.

Next, as planned, he walked into the underground mansion. He searched each room. Kitchen and dining room staff, secretarial and administrative personnel, housekeepers – no one was conscious. A feeling of grief-laden horror froze him in the midst of such carnage. All his doing… No survivors. For decades, the 'Seven' and its lust for greed and power had devoured a greater number than these. Did their dead legions now know vengeance? Has he and the Alliance severed the head of this huge monster? These thoughts and many like them raced through his mind until the urgency of his mission shook him free.

His mission complete, he returned to the chopper. The hangar door lever was obvious. As fresh air rushed in, he kept his mask in place. He pushed the first pilot from his seat, started the engine and gently backed the chopper into the night. Once outside, he closed the huge doors and ran to the place where he'd hidden out. Everything was as he'd left it. He cleared his gear and placed it into a small duffel and snapped it to his back. He slipped a sport-type parachute over his back and quickly returned to the chopper. No evidence of his camp remained. Without running lights or any lighting systems activated, he climbed the chopper to five thousand feet, flipped on the navigation lights and radios, and aimed the bird in a nose-down dive to the helipad. Controls locked into the descent, he jumped to safety into the night air. Moments later the bird crashed with all aboard, neatly into the hangar doors. The explosions were monumental – storage fuel tanks, fire igniting the mansion lobby, the helicopter itself. It would take a long time to identify the 'Seven,' its staff and crew. The explosions would draw immediate attention… Q's task was done.

*

Far, far away… breezy tropical air danced atop golden tips of water cresting in the light of the yellow Asian moon. Poised as a ship at sea, the Agency's private island appeared to float adrift, miles from the nearest Indonesian habitat. Midnight, and the waters slept, but for the silent swimmer whose stealth awakened neither fish nor posted guard. Not the gold of the waves nor the black of night revealed the dark shadow as it inched quietly underwater toward the thatched cabana's most seaward pylon. Serpent-like, it pulled itself from the sea onto the darkest corner of the deck and, as if frozen in time, began to match the breathing of the man asleep across the room, conforming its presence to the other – so synchronous were the movements that Q lay motionless and apparently unaware.

Sleep would not come easily to Q these nights. All his life, even after the most life-threatening and harrowing case-experiences, his conscience was clear... Duty first and always. He slept on command. This last mission was different – so many dead, such universal evil; throughout it all, the loss of Dianna – had she really survived? How? Awake, his thoughts recounted back-briefings to the Director, journaling the Salzburg affair, and closing the books on an evil so invasive that it had accounted for worldwide carnage, treachery, greed and murder. He had no regrets. The Austrian police and the press assumed that the helicopter crash happened in an attempted night landing; all passengers and crew were dead at impact. The Agency mission went down as planned, but this one was the death of a viral monster that only its utter antithesis, awakened in time, could destroy it. He'd never experienced anything like it before. Dianna...

The evil ones, on the other hand, had lost everything. The Group of Seven all dead, including Peter Marlin and three women identified with the last name of Jay, a tragic chopper crash. Their power gone, their massive fortunes now in government treasuries, no longer theirs by default, everything went in a flash of fire.

Q finally slept. Dianna. But a different feeling was edging into his conscious. Deep sleep disturbed sensually with the scent of perfume arousing him into deep breaths.

The silent figure stood beside the bed and delicately pulled the screen netting aside. "Shush, Q, shush... it's just me, your friend from Guincho... Shush, don't open your eyes... sleep... shhhh..."

He heard the softness of life whisper to him in half-sleep... the perfume he could not forget.

"Shhhh… Don't awaken, my sweet one, please feel me near you… Shhhh, can I bring you back to our night in Portugal, Guincho? Shhhh, no, do not move…" A gentle pressure on his navel caught his breath and as it did, the room immediately burst into light and his fist trapped the groping hand in a painful vice!

"Oh!" She almost shouted. Q was out of bed

"Dianna, I… I presume. Same touch, wrong face! Guincho?" He pulled her to him. "You smell like the sea. My Dianna would never wear a scent, except…"

"Yes." She interrupted. "Yes, except when I am with you, especially in a darkened room like Guincho. I left my calling card. My perfume."

"Joy." He paused, "Why Dianna? Why the deceit, the… gaming me in Portugal?"

"It's not complicated. There was so much I had to do. When I was in danger of losing everything, I knew I had to devise an alternative life hidden from the Agency. What I'd need to do would be considered traitorous – you and everyone would believe me to be a traitor. The operation to change my appearance was in part to change my identity. I took the assumed name of…"

"Marjorie Margaret Harrington, Maggie." Q smiled. "I learned your name through an old woman I knew as Elizabeth. You saved her great-grandson, Albert!"

"All for this very moment, Q. I risked my life, everything I have just for this moment. I knew it would come, the Indonesian sea at night, and awakening you. The 'Seven' endgame is over. Now, all of this is my private endgame; it was Alexandria who commanded me to be here."

She put a finger to his lips before he could question; afraid, she changed the subject "Oh… You were very impressive in Austria."

"Dianna, I have come to know that you are an extraordinary woman." She interrupted again: "No… I…"

Firmly, Q continued, "Stop interrupting and please listen to me! It's my turn to be heard. Ever since we became agents, since the first very, the very beginning, it seemed to me that you live as a person in constant déjà vu … like an echo. You know what's about to happen before it does happen. Either you are a mind reader – you deduct, cross-deduct and play seven-deep chess with everything you see and hear; or your perception is truly beyond any norm we know. And I say we, because the Director and I often were amazed with your insights, your intuition! Your IQ and memory are way off the charts. You read people so well that you can get them to agree with almost anything. Hmmm, yes of course you know what I did in Austria. You even know when I pleasure myself!

"You were the awkward nurse in the background when Peter Merlin was being interrogated. Your brogan-style high heels gave you away… no limp can ever give that ass of yours away, lady. When you walk, you move like no other woman on the planet! Of course you know what I did in Austria. You know everything. And yet at times, you almost had me convinced you were dead.

"I didn't scare any fawn, it was you, not a fawn. And, of course, someone else was with you. Carlos. He's been your backup all your life. At Salzburg, Austria you were both there to back me up. Right?"

"Yes." Dianna answered.

"The Director! You, Diana, were my redundant operative. See

what I mean? It was just hours between Ms. Atterby's arrival and my departure for Austria; only hours between your conversation with Atterby and getting to the Director. And now, you find me sleeping. Who is Alexandria?"

Dianna slipped onto the bed and pulled him down beside her. "No, beautiful Q. It is you who are the smart one. The Director recognized you from the beginning. He tracked IQ student-athletes. His files show that you were one in hundreds. He made sure that three of his 'protégés,' of his 'Q candidates,' received scholarships from multiple universities – the other two candidates chose well. You did not. They watched you choose private tutors. You went through them like cotton candy – sciences, physics, languages, physical arts, psychiatry and endless more. Your appetite devours fat text books within hours; you are a voracious reader. He had to recruit you. You are unmatched; in fact, one day you are to replace him as Director." She tickled his chest.

"There was a small chance that I would be blamed for the death of Ursula Rhue. You recall, I disappeared as a lost agent. You are correct, Carlos has and always will be my trusted accomplice... He is my personal operative known only by the Director, and now you, of course. Carlos resuscitated me and pulled me from the cottage bedroom back in Cuenca, Spain. He left Ussie Rhue and a woman who looked very much like me on the bed. Once in the fresh air recognition returned; everything at once came clearly into complete focus for me! I had survived. I was free and only Carlos knew I was alive. The Director and you, Q, thought me dead. No. Everything had gone precisely as I'd planned. I guess, in a way, I sacrificed myself for the sake of the Agency.

"It was necessary, I believed, to work outside the Agency for three reasons. The first was to protect Albert's child from the person or persons I referred to as the Candidate, now known as the 'Group of Seven.' The child is to inherit the Williamsburgh fortunes. The second was to uncover and destroy the 'Seven;' and the third, as I said earlier, is to complete my personal endgame. You and Carlos are my safety net for everything, even the last.

"Three children were in danger. The absolute imperative for me is them – now, and always – their safety, their happiness and their security, Hosea, Albert and Alexandria!"

Q pondered. "Albert is the Williamsburgh and Princess Anna's son, yes?"

"Yes."

"Hosea is Miss Lilly's grandson."

"Yes."

"And Alexandria is…"

"Our baby girl," Diana's tears fell unquenched. "Our daughter."

"Guincho!"

"Yes…" She sighed so very deeply. "I, we… I have no other endgame…"

Dianna pulled away and sat up. "So now, please hear my confession."

"No confession, Dianna. No."

"No matter what you decide, I will always have a part of you. Do you know that I have loved you from the moment I saw you? Because of all the reasons you and I know, our work could not allow any intimacy. So, I constructed a scenario that a pregnant Maggie Harrington could serve two objectives: one that could tie me to you forever – how selfish I was not to include you in making that decision, but I could take no risk; and the second was to become a nurse to Albert Williamsburgh's child – thank God I reached them in time to save their baby."

Q reached to touch her face. "So, you and I had sex in Guincho and you became pregnant."

"Yes… our daughter is so much like her father. It is she who sends me to you tonight, Miss Alexandria Margaret Harrington, our baby." Dianna sobbed, "Oh, Q, I've come to see if you will bring us home and make us yours." She held up her hand to stop his answer.

"But if not, we know that I tricked you. We have no right to you and your future. Can we be together until dawn? And then, I will disappear into the sea from where I came and return to Alexandria and Albert. We will always live, never to intrude on you. No one need know what happened or, or that I love you." Dianna stood. As she did, Q stood before her.

"Dianna, we will be married on this island as soon as it can be arranged. Somehow, somehow, I knew that Guincho was more than a night with you. I know now, as I knew then, that my beautiful Dianna took a part of me away with her – a forever part…"

The End

Until we begin again, with Dianna…